The
LAST SOVIET

A James Acton Thriller

Also by J. Robert Kennedy

James Acton Thrillers

The Protocol	*The Riddle*	*The Cylon Curse*
Brass Monkey	*Blood Relics*	*The Viking Deception*
Broken Dove	*Sins of the Titanic*	*Keepers of the Lost Ark*
The Templar's Relic	*Saint Peter's Soldiers*	*The Tomb of Genghis Khan*
Flags of Sin	*The Thirteenth Legion*	*The Manila Deception*
The Arab Fall	*Raging Sun*	*The Fourth Bible*
The Circle of Eight	*Wages of Sin*	*Embassy of the Empire*
The Venice Code	*Wrath of the Gods*	*Armageddon*
Pompeii's Ghosts	*The Templar's Revenge*	*No Good Deed*
Amazon Burning	*The Nazi's Engineer*	*The Last Soviet*
	Atlantis Lost	

Special Agent Dylan Kane Thrillers

Rogue Operator	*Black Widow*	*State Sanctioned*
Containment Failure	*The Agenda*	*Extraordinary Rendition*
Cold Warriors	*Retribution*	*Red Eagle*
Death to America		*The Messenger*

Templar Detective Thrillers

The Templar Detective	*The Sergeant's Secret*	*The Black Scourge*
The Parisian Adulteress	*The Unholy Exorcist*	*The Lost Children*
	The Code Breaker	

Kriminalinspektor Wolfgang Vogel Mysteries

The Colonel's Wife	*Sins of the Child*

Delta Force Unleashed Thrillers

Payback	*The Lazarus Moment*	*Forgotten*
Infidels	*Kill Chain*	*The Cuban Incident*

Detective Shakespeare Mysteries

Depraved Difference	*Tick Tock*	*The Redeemer*

Zander Varga, Vampire Detective

The Turned

THE
LAST SOVIET

A James Acton Thriller

J. ROBERT KENNEDY

ISBN: 9781990418280

First Edition

For Walter Gretzky.

A nation misses its hockey dad.

THE
LAST SOVIET

A James Acton Thriller

"Comrade Stalin, having become Secretary-General, has unlimited authority concentrated in his hands, and I am not sure whether he will always be capable of using that authority with sufficient caution."

Vladimir Lenin
As written in Lenin's Testament
Written Circa 1922-23
Presented Posthumously May 1924 to the 13th Party Congress

"Stalin is too coarse and this defect, although quite tolerable in our midst and in dealing among us Communists, becomes intolerable in a Secretary-General. That is why I suggest that the comrades think about a way of removing Stalin from that post and appointing another man in his stead…"

Vladimir Lenin
As written in Lenin's Testament

PREFACE

Under the leadership of a former KGB agent and now Russian president, the image of Joseph Stalin has been rehabilitated within Russia, with a 2019 poll of its citizenry indicating a 70% favorable opinion of the brutal dictator. This is up 16% in just four years, illustrating how successful the rewriting of history has been.

In 2005, in his State of the Nation address, he is quoted as saying, "First and foremost it is worth acknowledging that the demise of the Soviet Union was the greatest geopolitical catastrophe of the century." Even at the beginning of his tenure as the longest-serving leader of Russia *and* the Soviet Union, it was clear he admired the past glory of the USSR. Since then, he has reinstated the Soviet national anthem's melody, replacing that chosen after the collapse, brought back Soviet-era-style military parades, and even brought back the Hero of Labor award that Stalin himself introduced in 1927, the lapel pin remarkably resembling the original.

This is a man desperate to recreate the glory years of an empire that was far from glorious, and that history has shown was not only a brutal dictatorship, but an ultimate failure. Yet by rewriting that history and invoking the fading nostalgia in a weary populace, he is successfully guiding his country back to the old ways, with the ignorant citizenry cheering him on.

Should he succeed, as it appears he will, the world might once again face its old enemy. A Soviet Union 2.0, if you will.

And if there were a hidden piece of history that could shatter this image of the great dictator who led the Soviet Union during its glory years, what would a man like the Russian president, and former KGB officer, do to stop it from becoming public?

Black Forest, Germany

Tomorrow

Archaeology Professor Laura Palmer grabbed at her ears as her Glock clattered to the floor. The ringing in her ears went almost unnoticed as the spots pulsing behind her eyelids overwhelmed her, the effect of the flashbang tossed in a moment ago making its presence felt. Gunfire pounded the area as she curled into a ball, struggling to regain her senses, the battle almost over, the overwhelming odds proving too much.

We never stood a chance.

She forced her eyes open to see her beloved James firing at the blown doorway, his MP5 belching lead at anyone who dared attempt entry, but it was a lost cause. He and the others were merely delaying the inevitable.

They were going to die.

The Russians had won.

And it pissed her off.

She pushed to her knees, staying low behind the half-height wall they had taken cover behind, and picked up her Glock.

3

"Are you all right?" asked James, and she nodded.

"No permanent damage."

"Thank God. Next time someone yells 'flashbang,' you close your eyes and cover your ears."

"Rookie mistake, I know. Don't tell Leather. He'll be ashamed."

"I'm ashamed." James flashed her a grin then his face turned to horror. "Grenade!"

Not a flashbang, but a grenade. She lifted her head above the wall to see the explosive sail through the air and into the room with the young victims they were protecting. "No!" she cried as James leaped to his feet, surging toward the door in a futile effort to save the others.

She rose to stop him, breaking the cardinal rule just read to her moments ago, and cried out as something slammed into her shoulder, spinning her around so she couldn't see the massive explosion that tore apart the room her husband had just run into.

And as she blacked out from the pain, she prayed for death.

For life wouldn't be worth living without the man she loved.

State Archive of the Russian Federation

Moscow, Russian Federation

Today

He's wrong!

Dmitri Volkov flipped the folder shut rougher than he should have considering the age of the documents it contained, but he was frustrated and tired. He leaned back in the unforgiving wood chair, stretching his arms over his head as he yawned, covering his mouth with a fist. It had been months of work, months of sacrifice. He had barely seen his family and friends, and his girlfriend, Katarina Rozhenko, had long since given up on him, their relationship over. But the work was worth it.

Or at least he thought it was until this very moment.

The professor had been wrong. The proof of the theory didn't exist. To say he was disappointed would be understating things, and it wasn't only because of all the time he had wasted, all the sacrifices he had made—it was because it was an opportunity lost, an opportunity to perhaps save his country from continuing down the rabbit hole its iron-fisted ruler would have them travel.

The president was a man stuck in the past. Former KGB, he believed the greatest tragedy of the twentieth century was the collapse of the Soviet Union, and was doing everything in his power to restore the former glory of the USSR. But what was most disturbing, and something he hadn't noticed until his mentor, Professor Arseny Orlov, had pointed it out in a conversation they had before his disappearance, was how history was being rewritten surrounding the Soviet Union's most famous and brutal leader.

Joseph Stalin.

Stalin had been a mass murderer, perhaps even psychotic. Tens of millions had died under his watch through policies he had initiated, but it was also under his watch that the Soviet Union became a superpower, winning the Great Patriotic War, or as the West called it, World War II. He had converted the country from a primarily agrarian society into an industrial one that developed nuclear weapons and rivaled the mighty United States, but more impressively, had kept control of a population made up of 15 republics, often with little in common, by stifling any dissent with a simple signature at the bottom of a page.

Outright executions as well as deaths in the gulags and by other policies instituted by Stalin were estimated to be over three million. And that didn't include the famine he could be blamed for—another 5.5-6.5 million people. And there were so many more.

When he had died, those that followed attempted to maintain his level of control, but most failed for various reasons, not the least of which was the fact they couldn't replicate Stalin's viciousness, they couldn't command the fear that the man from Georgia could, they couldn't embrace the joy the man had in his brutality.

According to Professor Orlov, it was the ideals of Stalin, his uncompromisingly focused leadership style, that the current president ultimately wanted to replicate. It was Orlov's theory that the long-term goal was to reestablish a version of the USSR with the president as the undisputed head, all semblance of democracy removed, with the military might to strike fear in the hearts of any nation of the world, including the United States. He wanted the power, the fear, the glory, the respect the Soviet Union once had, restored upon a nation that had almost collapsed in upon itself after the dissolution of the USSR.

By embracing a revised version of Stalin, embracing the nostalgia surrounding a false history of life in the Soviet Union, the man was achieving his goals. A significant portion of the population worshipped the man, and were willing to embrace whatever reforms he proposed, in part because the population was eating up the revisionist history surrounding the last iron-fisted ruler of the Soviet Union. Orlov had expressed his concerns that his fellow Russians were embracing a past few remembered, a past that was a lie.

"There's only one person that those who embrace our past revere more than Joseph Stalin," Orlov had said at the time.

"Who?"

"Lenin."

Volkov's head bobbed. "I suppose, though the president is certainly doing whatever he can to change that."

"He is, and I believe he's starting to succeed. You are, of course, aware that Lenin and Stalin were bosom buddies, on a first-name basis, and, of course, Stalin was Lenin's choice to succeed him upon his death."

"Yes, pretty much everyone's taught that in school, though most things are glossed over these days so nothing taints our perfect country."

Orlov regarded him. "What if I told you it's all lies? That almost nothing about that period was true?"

Volkov remembered leaning back and folding his arms, wondering if his favorite professor was playing games with him once again. As Orlov's star pupil and prized graduate student, Orlov would often propose something outrageous in the hopes a spirited debate would ensue, allowing him to probe his student's knowledge of the subject matter by forcing him to state facts that challenged the outrageous contradiction.

And he had assumed that was precisely what had happened that day, for what he had been told was so shocking, so outrageous, he had refused to participate in an argument so obviously false. For what Orlov had told him had him doubting history, had him questioning everything he had been taught, everything he had believed in.

And the proof was supposed to have been here in this archive, among the personal papers of Stalin and the inner sanctum that had surrounded him for decades, an archive so secret, it hadn't been opened until 1995 after the collapse of the Soviet Union. Its contents had rewritten the Soviet-style thinking surrounding Stalin, revealing the extent of his brutality and how he had orchestrated it all. The official Communist Party line before the collapse had been that local officials had gotten out of control, murdering millions, and that Stalin had no idea it was happening, though once he did find out, he put an end to it.

A lie, of course. It had only ended when he died.

Yet it never really did. It only slowed.

According to Orlov, there was something in the archive, something he had seen in the early days of its opening that had never made it into the new biographies and the corrected history being rewritten by scholars. It was here, according to Orlov, and Volkov had been convinced it was as well.

Until now.

And he wished he could confront his mentor, face to face, over what he now feared was indeed another of his infuriating games. Yet that was impossible. It had been a couple of years since Orlov had disappeared abruptly. A set of artifacts had arrived that Moscow wanted identified. He wasn't sure what it was all about except that it was related to the incident that almost resulted in war between Russia and Japan. The authorities had arrested Orlov, and his office and labs were emptied of all their contents.

And then no one had heard from him again. Until three months ago. Volkov had received an email to his personal address. It was from someone he had never heard of and had contained a link with a simple message.

Do you remember our last conversation, my young friend?

Normally, he would have deleted it as a phishing scam, but there was something in the phrasing, in referring to him as 'my young friend.'

Usually, spam messages were so laughably misaddressed, they were easily identified, yet this was how Orlov had always referred to him.

He had clicked the link after taking precautions, and it didn't work. He was going to delete it when Katarina, someone with far greater computer expertise than him, had suggested he use a different type of browser that could access the Dark Web. They had installed one that would take them off the regular Internet and onto the Dark Web, the completely unregulated side of the Internet that few with good morals would ever visit. It was where the criminal element congregated. Pedophiles, sex traffickers, arms dealers, drug dealers, terrorists. It was also where conspiracy theorists and others who didn't want to be tracked by the government found refuge, and if that message were indeed from Orlov, it made perfect sense that this would be the way for him to reach out.

When they used the link in the new browser, communication had indeed been established with his old mentor, and the request had been made to search the archive for the documents that would prove the unfathomable piece of history was true.

Yet it wasn't.

And it had him angry, months wasted on a wild goose chase. But it also had him disappointed. He worshipped that man, and for him to be so wrong, it shook his faith in his mentor's infallibility.

He packed up the files, returning them to the box from which they came, then carried it over to the file clerk, Morozov, a man he had come to know over the past several months.

"Judging by the expression on your face, I take it you didn't find what you were looking for?"

Volkov shook his head. "No. And that was the last set of files."

"Like I said before, if you told me what it was you were looking for, I might be able to help."

Volkov delivered the rehearsed lie Orlov had provided. "You know I can't. My professor was very clear on that. He's writing a book and he doesn't want to risk anyone else stealing his idea before he can publish."

Morozov leaned back and laughed. "If he is worried that I'm going to write a book before he does, he needn't worry." He frowned. "So, I won't be seeing you again?"

Volkov sighed. "Not unless there are files you haven't told me about."

The old man shifted in his chair, staring at him, his lips pursed as if debating whether he should say something.

Volkov glanced about to confirm they were alone then lowered his voice. "Are there more files?"

Morozov did his own check. "You didn't hear this from me."

Gorki Estate

South of Moscow, Russian Soviet Federative Socialist Republic

December 22, 1922

Anatoly Bazarov leaned back in the utilitarian chair. Anything more would be luxury, and if all his people couldn't enjoy a padded leather chair, then none should, including the elite. Unfortunately, while the ideals of the revolution still stood in principle, too many had been forgotten. Those who now led lived a far better life than those they ruled.

Yet it was a necessary evil. Decisions, well thought out, were difficult to make on an empty stomach, or in a chilly room. Lenin, Stalin, and the other members of the Politburo, were guiding a new nation with a sometimes-unwilling populace toward a greater destiny.

And they needed to be comfortable so that one day, they all could be.

He eyed the luxurious chair that sat across from him, behind the great man's desk. Vladimir Ilyich Ulyanov was the man who had made it happen. He had corralled the Bolsheviks into the October Revolution, and now the Tsar and his family were gone, and the people ruled themselves for the first time. Bazarov had been on the streets, fighting alongside the others, and still had the scars to prove it. They were a constant reminder of the price sometimes demanded for a better future.

And the daily pain he suffered was well worth it to see the socialist dream take form.

The door opened and the orchestrator of it all, a man no longer known by his birthname, but by the alias he had given himself decades before, entered. Bazarov rose and bowed, and his friend, for he was his friend, smiled, waving him back into his seat.

"How many times do I have to tell you, that when you bow to me, you make me feel like a tsar, and you know what happened to him."

Bazarov chuckled, returning to his seat. "You honor me by calling me friend."

"Because you are my friend, as I hope I am yours."

Bazarov smiled at his friend as he sat behind the desk, the leather sighing as it embraced him. "You know you are. We've been through too much together for us not to call each other so."

"I'm happy to hear that. Then I have a question for you."

"Anything."

"What are we to do with Comrade Stalin?"

Bazarov's eyebrows rose at the mention of arguably the second most powerful man in the newly minted Union of Soviet Socialist Republics. "Is there a problem?"

"He spoke to my wife on the phone earlier today in a most egregious manner. Downright rude. It is inexcusable!"

Bazarov frowned. His friend's cheeks were red, his eyes aflame with rage at the mistreatment of his spouse. And Bazarov didn't blame him. It was bad form to take one's frustrations out on the partner of another. It *was* inexcusable. "I would demand an apology."

"I plan to, I assure you. I will be writing him a strongly worded letter as soon as you leave." His friend wiped his brow with the back of his hand, wincing before leaning back and closing his eyes.

"Are you all right?" asked Bazarov, concerned. His friend hadn't been well for some time, and many feared he wasn't long for this earth. It would be a shame for this great man to die before he could see his vision achieved.

"My condition continues to ail me, though I believe I have more good days than bad, which is an improvement, I suppose." He pursed his lips and leaned forward, his strength apparently returned. "We must do something about Stalin, especially as a successor for me will likely be needed sooner rather than later."

Bazarov sighed, shaking his head. "My heart aches when I hear you speak like that. I'm sure you have many more years left in you."

His friend chuckled. "You are an optimist. I like that, however one must also be a realist. Should something happen to me, we must be prepared. The country must go on, the experiment must go on, and I fear that should I not be around to rein him in, Comrade Stalin could run roughshod over the Politburo and take control. I never meant for this to be a dictatorship. We were supposed to rule by committee, for the betterment of our people, and eventually, all mankind."

Bazarov leaned closer, perched on the edge of his seat. "What do you have in mind?"

"At the upcoming Congress, I intend to demand Comrade Stalin be stripped of his position as General Secretary of the Party."

Bazarov gulped as his eyes bulged. "But, Comrade Lenin, he'll kill you for sure!"

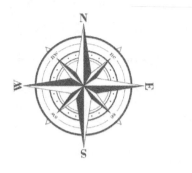

Shokolodnitsa Coffee Shop

Moscow, Russian Federation

Present Day

Volkov's heart fluttered and butterflies filled his stomach at the sight of Katarina Rozhenko stepping into the cafe. He raised a hand and waved at her, then pointed at her favorite tea already sitting across from him. She smiled and he took that as a good sign. It hadn't been an acrimonious breakup, though it hadn't been easy on either of them, he was certain.

As soon as the Stalin archives clerk Morozov had revealed his secret, Volkov had left and texted Katarina, arranging this meeting. It would be the first time they had seen each other since the breakup, and though he desperately wanted to beg her for a second chance, that wasn't why he was here.

Only two people in the world were aware what he was working on, and Professor Orlov was biased. Volkov rose and reached out to hug her, but she instead extended a hand. It broke his heart, but he took it, just that brief contact with her bringing a flood of memories back. She regarded him, concern on her face.

"You look tired."

The mere mention of his fatigue had him yawning. "You have no idea," he said as he indicated for her to sit.

She sat across from him, placing her oversized purse on the seat beside her. "Your message said it was urgent."

"It is. I need your advice about something."

She leaned back and folded her arms. "I'm not sure we have that kind of relationship anymore."

"If that's the way you feel, then why did you come?"

She frowned then leaned forward and wrapped her hands around her cup of tea. "I guess I was concerned. I haven't heard from you in a while, and Irena saw you the other day on the street and said you looked terrible. And now that I see you"—she hesitated—"I see she was right. When was the last time you shaved or had a haircut?" She leaned in and sniffed, lowering her voice drastically. "When was the last time you bathed?"

His cheeks flushed and he stared at his coffee, too ashamed to say anything. No wonder she had left him. He was a wreck. He had been so obsessed in his search for the proof Professor Orlov needed, he had neglected not only her, but himself, his friends, his family—everyone and everything. His eyes burned and he squeezed them shut before the tears flowed. Her cool hand gripped his wrist, and the comfort it provided reminded him of what he had lost. His shoulders heaved at the flood of memories. "I'm so sorry," he said, his voice barely a murmur.

She squeezed his wrist. "It's all right. I forgive you."

He opened his eyes and with a knuckle and the thumb of his free hand wiped them dry. He sniffed and stared up at her. "I never deserved you."

She patted his hand and smirked. "The way you are now, you certainly don't."

He grunted. "No, I suppose I don't deserve anybody."

She frowned. "That's not true at all. Why don't you go home, have a shower and a shave, do a load of laundry that I'm guessing you've been neglecting, then go see the barber." She leaned closer, squeezing his wrist again. "And get some sleep. I've never seen circles under your eyes like that."

He gripped his temples and squeezed, closing his eyes once again. His shoulders slumped. "I'm so exhausted. And you're right about everything. That's exactly what I'm going to do. I can't think straight, and I disgust even myself. But before I do, I really do need your advice."

She leaned back, letting go of his wrist, her arms once again folded defensively. "Fine. What's going on?"

"You know how I've been searching the archives for the proof the professor said he saw years ago when they were first opened?"

"Of course. It's why we're no longer together."

He flashed a weak smile. "Sorry, like I said, I'm not thinking straight."

She lowered her arms and took a sip of her tea then returned the cup to its saucer. "Did you find what you were looking for?"

He shook his head. "No. I went through the entire archive. The documents the professor said he saw aren't there."

Her eyes narrowed. "That's odd. Could he have been mistaken?"

He shrugged. "It's possible. And believe me, I thought worse until I talked to the archive clerk."

Her eyes narrowed further as she leaned in. "Why? What did he say?"

He lowered his voice to barely a whisper. "He said there was another archive."

Her eyes shot wide as she jerked back. "Another archive?" She slapped a hand over her mouth at her outburst then leaned in closer. "What do you mean another archive?"

"According to the clerk, the entire collection of Stalin papers was made public after the collapse of the Soviet Union, but shortly after our president came to power, the archives were shut for a week. The official excuse was upgrading the facility to better preserve the contents, but in reality, a team of researchers came in and went through every box of papers, every film, and took away a couple of dozen boxes. They refused to say what was in them, and he was told not to ask any questions or say anything about what had happened. The archive reopened, and that was the end of it."

"So, the documents that Professor Orlov saw might actually exist and be among those that were taken away?"

"Exactly."

She slumped back, slowly shaking her head. "If that's the case, then you're never going to find them."

He shifted in his seat slightly, then leaned halfway across the table. She leaned in, cheek-to-cheek, the warmth of her breath on his neck sending chills through his body. "The clerk told me where he thinks the files have been taken."

Her quick inhalation suggested fear, excitement, or a little bit of both. "Where?"

"In the basement of the archives. He said at the same time this purge of information was being conducted, a small room in the basement was cleared, a new lock was installed and a sign put up indicating no access was permitted without written authorization from the Presidential Executive Office. He believes this is where they put the documents."

She leaned back and he turned his chin slightly so their cheeks rubbed for a split second, and in that split second, he could have sworn she turned hers toward his, increasing the intimacy of that brief contact he had stolen. "And what do you want to talk to me about? What possible advice could I give?"

"He says if I wanted to, he could get me in the room."

Her eyes bulged. "How? There's no way he has a key."

"He doesn't, but right beside it is a maintenance room that he does have a key for. Apparently, it was added a few years before they moved the files in and shares a drop ceiling with the new file room. He can get me into the maintenance room, and then all I need to do is push the ceiling tiles out of the way and I can climb over and into the archive room. He says no one would ever know."

She paled slightly. "This sounds too dangerous."

"I agree, but if the professor's theory is true, don't you think it's worth it to prove it? It would rewrite history. It just might change people's attitudes about what's going on now in our country. It could save our country."

She stared into his eyes, tears filling hers. "But if they catch you…"

He shrugged. "Then they catch me. I'll just tell them that the professor told me to do it and that my blind loyalty to him compelled me to obey his orders. The leadership is so paranoid, they'd probably believe I was brainwashed."

She eyed him. "And they might not be wrong."

He chuckled. "Perhaps."

She took another sip of her tea, the cup rattling as she returned it to the saucer, betraying her nerves as she squinted at nothing. He waited for her to form her thought. "There's something I think we're forgetting here."

"What's that?"

"Why is the clerk willing to help you?"

He leaned back and scratched at his unkempt beard. "I don't know. I know he didn't seem pleased when he told the story of what had happened. I got the impression he felt the archive should be public, and none of it should be hidden away."

"But can you trust him? Maybe he's setting you up."

"Setting me up for what? It's not like going through the archives is illegal. They're supposed to be public."

"Climbing through the ceiling into a room that requires permission to enter from the President's Office, you don't think that's illegal?"

He chewed his cheek for a moment, tugging at his lengthy beard. "You're right, of course. I guess *that* would be illegal. But wouldn't he get in just as much trouble for letting me into the maintenance room?"

"I'm sure he would unless he's setting you up. What if he's working for them?"

He regarded her. "Who's 'them?' You're talking as if there's some conspiracy here."

"Isn't there? You just told me that they shut down the archive for a week, lied to people about the reason, combed through every page and every film, removed some of it, stored it in a secret room, sealed it shut, then put up a big sign forbidding access without the permission of the President's Office. That doesn't sound like a conspiracy to you? And don't you think they know what you're looking for?"

His eyes narrowed at that statement. "How could they possibly know what I'm looking for?"

She sighed, shaking her head. "You're too close to this. And you're too tired. You need to clean up and get some rest so you can think straight. It should be obvious. You've told him that what you're looking for isn't there. That means that what you're looking for has to be part of the files that were taken away, and whoever did that, knows exactly what was taken away. So, they know you're looking for something that's in those boxes. They might not know specifically, but they know you're looking for something that they don't want you to see, that they don't want the public to see. And if there's anything the past two decades under our president's rule has shown, it's that he's an admirer of Stalin.

Anything that would make the man look truly bad, he would want to hide."

He took a sip of his coffee. "You wouldn't believe some of the stuff I've read. It's truly shocking, eye-opening stuff. If they were trying to hide anything that made him look bad, they did a poor job of it."

She smirked. "I suppose if they truly did remove *everything* that made him look bad, there wouldn't have been much left." She frowned as she leaned forward and lowered her voice. "Which means whatever they did remove must be truly shocking."

"Well, we know what the professor says he found, and if that's not damning, I don't know what is."

"Agreed, but think about it. If they only took out the truly horrible stuff, the truly dangerous stuff, then they don't need to know what you're after specifically. The fact that you're after any of it could see you in prison for the rest of your life."

Weakness swept through his body as the muscles in his face slackened.

She squeezed his hand. "Breathe."

He sucked in a breath, taking several more as he regained control. He exhaled loudly, scratched, then smiled. "I'm all right, thanks."

She nodded at him. "That should be a warning to you. Even your subconscious is telling you this is too dangerous."

"You're still assuming that the clerk is part of a conspiracy. If he were, why would he tell me?"

"To entrap you."

"But why entrap me? What would be the point? I'm nobody."

She let out an exasperated sigh. "You really need to get some sleep. You're not nobody. You're the prized student of a wanted man. They could be trying to get to him through you."

His jaw dropped at the suggestion. Could that be it? Could his activities have been reported and a trap laid? His search had been thorough and exhaustive. It certainly hadn't gone unnoticed by the clerk, and if the clerk were involved, he would realize what he might be looking for, and when his search had failed, that would have been the confirmation. Could they have been playing him the entire time just to get their hands on Orlov?

He stared at her, fear gripping him. "What should I do?"

"You really want my advice?"

He snapped out a nod.

"My advice is to walk away from this, delete all your notes, remove anything that links you to the professor, then pray they don't come asking questions."

Banks of the Moskva River

Russian Soviet Federative Socialist Republic

December 23, 1922

Anatoly Bazarov ambled back to his humble apartment, outside the walls of the Kremlin where the new leadership lived. His mind reeled with the implications of what his friend intended to do. Lenin was mad, and perhaps in his prolonged illness that included two strokes, his mind had been affected. To challenge a madman like Stalin in such a public manner would be suicide.

Unfortunately, Lenin was right in his assessment of the man quickly taking over. Stalin was accumulating too much power, his troika, which excluded Lenin, the founder of everything, essentially ruling the country now. Lenin still had respect, however, and there might still be time for him to bring what would in a week be called the Soviet Union back from the brink of a dictatorship that might prove brutal.

After all, despite his illness, they had named the man leader of the newly formed union.

The question was who would replace Stalin? If his ambitions were checked by Lenin at the Congress in April, and Lenin were to die in the next few years, there could be a power vacuum left that might lead to another civil war. Could the country be torn apart again? Would foreign agitators influence the outcome? Could the communist experiment be destroyed?

He paused, staring at the Moskva River, the edges frozen. Something had to be done to save what they had built. This was the first communist state, the first nation to embrace socialism, and was to be the beacon to the world's masses of what could be achieved by taking power from the elites and giving it to the worker, of what could happen when everyone shared in the labors of others without any one man accumulating more than he deserved. The Soviet Union was the way of the future.

But it had been founded by a madman.

He had been there in Paris with Lenin in exile. Four long years they had spent, waiting for an opportunity to return to their homeland and bring freedom to their people.

And he had been there the night his friend had given in to the temptations of the flesh.

And there when the doctor had given him the diagnosis of syphilis, caught from the prostitute they had both shared.

Bazarov had been spared, but his friend had not. It was a shame that Bazarov had sworn would never be revealed. It was their secret, shared with no one, and his silence had proven his loyalty and trustworthiness over the years.

Unfortunately, he feared his friend's mind was now affected by the progressive disease so well hidden. Lenin had long suffered from multiple ailments, though his doctors always indicated most were from the bullets left over from the assassination attempt in 1918. The attack had left him a shell of his former self, and combined with the disease even his doctors knew nothing of, he was finally succumbing. The very notion that Lenin had years if not decades left was foolish, and they both knew it, and his friend was well aware the words were meant to be the comforting ones of an old friend.

Lenin would die soon, and his legacy couldn't be that of the man who, in his final act, tore down what he had built. He had to be stopped, but in such a way as to preserve his honor, his dignity, and his creation.

The question was, how could he, a lowly servant to the people, save a nation from the man who had founded it?

State Archive of the Russian Federation

Moscow, Russian Federation

Present Day

It had been good advice, sound advice, advice any sane person would take. And perhaps she was right. He wasn't thinking straight. But Volkov had to know if Orlov was right, and he had convinced himself that what he was doing, he was doing as a patriot. Stalin was a figure from the past, from a country that no longer existed, and hadn't in over three decades.

And more importantly, could never be allowed to exist again.

The Russian president had been in power longer than any Soviet leader, and had already set things up so that the only way he was leaving power was if he wanted to, or he was dead.

He was a dictator by every definition.

Finding the proof that Orlov claimed he had seen could at least show to his country that their current leader admired a monster who would stop at nothing for power. It would shatter this revisionist history being foisted upon the populace, where a false memory of the past was romanticized, and the architect of this fallacy made out to be not only a great leader, but the innocent victim of Western slander.

Volkov had left the cafe, promised Katarina he would take her advice, then headed home and broke that promise. He had contacted Orlov, informing him of everything, then taken a long shower, though not before stuffing a load of laundry into the stacked machines at the back of his kitchen. They were a surprise Christmas gift from his parents that had made his life so much simpler, yet apparently not simple enough to bother using it very often over the past few months.

He stared in the mirror, debating whether he should shave, but decided against it. This was how the clerk knew him, and this was the description that would go out if the authorities were after him. He switched out his laundry, checked to see if there was a reply from Orlov—which there wasn't—then was quite certain he was already asleep before his body flopped onto the bed.

He awoke in a panic, face down, enveloped in darkness. It took him a moment to realize he was in his own bedroom, in his own apartment, the blackout curtains doing their job. He stared at his clock. 5:32. He rolled out of bed and turned on the lights. He sat naked at his desk chair and logged into Orlov's secret corner of the Dark Web, sighing in relief at the sight of a message from his mentor. He opened it and his shoulders slumped.

You must do what your conscience tells you.

That was it? It at once disheartened him and pissed him off. What kind of advice was that? The man knew damn well that his conscience was telling him to do what they both thought was the right thing, which was to pursue the truth. And the only way the truth could be pursued was to take the clerk up on his offer, which meant putting his life in danger. This answer either meant Orlov didn't care about his student's life, or felt the truth was more important.

It was why he now stood in the basement of the archive building with the clerk Morozov, whose motivations couldn't possibly be known. He had convinced himself that the truth was indeed more important than his life, and the only way that could be true was if this were a patriotic duty, something he was doing for his country, not for himself, not for a former professor living in exile.

Morozov put the key in the maintenance room door and stared at him over his shoulder. "Are you sure you want to do this? Once you step through this door, there's no turning back."

Of course he wasn't sure, so he sought one last bit of advice from a man he barely knew. "What would you do?"

The old man eyed him for a moment. "Does it matter?"

"Of course it does."

Morozov regarded him. "I'm in the winter of my life. I've seen and done everything I'm going to. Taking risks is something I might have done in my youth, but even then, those were different times. You never experienced communism. You never experienced the Soviet Union, especially during the collapse. It was a life where you kept your head down, minded your own business, and cursed when you woke up the next day, still alive. You youngsters who are always complaining have no idea how good you have it compared to your parents and grandparents.

Take it from someone who lived through it. Anyone who glorifies the past is either ignorant or has an agenda."

Volkov processed the words so similar to those spoken by his mentor, and any doubts as to whether he could trust this man were erased. He drew a deep breath and held it for a moment before exhaling. "That's exactly why I need to do this. I need to help stop those who would rewrite our history into something that it wasn't."

Morozov stared at him. "What do you mean?"

Volkov opened his mouth to explain then thought better of it. "The less you know, the better," he finally said.

Morozov held a level hand to his neck. "I'm in it up to here, my boy. I doubt I can get in any more trouble than I'm already in."

Volkov chuckled. "You'd be surprised." He thrust his chest out, taking another breath, then snapped out a curt nod. "I'm ready."

"Very well." Morozov unlocked the door and pushed it aside, pointing at the ceiling panels. "The room is on the other side of this wall. I know there are no security sensors in this room, but I don't know about the file room. There weren't originally, but they might have put something in after they converted it. If you're lucky, the only sensor is on the door. My guess is you'll know fairly quickly."

Volkov stepped into the room then turned to face the man, finally asking Katarina's question. "Why are you helping me?"

"Like I said, I'm in the winter of my life, and as I watched you so eagerly searching for something that must be of importance, it made me realize I've done nothing with my life. I've never taken a chance. I've never done anything bold. I've been a file clerk my entire life with boxes of papers and shelves filled with administrative history as my only company. I never had the courage to ask a woman for dinner, to join colleagues for drinks after work. I lived with my parents until they died and still live in their same apartment. I've done nothing with my life, and when I'm gone, no one will ever remember me or anything I've done. It's been a life wasted, and now by helping you, perhaps I can die knowing that there was one time in my life where I took a chance and made a difference."

Volkov's chest ached at one of the most depressing stories he had ever heard, and even if the man were to urge him not to proceed, he would. He didn't want to grow old and live out his final years broken, filled with regret at not having done the right thing. He extended a hand and Morozov grasped it, the grip surprisingly firm for someone with no confidence in himself. "Thank you."

"No need to thank me. It should be I who thanks you. Now, remember, this door opens from the inside, so you can get out if you need to, however, I highly recommend you don't do so before six tomorrow morning. There are so few people in the building overnight, you'll be challenged. Mix in with the early risers, and you should be fine. Good luck."

Morozov let go of Volkov's hand then stepped back. Volkov shut the door, and the old clerk's footsteps echoed down the corridor, the door at the far end finally clicking shut, leaving nothing but the hammering of Volkov's heart and the hum of the HVAC system. He fumbled for the light switch he had spotted when he stepped inside and flicked it on, a lone bulb protected by a steel cage on the far wall flooding the small room with light. He checked his watch. He had ten hours to find what he was looking for, and with no idea how many files were on the other side of the cinder block wall, he had to pray it would be enough time. He stared up at the broken and stained ceiling tiles and steeled himself for the task ahead, praying that Morozov was correct and the only sensors were on the door.

For if the man were wrong, then this would be a short venture, and he might never see his own life's winter.

State Archive of the Russian Federation

Moscow, Russian Federation

Mikhail Morozov plodded up and down each aisle of the archive, straightening the occasional box. Few people came here now, not like in the beginning when there was excitement surrounding the declassification of the Stalin files by Boris Yeltsin's administration. Now, it was a smattering of academics and curiosity seekers. It did, however, give him the time to read the archive himself, and it was fascinating.

The sheer volume of the archive was overwhelming at first, though after almost 20 years working here, he had managed to read it all, perhaps even some of the documents taken away. What the young man was after, he wasn't certain, though Volkov's dogged determination suggested there was no doubt in the young man's mind that whatever he was looking for existed.

If it were in the secret archive, then it must be embarrassing somehow to the legacy of Joseph Stalin, one of the most brutal dictators in the history of the world. What had been hidden away likely had little to do with the viciousness the man was capable of. That was well known, though the Kremlin revisionist historians were attempting to deflect blame to subordinates. Yet the world knew the truth, and Russians never feared a strong leader. Whatever had been hidden had to be so embarrassing, so damaging to his legacy, that the current administration couldn't risk it being known by the general public.

Morozov finished his rounds then sat at his desk, lighting a cigarette and taking a long drag. He closed his eyes, enjoying the nicotine hit, though these modern cigarettes weren't what they used to be. He missed those from when he was young, from when the Soviet Union was something to be feared. It had been over 30 years, yet it was even further back than that. The last five or more years under Gorbachev hadn't been the real Soviet Union. He had to think back 40 years to truly recall the glory days.

He had been fortunate, finishing school and getting a job, a solitary one in the bowels of a depressing government building, retrieving files, returning files, all with very little human interaction. He slowly made his way to more important archives but never advanced in status, which was fine by him.

It had arguably saved his career.

When the Soviet Union collapsed, there was a purge, with many losing their jobs and positions. But he was a nobody, just one of the untold minions keeping the state functioning. His total lack of ambition due to his risk-averse way of thinking made him a threat to no one, so he had simply continued to report to work. And when the Stalin archives had been made public, he simply happened to be working here. He continued to do his job, that of a simple clerk with a simple life, a life with few colleagues and no friends.

And no disappointments, no heartbreak, no sorrow, no fears.

He flicked the ash at the end of his cigarette, a deep frown creasing his face.

No wife, no children, no love.

No excitement.

In fact, in his entire life, the only excitement he had experienced, the only time his heart had truly raced from emotion, were the past few weeks. Once a month, he filed a report that listed everyone that visited the archive. Two days after filing his last report, he received a phone call ordering him to report to his supervisor's office. Most people would be nervous, perhaps even terrified, but not him. He did his job and he did it well. He interacted with no one he could possibly offend, and he was past retirement age so didn't fear losing his job. He could leave at any time, but then he'd have nothing to do with himself, and the powers that be seemed uninterested in training a replacement. If he wanted to, he could probably work here until the day he died.

But the meeting hadn't been at all what he expected, for when he stepped through his supervisor's door, he didn't find the rotund administrator behind his desk. He instead found a fit, competent-looking man with a commanding presence. "Mr. Morozov?"

Morozov nodded. "Yes, sir."

The man indicated a chair, and Morozov closed the door then took the seat.

"I'm Deputy Director Alex Nikitin. I work for the President's Office." He held up a file folder. "I reviewed your latest report on those who have been accessing the archive."

Morozov's eyebrows rose slightly. In all his years, he had never once had anyone even mention the report, let alone admit to having reviewed it. "Is there a problem with it, sir?"

Nikitin waved his hand. "Not at all." He opened the file in front of him. "What can you tell me about Dmitri Volkov?"

The mention of the name surprised him. Volkov was a young graduate student of no importance, searching for something in the archives for his professor. He was a nobody. "Not very much, sir. I believe he's a graduate student doing some research for his professor."

"And what's this professor's name?"

Morozov shrugged. "I have no idea. I never asked."

"He's been coming to that archive, twelve hours a day for two months, and you've never asked him any questions?"

"It's none of my business, sir. I answer questions. I don't ask them."

"So, you've never asked him what he's searching for?"

"Only in the context of my job. I asked him if I could help him find anything specific. Other than that, no, I haven't asked."

"And what did he say?"

"He said he couldn't tell me, by order of his professor."

"Have you ever heard of a Professor Orlov?"

Morozov shook his head. "No. Is he Mr. Volkov's professor?"

"He was, but he's now a wanted criminal."

Morozov's eyebrows shot up as he recoiled from the dangerous assertion. "What did he do?"

"He betrayed his country. His actions almost led us to war with Japan."

Morozov's jaw dropped, and perhaps for the first time in his life, his heart pounded. Adrenaline rushed through him as the memories came flooding back about the incident on the high seas. "Is Mr. Volkov involved?"

"We don't know. We don't believe so, though because he's a former associate of the professor, his name has been flagged. When it appeared on your reports, it was brought to my attention. All we want you to do is file a weekly report with my office documenting all of his activities, including when he arrived and when he left, any interactions he might have with other people, what documents he looked at, and any questions he may have asked. Can we count on you for this?"

Morozov gulped. "Yes, sir, I'll do my best."

"Excellent. I'll expect your report by eight each Monday morning." A business card was pushed across the desk. "Use the email address at the bottom. Tell no one what you're doing, including your supervisor and your colleagues."

Morozov shrugged again. "No need to worry there, sir. I rarely speak to anyone."

Nikitin frowned. "You'll have to change that."

Morozov's eyebrows shot up. "Sir?"

"I want you to befriend the young man, engage him in conversation, gain his trust. He might loosen those lips."

The meeting had ended and he returned to his lonely desk, gripping the business card. And at the end of each day, he added to the email that he would send each Sunday night to Deputy Director Alex Nikitin of the Presidential Executive Office. At first, it had felt like a betrayal, but it had also been exciting. If this Professor Orlov were indeed responsible for almost causing a war, then he should be brought to justice. And if he could play some small part in that, he was doing his patriotic duty. After all these years, he was finally doing something outside his comfort zone, something out of the ordinary, something that might actually make a difference.

But today, he had taken a risk and gone out on a limb that just might snap off under him. He wasn't supposed to know about the secret archive. And in fact, he couldn't be positive it was there—it was an educated guess. When his newfound purpose was nearing its end with Volkov's unsuccessful search of the archive, he had informed the young man of the secret files. It was a foolish risk, one that might put him in prison for the rest of his life, or might earn him praise, for the trap had been laid and the prey had taken the bait. The young man had left, weighed his options, then returned willingly.

And now a crime was being committed that had to be reported.

He opened up his email and sent a message to Nikitin explaining what he had done, then turned off the computer and headed home, his entire body shaking from the adrenaline rushing through his veins. Fear, excitement, guilt—a confluence of emotions unlike he had ever felt before threatening to overwhelm him. He stepped past the security station, ignoring those behind the desk as he always did, and pushed open the doors, stepping out into the crisp evening air. He inhaled deeply, steadying his pounding heart, then headed down the steps on his journey home on the Metro, and as his foot cleared the final step, a police siren erupted, splitting the peaceful evening with its shriek.

He spun toward it, startled, his heart racing into overdrive. A jolt shot up his arm and he grabbed at it as his jaw clenched, lightning bolts of pain pulsing through it. And as the terror of what was happening set in, he collapsed to his knees then to the ground, his final thoughts filled not with patriotic fervor, not with satisfaction at having finally taken a risk and done something good with his life, but with the fact he had betrayed the trust of a young man merely searching for information at the behest of his mentor, information about one of the most evil men to have ever walked the face of the earth.

And now, thanks to him, the future of a young man he had entrapped then reported to the state, just like any good Soviet citizen would have done in a past that should have been forgotten, was finished. No, his final emotions, his final thoughts, weren't of the good he had done.

But of the young life he had just destroyed.

Beluga Restaurant

Moscow, Russian Federation

Alex Nikitin sat across from his wife, Tatiana. It was a rare night out for them. In fact, it was the first night out in almost six months. A newborn was to blame for most of it, though their daughter was merely an excuse. His job occupied far too much of his time. Tatiana was younger than him by seven years, the age gap at times an issue, but he had ambitions. Those who could show they were successful and stable required wives, and the more beautiful those wives were, the more virile one appeared.

Tatiana also had ambition. She wanted to be the arm candy of someone powerful, and though he wasn't yet, he was well on his way. Their marriage was mutually beneficial, and despite it sometimes appearing transactional, there was love there.

And she had turned out to be a wonderful mother.

Tonight, they had arranged for their daughter to stay with his parents, and he had cleared his schedule at work, leaving instructions that he was not to be disturbed while he blew half a week's pay on the type of dinner they both hoped would be commonplace in their future.

"I love this place," she said, taking a sip of chardonnay.

He leaned forward and smiled at her. "Oh yeah? What do you love about this place besides your date for the evening?"

She ran her fingers seductively along the tablecloth. "The linens."

He cocked an eyebrow at the unexpected answer. "The linens?" He cast a hand at their surroundings. "All of this, and you're impressed by the tablecloth?"

She leaned back, placing her arms across the back of the booth, revealing the assets that had attracted him to her when they first met. "As much as I like a good Big Mac and fries, there's one thing you can't do at McDonald's with their naked tables."

"And what's that?"

She smiled at him slyly. "This."

He grunted and stared down to see five painted toes in his crotch. His head spun from side to side to make certain no one had noticed, then sighed, a mix of relief and ecstasy, his favorite thing about this restaurant no longer the ambiance, but the low-hanging tablecloth that provided so much discretion. As her foot worked its magic, he gazed about the restaurant, controlling his facial expressions, wondering how many other tablecloths were being taken advantage of. He suppressed a moan, then groaned outright when his phone, sitting on the table to the right of his place setting, vibrated with a flagged message.

"I have to take this."

Her toes went into overdrive. "No, you don't."

He picked up the phone, saw who the message was from, then returned it to the table, leaning back slightly. "You're right, I don't."

An overeager clerk, filing a report early, could wait.

State Archive of the Russian Federation

Moscow, Russian Federation

Volkov sat at the lone chair in the small room, stunned. There were perhaps 20 boxes in the room, all on a single shelving unit lining the opposite wall from where he had made his entry. There were no indications of cameras or motion detectors, and when no alarms had sounded upon making entry, he had begun his search.

And what he had been looking for was in the very first box he grabbed.

He hadn't been there ten minutes, and he had already found exactly what he was seeking, the exact documents Professor Orlov had claimed to have seen in the early days after the archive had been initially opened. Volkov reread the most incriminating piece of evidence when he paused, cocking an ear. A wave of nausea swept through him at the wail of a siren.

They were coming for him.

He bolted to his feet, sending the chair skidding across the floor before it tipped over. He grabbed the pages and stuffed them in a file folder he had brought with him, then returned the box to the shelf. He grabbed the chair and put it back in place, then scanned the room to make certain there was no evidence he had been there, before climbing atop a filing cabinet underneath the ceiling tiles he had moved aside. He hauled himself over the cinder block wall that didn't go all the way to the floor above, and carefully pulled the tile back in place. He dropped down into the maintenance room, replacing the tile there, again, inspecting it. He was supposed to wait here until tomorrow morning, but that plan had been made with the belief it would take him most of the night to find what he was looking for.

Neither he nor Morozov had ever thought he would be successful so soon.

There were still people in the building, and he could perhaps make his escape now and mix with them. And if that siren he had heard were the authorities coming for him, he couldn't be found down here. He stuffed the file folder under his jacket rather than in his bag, as it was more likely to be searched. He zipped up his coat then gripped the door handle. He drew a deep breath in a failed attempt to steady his nerves, then turned the knob and pulled the door open. He poked his head out to make sure the corridor was empty, then flicked the light off inside the small room. He pulled the door closed and hurried toward the far end of the corridor. He opened the door and made his way up the stairwell to the ground floor.

The sirens could be heard plainly now, and with the proof tucked under his jacket that could change even the most fervent Stalin supporter's opinion of the man, a secret so shocking the current president's people had hidden it away from the public, he likely would never be seen again if he were caught.

He again inhaled deeply and again it failed to calm his nerves. He pulled open the door and stepped into another corridor. To his left was the lobby, to his right, he had no clue. He could hear shouts echoing off the marble floors coming from the direction he had to head, but he had no choice—the longer he stayed, the more likely he would be captured. He willed his legs to move and they finally complied.

Somebody came up from behind him, their footfalls heavy and quick. They raced past him as he almost fainted, but they paid him no mind. He opened his eyes that he had squeezed shut involuntarily. It was someone in a security uniform, and if they had ignored him, then something more critical was happening. What that could be, he had no idea, but it didn't matter. Instead, he rushed forward, running toward the lobby with the same urgency as the security guard.

He reached the large, marbled space and skidded to a halt. His eyes swept from left to right, taking in everything. At least a dozen people were there, all clustered against the front doors, staring outside at something. Red and blue lights flashed outside, yet from his vantage point, there was no indication as to what was happening. He glanced over at the security desk to find it abandoned.

This was his chance.

He headed toward the crowd, and as he neared the doors, one of them opened, a police officer entering. Volkov nearly soiled himself.

"Does anyone know who he is?" asked the officer as he stepped inside, the crowd spread across the multiple doors now encircling the man.

Volkov made a beeline for the exit on the left now that no one was in front of it.

"I think he's the senior clerk for the Stalin Archives," said someone.

Volkov forced himself forward at the shocking revelation. Could they be referring to Morozov? He pushed open the door and stepped out into the brisk evening. A police car and an ambulance were there, the source of the flashing lights and the sirens that had him in such a panic. They weren't there for him at all—they were there for the man who had helped him.

He descended the steps and his chest ached at the sight of Morozov on a stretcher being loaded into the back of the ambulance.

"Do you want an escort?" asked one of the police officers.

The paramedic shook his head as he closed the doors. "No, he's already dead. It'll be officially declared by a doctor at the hospital."

"How did he die?"

The paramedic shrugged. "No idea. Probably a massive heart attack."

Volkov continued to walk away from the scene, the conversation fading as he headed for the Metro. He reached the sidewalk as four unmarked black SUVs, emergency lights integrated into their front grills flashing, sped past him, screeching to a halt in front of the building he had just left. He glanced over his shoulder to see a dozen men in suits

47

swarm out. He directed his eyes forward, away from the new arrivals, and fought the temptation to sprint from the scene. Those men were agents, likely federal agents, and he had no doubt they weren't there for an old man having a heart attack.

They were there for him.

He rounded the corner but held his pace until he was out of sight of the building, then collapsed against a streetlight, squeezing his eyes shut as his heart hammered. He wasn't sure what to do. The government knew what he had done. The question was whether they knew *he* had done it. Was there an alarm he hadn't seen and they were responding to that, or had he been betrayed by Morozov, just as Katarina had feared he might be? Had Morozov died on those steps racked with guilt over turning him in, or had he died from the excitement of turning him in.

Or perhaps it was none of the above, and the man had simply died because it was his time and was innocent in all this. That part of the truth would have to wait, and it might be something that would never be answered. Right now, he had the proof tucked inside his jacket of what Orlov had told him, and it was something the world needed to be made aware of, especially his country, especially those who would worship a leader who aspired to be the revised version of the Soviet Union's most brutal dictator.

If those agents didn't know who he was, they soon would. There were cameras in the lobby he had just crossed, and his name was on the sign-in sheet every single day for three months. It meant he couldn't go home. There could be agents already there waiting for him, and even if there weren't, there would be in short order. He had planned for not going home, but not much beyond that.

Yet this was no place to plan his next move.

He pushed off the streetlight then continued toward the metro station, uncertain as to where he was going, though quite certain he had gone beyond the point of no return.

State Archive of the Russian Federation
Moscow, Russian Federation

Nikitin pulled up to the scene, struggling to control his rage. His wife's inappropriate ministrations had been a delight, the release he needed to enjoy the evening free of the stress building from the job. But when he had brought up the ignored message, the dinner had ended abruptly.

Morozov had overstepped his authority.

The entire operation was designed to catch Orlov. The official record on the man indicated the professor's interest in Stalin, yet in the years he had been missing, his former graduate student had never shown the slightest. Yet suddenly, for three straight months, he was at the archive from dusk to dawn. It had to mean contact had been made. The question was, what was he looking for? Nikitin had no idea what was in the secret room in the basement of the archive. All he knew was that it was strictly forbidden, and for Morozov to have left the young man inside, it had turned what had been a manhunt for a traitor who had escaped justice, into a national security issue.

He had immediately called in a team to secure the area before making his apologies to his wife who was none too pleased with his sudden departure. And now he was here, ten minutes later than he should have been, and those precious minutes could be all that was needed for Volkov to escape with whatever information he might have found. If they were lucky, he was still in the room searching.

They would know shortly.

He spotted an ambulance, its lights flashing, and he strode toward it with the idea that security might have already caught Volkov in the act. A sheet covered the patient's face and he frowned. They needed Volkov for questioning, and if he had been shot attempting to escape, that would be most unfortunate.

He hailed two of his men questioning the paramedics. "What do we have here?"

"Apparently, one of the employees had a heart attack just over there on the steps," replied Agent Ilya Zaitsev, a man he had worked with for years.

Nikitin glanced over to where Zaitsev's thumb had jerked. "Name?"

"Mikhail Morozov. He was apparently a senior clerk for the Stalin Archive."

Nikitin's shoulders slumped at the revelation, despite the man being a source of information that was no longer useful. Whatever Volkov was up to, this would be the last day he ever came into contact with Morozov, making the dead man useless regardless. Nikitin did, however, feel some guilt. This was an old man, and the stress and the excitement of what he had been put through likely had proven too much for a weak heart.

He was dead in part because of Nikitin's ambition. He was desperate to capture Orlov because he was fully aware the president wanted the man in prison. Catching him would be a feather in his cap that could mean a promotion, and certainly would curry favor with his country's leader.

Yet he shouldn't feel guilty. What had likely killed the man was his own actions taken tonight. Helping Volkov gain access to the secret archive was never part of the plan. The contents of the email Morozov had sent only minutes before his death revealed it was his own idea, and he thought it would allow them to identify what the young man was searching for, and by arresting him in the act, they would have the leverage to use against Orlov.

The unfortunate thing was that Morozov was probably right, but it was a plan that needed to be approved by someone far up the chain in the President's Office, not by a lowly clerk who had been recruited to simply provide reports.

Nikitin stepped into the ambulance and flipped the sheet aside, confirming it was indeed the man he had met only once. He said a silent prayer for him and stepped back down.

One of the paramedics standing impatiently nearby approached. "Can we go now? This was the last call of our shift and we don't get paid overtime."

Nikitin flicked his wrist at the ambulance and the body it contained. "Take him." He indicated Zaitsev. "But tell him where you're going. Somebody will be by later. And make sure nobody touches the body."

He headed for the main entrance and a man, perhaps in his fifties, approached.

"Are you in charge?"

Nikitin nodded. "Yes." He didn't bother providing his name, he simply flashed his ID. "And you are?"

"Director Pasternak. I'm the most senior person still in the building. Can I ask why we're being detained?"

"No, you may not."

Pasternak appeared taken aback, apparently unaccustomed to someone twenty years his junior not answering his questions. He gathered himself and phrased his response carefully, no doubt aware who Nikitin's office ultimately reported to. "We're happy to help in any way. I just need to be able to tell my people something. It's a Friday night, and they have families, they have plans. How long do you think they'll be detained?"

Nikitin thought of his own waylaid plans for a moment and felt no sympathy. He glanced at the several dozen men and women of varying ages, some angry, some scared, some tired, and he put himself in their position for a moment. A coworker had just died, it was the end of what was likely a hard, thankless week, and even if their delayed or canceled plans were merely to relax in front of the television alone, they were still plans. He softened slightly. "Tell them we'll have them out of here as quickly as possible. And figure out who here worked with or knew the man who just died. Also, identify any of them that has access to the basement or the Stalin Archive. That will help expedite things for when I return."

Pasternak snapped out a curt nod. "I'll see to it personally. Thank you."

Nikitin turned to one of his men. "How do we get to the basement?"

The man pointed to their left. "There's a stairwell over here, sir."

He followed his men down the corridor and into the stairwell as Zaitsev joined them. "Have we received the entry code yet?"

Zaitsev shook his head. "No, and we're not going to. They're sending somebody."

Nikitin cursed. He pushed through the doors at the base of the stairs then headed swiftly toward a door at the far end of the hallway, two of his men flanking it. "Did you hear anything inside?"

Both shook their heads, the more senior one replying. "No, sir. Nothing."

One of the building staff stood next to another door, holding it open with his foot.

"Is this the maintenance room that was used to gain access?" Nikitin asked.

"Yes, sir. It's clear. No indication he was in there, but without sweeping it for prints, there's no way to truly say."

Nikitin pointed at the ceiling tiles. "Did you look over the wall?"

Both men rapidly shook their heads. The senior man pointed at the sign indicating access was forbidden by order of the Presidential Executive Office. "There's no way in hell I'm looking in there without permission from the man himself."

Nikitin frowned but understood. In today's Russia, you didn't do anything that went against the president's orders. You could find yourself demoted, without a job, jailed, or worse. He pulled out his phone and dialed the number at the bottom of the sign, a cranky switchboard operator answering on the third ring.

"President's Office. What do you want?"

"This is Deputy Director Nikitin of the Investigations Branch of the Presidential Executive Office. I need a door unlocked and I need it unlocked now."

"Yeah, yeah, one of your people already called here. Someone's on their way. You'll have to wait for them to arrive."

Nikitin could sense the woman was about to end the call. "Hang up on me and I'll put your entire life under my microscope." The line remained connected, but the woman said nothing. "On the other side of the door I need opened, there could be a man actively reading classified files. The longer he remains behind that door, the more classified information he's exposed to. He could be taking photos of the files and transmitting them to a third party as you and I waste time talking. The longer he's allowed to do that, the longer Russia's secrets are exposed to the world, and these are secrets important enough to require permission from the President's Office to even access the room they're in. Do you think the president wants that information exposed? This is an emergency situation, and we need immediate access!"

"I'm sorry, sir. I'm only following procedure. The procedure is if someone wants access to that room, they have to be personally escorted by someone from the President's Office. All I could do was call the number the system indicates for me to call and leave a message there telling them that you needed access."

Nikitin's grip on the phone tightened as rage built. "Are you telling me that you left a message? You mean you didn't speak to anybody personally? You mean we're waiting here for someone who might not even be coming until Monday morning?"

Her voice trembled with the realization she had been dismissive to the wrong person. "Y-yes, sir."

Nikitin slammed the bottom of his fist against the door he needed to get through, growling in rage. "Forget about saving your job. That's done. Now you need to worry about whether you have a life on Monday morning. You have one chance to get yourself out from under the microscope. You are going to do everything it takes to get my door opened. You have my number?"

"Yes, sir, it's on the system."

"Then you call me back with the code or someone who can give me the code."

"Yes, sir."

He ended the call and stared at the others, dumbfounded. "She left a message. Can you believe that? There's nobody on their way!"

Zaitsev frowned. "Do we even know if he's inside?"

"No." Nikitin stared at the ceiling tiles of the still open maintenance room. All it would take would be one quick look, but that quick look could end his career, yet it could also propel it forward. He stared at Zaitsev, debating what to do.

"I'll do it," said the man, stepping forward.

Nikitin shook his head. "No. If anyone's doing it, I am. If he's inside, he's not getting away with anything, but he could be transmitting what he's finding. If he's not in there, then we're wasting time. We have to know." He pointed at two of his men. "Record everything I do." Both men pulled out their phones, holding them up. He entered the maintenance room and grabbed a step ladder, climbing it far enough to move aside the ceiling tiles. Footfalls echoed in the corridor.

"Where's Deputy Director Nikitin?" echoed someone's voice behind him.

"I'm in here. What is it?"

"I found him on the cameras. He walked through the lobby and left the building just after the old man had his heart attack."

Nikitin retreated from the ladder and stepped into the hallway. "Show me." The man handed him a tablet and tapped on the screen. Video footage from one of the lobby cameras played, showing their subject Volkov crossing the lobby as everyone was gathered at the doors, then leaving the building.

"All right, he's not here. I want two men on the door. When the representative from the President's Office arrives, contact me, but only he enters that room. I don't want any of you setting foot inside. I don't want anybody even *looking* inside. This is a room that's not supposed to exist." Nikitin pointed at the ceiling tile he had moved aside as he turned to the maintenance worker. "Put that back in place, then lock this door."

"At once, sir." The man set about the task as Nikitin marched toward the stairwell.

"I want a net thrown across this city. I want everyone on the lookout for him. This is a national security matter now, and we need to find him fast. Morozov said he would be in that room until tomorrow morning when the day shift arrived for work. If he left so quickly, it means he found what he was looking for. We need to find him before he can get those documents into the hands of others."

"But wouldn't he have already transmitted it?" asked Zaitsev.

"He may have, but images are just that, and they can be manipulated and their validity denied. Original documents? That's a lot harder to fake."

He rushed up the stairs, eager to get on with the investigation. Until this point, Volkov had committed no crime, but now he had, and it was a serious one. This was something that could land him in prison for a long time, and if Nikitin's team could find the young man, it could propel his career forward.

But he had to catch him first.

Outside Katarina Rozhenko Residence

Moscow, Russian Federation

Volkov stood across from Katarina's apartment building, his heart racing, sweat beaded on his forehead, his back drenched. He had never been more terrified. His biggest fear the entire way here was that the documents might slip out from under his jacket, spilling their contents onto the subway floor for all to see. He had managed to transfer them to his bag, and now gripped it tight to his chest. He needed to scan everything and send them to Orlov, or at a minimum, take a photo of each page and send them. But he didn't know how to use the phone with the new browser that was on his laptop. He needed to find some place secluded, away from prying eyes and CCTV cameras, but he had no doubt the authorities would be at his apartment, and anyone he was close to could soon be under observation.

Though only if they knew about them.

His family and coworkers at the university were out of the question, but they would have no way of knowing about Katarina. He rushed across the street, his stomach churning with the guilt of involving her further, but the fact was, she was already involved. She had installed the browser, she had shown him how to use it, she was aware of what he was seeking.

He entered the lobby and pressed the buzzer for her apartment.

"Who is it?"

"It's me."

"Dmitri? You really shouldn't be here."

"I need your help."

"You didn't do anything foolish, did you?"

He glanced around. "Whatever I did do shouldn't be discussed on an open speaker."

She muttered a curse then the buzzer sounded. He yanked the door open then crossed the familiar lobby, pressing the button for the elevators, and moments later was knocking at her door. It opened and she beckoned him inside, closing it then locking it.

"Please tell me you didn't go in that room." One look at him and she knew the answer. "You did, didn't you?"

He nodded.

Her jaw dropped. "And you're already here." Her eyes shot wide as she leaned closer to him, lowering her voice. "You found it, didn't you?"

He smiled, unzipping his bag and pulling out the folder. "It was in the first box. I don't think I was in there fifteen minutes."

She led him into the living area and sat on the couch, curling up a leg underneath her as she turned to face him. He sat in his customary spot, opening up the file folder.

"Weren't you supposed to wait until tomorrow morning to leave?"

"I was, but I heard sirens. I thought they were coming for me so I figured I should try to escape."

She paled slightly. "Are they after you?"

He shrugged. "Probably, but that's not why there were sirens. Morozov is dead."

Katarina gasped as she jerked away from him, her hand darting to her mouth. "Did they kill him?"

"No, I think he had a heart attack as he was leaving the building."

She frowned as her head slowly bobbed. "Well, he was old. Maybe the excitement of all this was simply too much for him."

"It could be, but none of that matters right now." He tapped the file folder. "I found it. Everything that the professor said would be there."

"Can I see it?"

"Are you sure you want to?"

She chewed her lip. "Part of me wants to, part of me doesn't."

He grunted. "I know what you mean. Before, I wanted to find it, but I never really thought it was real. Now that I know it is, I'm kind of terrified, if I'm being honest."

"What are you going to do now?"

"I have to get copies of these to the professor right away."

"And you came here for that?"

"You have a scanner. You can make the copies faster and better than I can with just my phone and laptop."

"You've got a scanner at your apartment."

"Yes, but I can't go back there."

She was about to ask why when she stopped herself. "No, I guess you can't." Her eyes bulged. "What if they track you here?"

"Just tell them I asked you if I could use your scanner, you said yes, then left the room because you weren't happy I was here." He pointed toward her corner desk. "May I?"

Her eyes darted toward her set-up, and it was a moment before she finally nodded. "Go ahead."

He retrieved his laptop and plugged the scanner into it, then began the process, setting each completed page aside. She rose from the couch, apparently unable to resist her curiosity, and went through each scanned page, her mouth widening with each one.

"This is unbelievable," she whispered. "I always thought your professor was playing a game with you, one he had taken too far. Are we sure these are genuine?"

"If they were fake, why would they hide them?"

"Yeah, I guess that wouldn't make sense." She continued reading. "Anyone who worships at the altar of Stalin would kill to make sure nobody ever saw these."

"That's what I'm worried about." He cursed. "I never should have come here."

She placed a hand on the back of his neck and gently squeezed several times. His head slumped forward and he had to suppress his moan of ecstasy. He missed her touch. He missed her caring about him. He was so tense, so scared, that if it were anyone else touching him, he probably would have jumped from his chair.

He still loved her, loved her desperately.

"Back to work," she whispered.

"Sorry." He resumed scanning, wishing he didn't have to, for it meant her soft touch was about to end, but instead, to his delight, she took both his shoulders in her hands and kneaded them, her thumbs pressing into his neck. This time he moaned, but continued scanning.

"You have no idea how much I needed that."

She chuckled. "I'm glad you took my advice and cleaned yourself up." She leaned forward and tugged at his beard. "Planning on keeping this?"

"Why, do you like it?"

"Hell no." She returned to working on his shoulders. "I can't imagine kissing a man with a scruffy beard like that."

His heart leaped at her words, and he chastised himself for reading too much into what was likely an innocent comment. "I kept it for the cameras," he explained as he placed the last page on the scanner. "My plan was to shave it as soon as I got the information out. If the police put out a description, they'll be looking for a bearded man, and I'll be clean-shaven."

"Good thinking."

The scanner completed its cycle. He launched the browser and her massage stopped.

"Zip them first. It'll take less time to upload if you compress them."

"Of course." He selected all the files then right-clicked and sent them to a new compressed folder. The computer indicated it would take almost ten minutes to zip all the files, and Katarina released his shoulders, much to his disappointment.

"Why don't you go shave that thing off while you're waiting."

He tugged at the beard he had become accustomed to. "Yeah, I suppose you're right." He grabbed his bag and headed for the bathroom, the necessary supplies already inside. Katarina squeezed into the small room with him, staring at him in the mirror.

"Can I watch?"

He grinned. "Kinky."

She smacked his ass, which just made things worse. "Don't get any ideas. I've just never seen a man shave a beard like that off before. Are there any tricks?"

He shrugged. "I have no idea. I've never done it before. In fact, I didn't even know I could grow a beard until this whole thing started." He pulled out his electric razor and clicked it on, the tiny machine buzzing happily as he stared at it.

Katarina shook her head. "There's no way you can shave a beard off with that thing. You need clippers or scissors to get it short enough before you can use that."

"I don't have time for scissors. Do you have clippers?"

She shook her head. "No." Her eyes shot wide. "Wait a moment." She darted from the bathroom with no explanation. He pulled open one of the familiar drawers and retrieved a pair of scissors she kept there. He hacked at the beard. There was no time for whatever she wanted him to wait for. As soon as the files were transmitted, he was out of here, though he had no idea where he should go. He should have planned for this. Orlov should have planned for this. The only way a plan wouldn't have been needed was if he were to fail in finding the documents Orlov claimed existed.

So why had there never been talk of what would happen if he found them?

He sighed as he continued to trim the beard.

Because they were supposed to be in the public archive, you idiot.

There never was supposed to be a need to steal the documents. They were supposed to be public. Instead, he had stolen classified documents and was now a criminal. If they weren't after him yet, they soon would be, and this was Russia, and his crime involved the president.

He stared in the mirror, his hands frozen in mid-cut. "What am I going to do?"

"You're going to use these," said Katarina as she rejoined him. She handed him a pair of clippers.

"Where did you get these?"

"My neighbor. She's a stylist."

He flicked on the clippers and made quick work of the lengthy beard before switching to a blade to complete the job. He was soon finished and stared at the stranger in the mirror. Katarina leaned over his shoulder and gripped his chin between her thumb and forefinger as she stared at him in the mirror.

"There's the handsome man I fell in love with."

He smiled at her and his eyes glistened, but he said nothing, instead merely giving her a weak smile. He stared down at the mess and she patted his shoulder. "Don't worry, I'll take care of it. You go check on the computer."

"Thanks." He headed back to the desk and found the file compression had completed. He opened up the Tor browser, then selected the bookmark for the site he and Orlov used to communicate. He logged in then sent a message.

I found what we're looking for.

He clicked an icon on the left of his screen that would allow him to upload the large file. He selected it from his hard drive then clicked to upload it. He cursed at the two-hour estimate then breathed a sigh of relief as it bounced up and down between five minutes and 15, Katarina's Internet connection never very steady. There was a beep indicating a message had arrived.

You need to send me copies right away.

He clicked reply.

I'm uploading them now. You should have them in the next 10 minutes. I think they know the files are missing, and I think they know I'm the one who took them.

Why?

The clerk who helped me had a heart attack on the steps as he was leaving the building. I left as soon as I heard the sirens because I thought they were coming for me, but as I left, four vehicles with men in suits arrived. I don't think they were there for a heart attack.

I agree. Where are you now?

I'm at my ex-girlfriend's sending you the files. I'll be leaving as soon as I'm done.

She's now in danger. They'll assume she's seen the documents. She has to leave with you.

Volkov gulped, glancing toward the bathroom. Orlov was right. The idea of pleading ignorance wouldn't work, or at least couldn't be relied upon.

I'll let her know, but where should we go?

Does Yegor's sister still work at that hotel?

Volkov's eyes shot wide. Yegor was a fellow grad student. His sister, Alina, was the night manager at a mid-range hotel—or at least she had been the last time it was a topic of conversation. Unfortunately, like most people in his life, Yegor had been ignored for the past three months, and his sister probably hadn't been spoken of in twice that.

I believe so.

Then find out if she can get you into a room without either of your names being on the register.

His heart hammered. With each passing moment, the hole in which he found himself was getting deeper, and he could see no way out. Hiding in a hotel room under someone else's name he assumed was a crime, though nothing compared to the theft of state secrets. He cursed at himself for not having thought this through, and he cursed Orlov for not having been a source for sober second thought. He was supposed to be his mentor.

You must do what your conscience tells you.

It was bullshit advice. As soon as Orlov had been made aware that the documents had to be stolen rather than simply found, he should have immediately called everything off, at least until they could come up with a better plan. What that plan might have been that didn't involve him fleeing the country he called home, he had no clue.

Orlov had clearly changed in the years since he was missing. Perhaps living in exile, afraid for your life, did that to a person. But to essentially encourage him to commit treason wasn't right. If he were still the man he once knew, Orlov would never have left the choice up to his student.

His primary concern should have been for the safety of those for whom he was responsible.

But it was too late for that now. Assignment of blame wasn't the priority—his and Katarina's safety was. He tapped at the keyboard.

I'll try. Do you have the files yet?

I'm downloading it now. I should have it in a few minutes. As soon as I've confirmed I've received them, I'll send you a message. I want you to delete everything related to this once I've confirmed I have them.

Understood.

He hopped onto Facebook and sent a private message to Alina, and she replied immediately.

Dmitri! I haven't heard from you in months. How have you been?

I'll explain everything when I see you. Are you still working at that hotel?

Yes, actually, I'm working now.

I need a room with two beds.

He deleted the last three words.

It can't be under my name, and if at all possible, it needs to be kept off the books. It's really important. Can you help me?

There was a pause, the three pulsing dots indicating a message was being typed, disappeared and reappeared, suggesting a debate was happening at the other end. Finally, a reply came through.

Are you in trouble?

His shoulders slumped. He had to tell her the truth. He couldn't put someone else in danger without at least giving them a choice.

Yes. It involves Professor Orlov. I think the police might be after me and I accidentally got Katarina involved. We just need someplace to hide until we figure out what to do.

The people who are after you. Moscow police or state?

He smiled slightly at the question as he recalled something he had forgotten. Alina hated the current leadership. She had been tear-gassed several times at protests and apparently arrested on multiple occasions. Her parents were activists, though her brother could never be described as such. He replied back.

State. Probably the President's Office itself.

A smiley face emoji returned.

I can help you. Just make sure you both get rid of your phones and any other devices that can be tracked.

He eyed his phone sitting on the desk, charging, and paled. He reached over and turned it off, then replied.

Understood, we'll be there in less than half an hour.

Come to the back entrance. I'll be waiting for you in 30 minutes.

He sent a thumbs-up then deleted the conversation as Katarina emerged from the bathroom.

"I can't believe how much hair was on your face." Her smile disappeared as she noticed his serious expression. "What's wrong? Did you hear from the professor?"

He nodded. "He's downloading the files now. But we've got a bigger problem. We need to go into hiding immediately."

"We?"

"Yes. He thinks that because I came here, you're no longer safe."

She collapsed onto the back of the couch, her arms dangling loosely between her legs. "Can't I just deny knowing why you were here?"

"No, it's too big a secret. They won't risk anyone knowing it."

"Then what *are* we going to do?"

"You know my friend Yegor?"

She bit her lip for a moment. "The mousy one with the tattooed-up sister?"

He chuckled. "Yes. Alina works at a hotel nearby. She's the night manager. She's agreed to give us a room under false names."

Katarina regarded him. "Why would she agree to help us? Doesn't she know she's putting herself in danger, or are you doing to her what you just did to me?"

His heart ached and his face sagged at the completely accurate assessment of what he had done by coming here. She rose and stepped forward, then took a knee in front of him, clasping his hands.

"I'm sorry, I shouldn't have said that. It wasn't fair. I don't blame you for coming here, but from now on, we have to be careful who we involve."

He wiped a tear away that threatened to escape. "I told her who I thought was after us, and she still wants to help. She hates the president. It could buy us time to figure out what to do."

Katarina rose. "What *are* we going to do?"

He shrugged. "I think the only safe place for us now is out of the country."

"How the hell are we going to get out of the country?"

The laptop beeped with a message from Orlov.

Download complete.

Volkov immediately replied.

Accommodations arranged. Heading there now, will not have our phones.

Understood. Contact me when you can. Good luck.

He logged off then glanced at Katarina. "I'm going to delete everything from the laptop. Pack a bag with the essentials."

"How many days do you think?"

He shrugged again. "If it's more than three, my guess is the prison will be issuing us whatever we need."

She gave him a look, not amused. "What about you?"

He pointed at his bag already packed with toiletries and a change of clothes. "I already knew I was never going home."

She disappeared into her bedroom and he set to work, eliminating everything from his laptop, wondering if any of this was necessary. There was a slim chance they had no idea the documents were missing and that he was involved.

Not bloody likely.

State Archive of the Russian Federation

Moscow, Russian Federation

Nikitin snapped his fingers, pointing at the screen. "That's him! Dmitri Volkov. He's the one on our watchlist. He's a former graduate student of Professor Orlov."

Zaitsev pointed. "Look how he's holding his left arm. It's like he's trying to keep something hidden under his jacket."

Nikitin cursed. "He'd only be hiding something if it came from the secret archive. We need to find him before he has a chance to pass those documents on to someone else."

"Orlov?"

"If his intention is to get the files into the professor's hands, I don't know how they think they're going to do it. Our intel indicates Orlov hasn't been in the country since his escape from prison."

"Could he be coming here? Would he take the risk?"

Nikitin scratched his chin. "It's a possibility. A foolish one. Get Volkov's image to the airports and borders, and get our people tracking him. There are enough cameras in this area, we might be able to find out where he went. There's no way he's going home, not if he found something." He headed for the door. "We need more personnel on this. I'm going to get approval to widen the net and get his face on the newscasts."

"Maybe we should offer a reward," suggested Zaitsev. "This is just a student. I can't see him having anybody helping him beyond friends. Offer them ten million rubles and they might question that friendship."

Nikitin smiled slightly. "I like the way you think." He headed down the corridor from the security office toward the lobby, his fingers flying furiously over his phone as he sent multiple messages. His pulse raced with excitement with the possible confirmation that documents had indeed been stolen from the classified archive, as it meant he hadn't been wasting his time.

He paused just before entering the lobby as a thought occurred to him. Whatever was stolen was something the president didn't want seen by anyone. It meant failure wasn't an option. He had to retrieve those files before it was too late, otherwise *he* might be occupying a prison cell rather than Volkov.

A wave of nausea swept through him when his phone vibrated with a message. He brought it up and smiled.

Public release of suspect's information approved, reward approved. Release must be vetted by President's Office first.

The nausea was gone, replaced with the possibilities for his career should he be successful. This was about to become the highest-profile case in Russia, with the top echelon of the leadership, including the man himself, following his every move. If he failed, it could be the end of his career or worse.

But if he succeeded, the sky was the limit.

Gorki Estate

South of Moscow, Russian Soviet Federative Socialist Republic

December 29, 1922

Bazarov removed his glasses, his head slowly shaking as he looked up at his friend, sitting behind his desk, appearing more full of life than he had seen in months. Bazarov shook the pages he had just read. "Brilliant!"

"You think?"

"Absolutely. You know I would never lie to you, however..."

Lenin leaned forward. "However?"

"These are dangerous words. They could cause chaos. At a minimum they will cause great controversy. There could be consequences. Severe consequences."

Lenin tossed one arm up, the other still affected from his stroke. "Good! It's meant to have consequences. Comrade Stalin must be removed from his position as General Secretary of the Communist Party. If he is not, he will continue to gain power, and eventually even I won't be able to stop him from taking complete control. And that man"—he

75

stabbed a finger toward Moscow—"is a madman. If he leads this country after I die, millions will suffer for it. Mark my words, if Stalin takes over, it will be a dark day for our people."

Bazarov had no doubt, though a darker day would be the civil war that could result if these words were made public. He was torn as to what to do. Everything his friend was saying was true, yet in the back of his mind, he had to wonder if the actions the man was taking were affected by his illness. Was Lenin himself mad? It was possible, yet the words written were eloquent, well thought out, though blistering.

"And I'm writing more! I'm going to point out all their flaws. Each and every one of them. If they see them written down, if they hear them read to the Congress, they might take a step back for some self-examination and come out the other end better men, better able to lead us into the future."

Bazarov paled slightly. "All of them?"

Lenin slammed his fist on the desk. "All of them! Even that bastard Trotsky, despite the fact I'm going to recommend he take over from Stalin. At least Trotsky is an intellectual. He understands what it takes to run a country. Stalin is a brute who thinks only power and violence accomplishes anything."

Trotsky!

It would never have occurred to him that Trotsky would be Lenin's named successor, though no name had come to mind since he had been thinking about this problem. Trotsky was a great man, but he didn't have Stalin's support in any way, which would mean those who supported

Lenin's rival would never support his named successor, even in the unlikely event Stalin were to recede quietly into the night.

"Do you think he could control the Troika?"

"Forget the Troika! It should be disbanded, or at least expanded, so the power is shared between more than just three men. The Politburo needs to be the ultimate holder of power so that no one man can control the country."

"Aren't most countries controlled by one man?"

"Monarchs, dictators, and elected men."

"And those are all equally repugnant to you?"

Lenin chuckled. "This is why I like you. You always ask questions and rarely give opinions. You draw out of me what I don't even realize I'm thinking. Yes, they are all equally repugnant. No one man, elected or ordained, should have sway over men. You need a group of men who debate the issues then come to a consensus on what is best for those they manage the country on behalf of. Only then can the collective good be the driving force, not the blind ambition of one man."

"Like Stalin?"

Lenin nodded firmly. "Like Stalin."

Bazarov shook the pages. "And you think this is the way to prevent our glorious nation from falling into the hands of another ambitious man?"

"I do, but not that alone. I have five months to finish my final testament, to lay out my vision for our grand experiment, that will guide not only our nation into the future, but all the workers of the world who have for too long been trodden upon by those who care not for their fellow man, but only for the accumulation of wealth and power."

"It could be the death of you."

Lenin smiled at him. "Better to die on my feet saving what I have built, than in a bed, a crippled man with no tongue to speak and no brain to think. This will be my final gift to my people, and to the Communist Party. The words to save them, and create the workers' paradise we have envisioned for so long."

Bazarov rose, beaming at his reinvigorated friend. "And I shall be at your disposal to make certain your gift is delivered to what I am certain will be a grateful nation."

Lenin rose and they shook hands. "I know I can always count on you, my friend. Now leave me. I have much work to do."

Bazarov bowed, apologized yet again for the gesture, then left his friend's *dacha*, strolling slowly down the hall toward his carriage that awaited him outside. A portrait hung at the end of the hall showing the members of the original Politburo, and his eyes settled on one of the men.

Joseph Stalin.

He was a fearsome man, and that fear commanded respect. He would stop at nothing to get what he wanted, and what he wanted was a strong Soviet Union, a country that could stand on its own two feet without fearing interference from those nation-states that disagreed with the socialist dream they were fighting to create.

The man who just might be the leader they so desperately needed after his friend was gone.

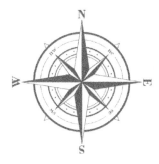

The Old Shades Pub

London, England

Present Day

Interpol Agent Hugh Reading leaned back, spreading his arms across the booth behind him. "We don't do this nearly enough."

Archaeology Professor Laura Palmer nodded in agreement. "Then you should move to the States with us."

Her husband, Archaeology Professor James Acton, hoisted a beer in agreement. "Sounds like a great idea. Why don't you quit your job and move in with us?"

Reading's eyebrows shot up. "If I recall correctly, that house of yours is barely big enough for the two of you. And you don't have any spare bedrooms that aren't being used."

Acton eyed his friend. "Bedroom? I was thinking I'd move the weight bench in the basement, set you up with a cot there."

Laura giggled. "James, you're terrible."

"Yet you still married me."

"I warned you," said Reading.

Laura wagged a finger at him. "Oh, no, you didn't. You were so excited about our wedding you were like a schoolgirl."

Reading's cheeks flushed, though he leaped to his own defense, raising a finger and jabbing it at her. "School*boy* maybe. Definitely not schoolgirl. There's no need to exaggerate here."

Acton roared with laughter. "All kidding aside, you're right. We do need to do this more often. But with all of us gainfully employed, it makes it difficult."

Reading shook his head. "I don't understand it. With the money you two have, you don't need to work a day for the rest of your lives."

"But we love what we do," protested Laura. "The work I do at the Smithsonian is fascinating. We still have our digs in Peru and Egypt. James loves teaching the students, I love giving my guest lectures. I don't think either of us could give that up."

Acton agreed. "Life wouldn't be worth living if I didn't have my students."

Reading regarded both of them for a moment. "If you had to spend the rest of your life doing one thing, which one would it be? In the classroom with your students, or at a dig site with your students?"

"Dig site," echoed both of them.

Acton grinned at Laura, and she returned it.

Reading waved a hand at them. "Seems like you have your answer there."

"What do you mean?" asked Laura.

"Step down from your teaching positions, split your time between your two dig sites and home, and you've got the best of both worlds."

Acton smiled at his friend, who only wanted the best for them, however was missing one vital point. "That's all well and good, buddy, but you're missing the all-important recruitment phase."

Reading's eyes narrowed. "Huh?"

"The students out in the field at the dig site. They're the best and brightest. They're the ones who stuck it out, who've already made the commitment to being an archaeologist. They've wanted to be there for years. In the classroom, that's where those future archaeologists are enticed to join a profession they might not have been considering. It's there where you capture their imagination, have them wondering could this be something for me?

"A lot of times they're there for what they think is an easy credit, and these days, sometimes they're there because they've heard of me on the Internet. But many of them have a genuine interest that they don't know can be turned into a career. If I didn't spend time in the classroom teaching those kids, they might never discover the profession."

Reading regarded him for a moment. "That makes sense, but you're forgetting one thing."

"What's that?"

"You're not indispensable. Someone else will take your place and teach those same kids."

Acton chuckled. "True, but if they're not as passionate about the subject as I am, then perhaps they're not as effective in recruiting new people into the field." He dismissed the conversation with a wave of his hand. "We love what we do, and the money allows us to fund our own digs and let kids who otherwise wouldn't be able to afford it get their hands dirty."

Reading grunted. "I suppose I see your point." He wagged a finger. "But I'm not moving into your basement."

Acton laughed and Laura fake-pouted before joining in. She drained her pint and waved for the server, indicating another round be sent over.

"She drinks like my son."

Acton's eyebrows shot up. "God, I hope not. Drunks don't last too long on the force."

Laura swatted him. "That was my first beer. You two are already on your third." She turned to Reading. "So, how is Spencer?"

"Good. He's loving the job, much to the annoyance of my ex-wife."

"I'm sure she's just worried about him."

Reading sighed and leaned back as fresh pints were delivered. "I can't really blame her. I'm worried about him, too. Today's London is not the London I served in as a young copper. It's far more violent than it was."

Acton grunted. "Everywhere is, but it's still no Chicago."

Reading took a sip of his beer. "No, we definitely don't have your problems, but we could be getting there if we're not careful."

Acton leaned back, putting an arm around Laura's shoulders. "I guess it's a matter of perspective. When I walk through the streets of London at night, I never feel unsafe compared to a big city back home. But then I guess, like anywhere, it depends on where you are in that city."

"There are parts of London, I guarantee you, you wouldn't feel safe in at night, just like there are parts of Chicago where you'd feel perfectly safe. I think part of it is that society has become a lot less friendly, a lot more selfish. Everybody only thinks of themselves instead of the greater good. In my day, when you saw someone in trouble, you either helped them or you got help. Today, everyone pulls out their phone and just records it, hoping they'll get their fifteen minutes of fame, just like those damn videos you see all over the Internet of people helping animals. They want you to think they're doing a good deed, but they insist on holding their phone as they do it. So, they're trying to help the animal with just one hand. If they truly cared about the animal, they'd put the damn phone down and use both hands to help the poor thing. The animal might be out of its predicament in five seconds instead of five minutes, but nooo, that won't give that so-called 'Good Samaritan' an opportunity to profit off of the creature's suffering. It disgusts me."

Acton had to agree. It was one of the many reasons he spent almost no time on social media. Everyone today was obsessed with going viral in an effort to get affirmation from strangers they would never meet, and they were willing to let animals and people suffer in order to do it. It was a new phenomenon brought on by a media-obsessed culture that had discovered a way for the average person to become a celebrity like those they worshipped.

Reading gulped down a third of his glass. "And don't get me started on that binary society theory of yours. I think you're one hundred percent right. This whole, yes-no, good-evil, left-right culture that's been ingrained into our young people by Facebook and the like, is tearing society apart." He paused. "How long did it take for the Roman Empire to collapse?"

Acton smiled at him. "Which one?"

"Huh?"

"Well, before Rome was sacked, the empire had been split administratively into the Eastern Roman Empire and the Western. So, the empire, as most people think of it, essentially collapsed with the sacking of Rome in AD 476. However, the Eastern Roman Empire continued for another thousand years as the Byzantine Empire, before its capital, Constantinople, was sacked in 1453." Acton leaned forward and smirked. "When you retire, I'll let you sit in on some of my classes."

Reading grunted. "Why bother when I can get the milk for free?" He sighed. "Something tells me the collapse of Western civilization isn't going to take a thousand years this time."

Acton frowned. "Unfortunately, I agree with you. I fear the students I'm teaching today may be the last generation to experience freedom and democracy as we know it."

Laura leaned forward, clasping her drink in both hands. "I think one of our biggest problems is that the art of compromise seems to be dead, and it fits into James' binary society theory. If everything the other side believes in or wants is absolutely wrong, absolutely evil, then why would you ever compromise and let any of their desires become part of a final agreement? It means you can never agree on anything. Take oil, for example. Is it dirty? Sure. Does it pollute? Absolutely. Should we as a society move away from it? Yes, eventually we should. However, if you talk to an environmentalist, they believe you should shut off the taps today, damn the consequences. They have no concept of how important oil is, not only to the economy, but to day-to-day lives.

"Or take natural gas. Environmentalists prevent pipelines from being built that could bring natural gas from North America to China. They want the natural gas left in the ground, but what they're ignoring is that China is building coal-fired power plants like crazy and reopening dozens of coal mines, whereas if they had a reliable natural gas supply, they could build natural gas power plants instead. Certainly, they're not as clean as hydroelectric or solar, but they're far cleaner than coal. But this whole entire attitude of good versus evil, absolute yeses or absolute noes, means you can't entertain the compromise, the entire idea of getting China off coal first with natural gas, then look at getting them off natural gas with something else. But no, it has to be all or nothing, keep the taps flowing completely or completely turn them off. There's no compromise in between, which means nothing gets done." She sighed. "I think the best thing that could happen for Western society is for social media companies to ban the Like button. It might get rid of this thinking in absolutes."

Acton gave a thumbs-up, grinning. "Where have I heard that before?" She swatted at him again as his phone vibrated with a message. He pulled up the text message, his eyes narrowing.

Urgent I speak with you. Arseny.

"Who is it?" asked Laura, noting his puzzled expression.

"Someone named Arseny. He says he has to speak with me urgently."

Reading ran his finger down his glass, leaving a line in the sweat. "Who's Arseny?"

Acton slowly shook his head. "I don't know. I can't think of anyone with that name that I'm familiar enough with for them to only use their first name and assume I knew who it was."

"It sounds Russian."

"In this day and age, it could be from the Bronx. Just text him back," said Laura. "Ask him who he is."

Acton exhaled loudly. "I hope I'm not about to really embarrass myself."

Who is this?

The reply was immediate.

We last saw each other in a hotel in Moscow.

Acton gasped as he realized exactly who Arseny was. "It's Professor Orlov!" he hissed.

Laura's eyes shot wide and Reading's narrowed. "Who the bloody hell is that?"

"You remember the incident with the Japanese imperial regalia?"

Reading leaned back, his beer forgotten. "Yeah, I remember now. He was the bloke that the Russian government wanted to determine whether what they had found was real or not."

"Exactly. He was arrested and imprisoned after he handed them over to us, and I haven't heard anything of him since. I made some inquiries through the university, but they've all gone unanswered."

Reading frowned as he rubbed his chin. "If he's in a Russian prison, then there's no way that's him. Is there something you could ask him that only he would know?"

Acton shrugged as he turned to Laura. "Can you think of anything?"

"I don't think either of us really knows him well enough. Questions like where we first met, the government could know. Why don't you just ask him how he can confirm it's him?"

It was as good an idea as any. Orlov was an intelligent man and should have anticipated the question, and perhaps had already figured out a way for them to confirm it was him and not some imposter.

How can I know it's you? You're supposed to be in prison.

The reply again was immediate.

You have a friend who would know. Contact him.

Acton slumped back, handing the phone over to Laura who read the reply before passing it to Reading.

Reading frowned. "Who's this friend?"

Acton shrugged. "Orlov knew very little about us. We were on friendly terms, but it was purely academic. We don't have any mutual friends."

Reading handed the phone back. "He doesn't say anything about it being a mutual friend, he says *you* have a friend."

"What friend of mine would know whether Orlov was in prison?" His jaw dropped, as did Laura's, and they both echoed, "Dylan!"

Acton launched the secure app on his phone that his former student, Dylan Kane, a CIA operative, had installed for emergencies. Acton's face was scanned and he entered an eight-digit code before gaining access. He fired off a message to Kane, praying the young man was somewhere in the world that he could receive it. Sometimes the Special Activities Division operative was able to reply within minutes, but sometimes it could take days.

87

And Acton had a sense if this were indeed Orlov, that the man didn't have that kind of time.

Chongqing, China

CIA Special Activities Division operative Dylan Kane stared through his scope, scanning the crowds in a futile effort to find his target. Langley had already tapped any cameras in the area it could access, and their computers would be processing the faces far faster than he could, but he wasn't one to sit idly by while others did the work, so he continued his search.

His CIA-customized Tag Heuer watch sent an electrical pulse into his wrist, undetectable to anyone but him. He pulled away from the scope on his Chinese-made QBU-88 sniper rifle and entered a coded sequence by pressing buttons surrounding the watch face. A message was projected on the crystal indicating he had received a secure communique from his old professor, James Acton.

"What now?" groaned Kane to the empty room. Acton was a man he looked up to, so much so that when the internal debate raged on whether to remain in college or join the military to fight terrorism, Acton was the only man he could think of to go to. His former professor had wisely not told him what to do, but had instead listened and asked the correct questions.

He had followed his heart, quit school—much to the annoyance of his parents, especially his father—and joined the US Army. He had set a goal and achieved it, first getting into the Rangers, then Delta Force, and from there, the CIA had recruited him into their Special Activities Division and into a job he loved. He was making a difference protecting his country, and far too often protecting his former archaeology teacher, a man he had met not because of an interest in the subject matter, but because it was an easy grade.

Or so he had thought

His laptop sat next to him, and he logged into his secure app and frowned at the message about Professor Orlov. Viktor Zorkin, a former KGB agent who had effected the escape of Orlov after the Russian-Japanese incident, had managed to get him out of Russia with a new identity. The rules had been simple. Orlov had to live out a quiet life, making no contact with anyone from his past.

And apparently the man had broken his promise.

Kane fired off a quick reply.

Our friend VZ rescued him. He's been living under a new identity in a safe location, therefore it very well could be him. Note that if it is, he is violating the agreement he made and put himself in danger. I recommend extreme caution.

His comms squawked, his best friend from high school Chris Leroux, Control for his mission, now in his ear.

Keep me posted.

He fired off the message then activated his comms. "Control, Tweedledee. What have you got for meee, over?"

"Tweedledee, Control. I can confirm that you are a poet and that we've located your target."

Kane grinned, repositioning himself and pressing his eye back against the sniper rifle's scope. His smile had nothing to do with the fact he was about to kill a man, and everything to do with the fact that once he did, he'd be heading home to his girlfriend.

Unless, of course, the professors interfered with his plans.

Unknown Location

Professor Arseny Orlov sat hunched over his keyboard, staring at the screen, impatiently awaiting a reply from Acton. Sweat beaded on his forehead and trickled down his back as he battled his chronic pain. His diabetic neuropathy had his feet aflame, and it seemed to be getting worse with each passing day. His arthritis had turned anything involving the hands into a twisted painful exercise, and it had spread to his toes as well. His legs were swelling, he'd been suffering from sciatica for over a year, and now he was convinced he had fibromyalgia. Even the touch of his pants sometimes caused agonizing pain

And he was alone, living in constant fear.

It was a miserable existence. It was a life he never thought would be his, and he hated every minute of it. He couldn't take it any longer. Life wasn't worth living anymore, and if he had any courage, he'd have ended it long ago. Was it wrong to pray to God to end one's life? If suicide were the ultimate sin, wouldn't the granting of such a prayer be sinful as well?

He was never a very religious man, but alone with his thoughts and constant agony, he needed someone to talk to, someone to beg for help, someone to end his suffering, and that had become God despite his doubts.

When Victor Zorkin, a man he had never met before, rescued him from the Russian prison he expected to spend the rest of his days in, he wasn't sure what kind of life in exile he would have, and if it weren't for the pain, he could probably live with the loneliness. He had few, if any, guests, as he still struggled to learn the language of the country in which he found himself. He had instead taken to perfecting his English, which had already been quite good, since most places he went to now had shopkeepers that spoke English rather than Russian.

And that was another thing he missed—the sound of his mother tongue. Some nights he would cry himself to sleep in his recliner, watching a Russian movie on Netflix, longing for a conversation in the beautiful language. Yet he was destined to never hear it again in person.

He sighed as he continued to stare at the screen, waiting for Acton's reply. What he had started three months ago had been foolish and impulsive, perhaps even self-destructive. It had been triggered by watching his former homeland's glorious dictator giving the annual State of the Nation address, his smug expression and arrogance infuriating. He wanted to tear the man down, to destroy him, but he had no power, no ability to do so.

That brought on another wave of helplessness and self-pity. He had done nothing wrong. He had merely tried to prevent a war by doing what was morally right, and instead he had been labeled a traitor, his life taken away from him. He hadn't seen his family in years and never would again. It was too risky. And those thoughts had led him into a near death spiral as he gripped the bottle of blood pressure pills he was certain if swallowed he would never wake up from.

His suffering would be over.

But as he continued to watch the diminutive former KGB agent, the thought of the man winning had pissed him off, and he had thrown the bottle across the room.

It was the presentation of the Hero of Labor award, the most Socialist, the most Communist of civilian medals from a bygone era there could possibly be, that had reminded him of just how much this man admired the Soviet Union and how twisted and distorted their fearless leader's image of that brutal empire was. The man wanted to bring back the old days and the old ways. He'd already convinced the population through a referendum surrounded by a massive propaganda campaign to essentially give him permanent power. What was heartbreaking was that the Russian population was eating it up, the vast majority worshipping the man, believing the garbage he and the state-controlled media spouted.

Russians loved strongman leaders, and they loved living in a country perceived as strong and feared by the world. Their Russian Napoleon had given them that. Russia was once again strong, once again feared, and its leader was loved. But for those who longed for the old days under a strong leader like Stalin, a man who had won the Great Patriotic War— single-handedly, apparently—who had guided the country from a poor, peasant farmer state to a massive empire the world trembled in fear of, there was one thing they weren't aware of, and that in all of his suffering, he had forgotten about.

And as soon as he had remembered it three months ago, he had done what he had promised he would never do.

He reached out to his past.

Volkov had been his prized student. The young man worshipped the ground his mentor walked upon and would do anything he asked of him. And just as Orlov had expected, the young man had readily agreed to begin searching the archives for the documents Orlov was fully aware existed, for he had seen them with his own eyes in his own review of the archive when it first opened. And now his former student had found what he had seen all those years ago as a much younger man, documents that would shatter the revised, softened version of one of the most brutal dictators to ever live.

But in so doing, he had put Volkov in grave danger.

There was guilt there. He was, after all, still human. Though sometimes the individual needed to be sacrificed for the greater good. But for that sacrifice to have been worthwhile, he needed the documents that Volkov had discovered. The scanned copies sent to him were useless. He required the originals so they could be tested to prove they were genuine. Yet just reading the words written had him feeling more alive than he had in years, and for a brief moment, he had forgotten the pain, whatever hormones that had briefly coursed through his veins washing it away.

But now the pain was back and growing in intensity as he awaited Acton's reply, and when it came, his pain once again disappeared.

201

Outside the Novinsky Hotel

Moscow, Russian Federation

Volkov reached out instinctively and took Katarina's hand before he realized what he had done. He prepared for the sting of her forthcoming rejection, but instead, she gripped his hand tightly. She was scared, and so was he. There had been an argument in the apartment as her fears and frustrations had boiled over and she expressed her anger at him for coming to her home and dragging her into his crime. She was right, of course, but it didn't change anything. It was too late. He couldn't jump in a DeLorean and stop his past self from committing a future idiotic act. This was reality, she was stuck in the middle of it, and they had no time to waste arguing. Fortunately, she had recognized that, and the frustration had only lasted a few minutes before they were out the door.

Now they were across from Alina's hotel. He checked his watch. They were supposed to be at the rear door in two minutes.

"Should we go now?" asked Katarina, her voice barely a whisper, yet the trembling clear.

He shook his head. "No, we want to time this perfectly. We don't want to be seen waiting by the door."

"What if she doesn't come?"

He didn't want to think about that possibility. Alina wasn't stupid. She was the most street-smart person he had ever met, and despite her political leanings, she had to know this was dangerous to get involved in. If she were wise, she'd stay at her post and leave that rear door locked, but if she did, they were screwed. All their electronics had been left behind at Katarina's apartment, wiped clean. They couldn't reach out to any other friends because every single person would then be in as much trouble as he had gotten Katarina into.

This ended with Alina.

He wasn't dragging anyone else into this mess, and her involvement would hopefully never be known if Orlov were successful in figuring out how to save them. Yet how could he save them? Orlov was a nobody. He was merely a professor before he became a fugitive. He wasn't a wealthy businessman with connections that could help. He wasn't some former government agent who could feed them into an underground railroad. What he could possibly do to get them out of the country, Volkov had no clue.

But first things first.

The door across the street opened and Alina poked her head out, searching for them, and he breathed a sigh of relief.

"Let's go." Still gripping Katarina's hand, he strode across the street as calmly as he could manage. Alina beckoned them to hurry, and he picked up the pace slightly, yet only slightly. He didn't want to draw attention, though Alina's waving hand urging them on was doing just that. Katarina pulled ahead of them, clearly in a panic, but he tightened his grip, drawing her back. "Everybody calm down," he said, loud enough for Katarina and the now close Alina to hear. Katarina slowed as Alina dropped her hand, realizing her mistake.

She receded back inside, the door closing behind her. And he cursed. Had she changed her mind? Had she finally realized the danger she was putting herself in? He kept moving forward as the door continued to close. He could make a run for it and grab it before it shut, but if she had changed her mind, that was her right. At the moment, she wasn't in trouble, for she hadn't actually done anything, and he shouldn't force anything upon her.

The door was almost shut now, only a sliver of light around the edges, but the sliver remained. She hadn't closed it. He reached forward and pulled open the door to see Alina's foot holding it open, and he breathed a sigh of relief at her bravery. She beckoned them inside and he let go of Katarina's hand, pushing her in by the small of the back. He followed, yanking the door closed behind them.

Alina held a finger to her lips. "Follow me. Don't say anything to anyone. You are VIP guests who don't want to be recognized. We do this all the time, so none of the staff will think anything of it."

They both nodded, remaining silent. She led them down a corridor and through a set of doors. Another set immediately to the left led to a service elevator. Alina pressed the button and the chime sounded, the doors opening slowly. They climbed on board and within moments were on their way to the fourth floor. The silence continued though Volkov was certain everyone could hear his pounding heart, the drumbeat now rapid. The elevator jerked to a halt and the doors opened, nearly causing him to soil himself. Alina stepped out into the small room hidden away from the general public. He followed Katarina out as Alina poked her head into the hallway beyond.

She turned to them. "It's clear. Third door to the right, room four-twelve." She stepped out of the hall and they followed. They reached the door and Alina slid the pass in the key reader, the light showing green on the first try. She pushed open the door and stepped inside. Katarina followed with Volkov holding his breath on her heels. The door closed behind them with a satisfying click and Katarina collapsed into his arms, sobbing, her entire body trembling. He held her tight as he struggled to control his own emotions, his own body joining in the shaking.

Alina slumped against the wall, her hand on her chest. "My God, I don't remember the last time that I've been so scared, and I don't even know what the hell is going on." She drew a deep breath and exhaled loudly before pushing off the wall and heading deeper into the room.

Volkov eased up on Katarina, staring at her. "Are you all right?"

She gently slammed both of her clenched fists against his chest. "Why did you get me into this?"

His heart ached. "Because you're the only person I could trust. And I'm a fool." He gripped her hands in his, clenching them to his chest. "Maybe it's still not too late. Turn yourself in. Tell them I came to your apartment and insisted on using your computer. I told you that I had done something, I had stolen something I shouldn't, but never said what."

She shook her head. "You and I both know they'll never take the chance that I didn't read those papers."

"What papers?" asked Alina. "I'm risking my neck for you two. I think I have a right to know why."

Volkov frowned. "The less you know the better."

A harrumph erupted from Alina, her fists shoved against her hips. "If just seeing whatever it is you took is enough for Katarina to be in danger, then don't you think I'm up to my eyeballs in this now by giving you a room? I deserve to know."

Volkov stared at Katarina and she nodded. "It's her choice. She deserves to know what she's getting herself into, and maybe it's not too late for her to change her mind."

Volkov agreed. "Very well." He picked up his bag off the floor and stepped inside the room, tossing it on the bed. As he unzipped it, he stared Alina squarely in the eyes. "Once you see this, you'll realize just how much danger we're in, and you might want to change your mind."

"Not bloody likely."

He waved a hand, dismissing her bravado. "If you do change your mind, we'll understand." He pulled out the folder containing the documents he had stolen and handed it to her. She opened it up and began reading, and as she skimmed the pages, her eyes bulged.

And the ruddiness in her cheeks abandoned her, her eyes now wide with fear.

The Old Shades Pub

London, England

Reading pushed Acton's phone across the table, having finished reading what was clearly a prepared message from Orlov—there was no way anyone could type that fast. It told of a set of documents dating back to the early days of the Soviet Union that would rewrite history. Yet there were no details as to what revelations these documents might contain, only that Orlov was traveling to Moscow to collect them from someone who would hand them only to him, and he needed an independent courier who could not only confirm their authenticity, but get them out of the country without being searched at the border. He had assured them there was nothing illegal or nefarious going on here, it was simply that he feared an over-zealous border guard might seize them for review.

As a fellow historian, I cannot stress to you enough the importance of these documents. What they reveal is so shocking, it rewrites the entire early years of the Soviet Union. I can honestly say I've never been so excited about any find, which is why I'm putting my life at risk by going there myself to collect them. I don't care if I'm captured after I've handed the documents over to you, all I care about is getting them safely out of the country so you can authenticate them, then reveal them to the world. History should not be hidden away. It should be exposed to the world so it can be analyzed, assessed, and judged by the people rather than those who would hide it away because they fear the effect it may have on their version of the truth.

It had Acton puzzled. Just what could this secret be? He desperately wanted to know. He respected Orlov, and if the man had indeed escaped the Russian authorities and was now willing to risk capture to get his hands on these documents, they must indeed be a revelation. But the butterflies in his gut indicated he was far too excited for his own good. Yet he had to know.

Reading eyed him. "Please tell me you're not considering this."

Acton exchanged a look with his own worst enemy, and it was clear she was just as excited and curious as he was.

Reading growled at his friends. "You two are determined to get yourselves killed, aren't you?"

Acton picked up the phone. "I wouldn't go so far as to say that, but aren't you the least bit curious as to what he's talking about?"

Reading leaned forward, jabbing a finger at the phone. "Yes, I can honestly say I am not the least bit curious, not if it means putting your lives at risk."

Acton's eyes narrowed. "Who said anything about putting our lives at risk?"

Reading threw up his hands, slamming back against the booth. "Are you really that daft? This is Russia we're talking about. Moscow. The heart of the enemy. You don't want to hear about what happened last time I was there. And to hell with that. Remember what happened last time *you* were there! Police were after you, the army was after you, helicopters, fighter jets, drones. Hell, I can't even remember what the hell was chasing you down. And it was all over something that this very same professor asked you to come to Moscow and authenticate." He jabbed a finger at him. "Fool me once, shame on you. Fool me twice, shame on me."

Acton frowned. Reading was right. It had been dangerous, though the Russians had been after them specifically. After the incident was over, Kane and his people had reached out through private channels and were assured that the Russians were burying their involvement. The official story now was that they had no idea how Orlov had managed to steal the Japanese artifacts, and were grateful that the professors had helped repatriate them. It was the typical nonsense that came out of Soviet/Russian thinking, worthy of any North Korean, Cuban, or Chinese press release. When one lived in a cocoon of disinformation, it was easy to not recognize how unbelievable one's own contributions to the lies sounded to the outside world. Yet if the Russians weren't interested in them and wanted to bury the truth, arresting them would be the worst thing they could do to preserve their secret.

Laura beat him to the punch. "Dylan has assured us that the Russians aren't interested in us, and that they've buried the entire incident. They wouldn't dare arrest us just for showing up, because then the truth would be revealed to the world when the first reporter asks why."

Reading stared at her for a moment, then his head slowly shook and his shoulders slumped. "There's nothing I can say or do that will stop you two from going to Moscow, is there?"

Acton grinned at him. "The fact that you even have to ask that question hurts my feelings. I thought you knew us."

Reading rolled his eyes. "If you two insist on going, then I'm coming with you."

"The more the merrier."

Reading sighed and pointed at the phone. "But we need more details. When, where, what the hell these documents contain. We need as much information as we can get before going in, and we want to spend as little time on the ground as possible. So that means rendezvous times have to coordinate with flight times." He turned his attention to Laura. "See what magic that travel agent of yours can work." He threw his hands up again, cursing. "We need visas!"

"Not a problem." Laura brought up their travel agent's number on her phone and dialed. "I assume none of your info has changed?"

Reading shook his head. "Just my blood pressure." Acton and Laura both laughed, then she became serious as the other end of her call connected. Reading jutted his chin toward Acton's phone. "You better start asking questions."

Acton's thumbs attacked his phone's screen as his heart raced with excitement and fear. This could be one of the more stupid moves they had made, heading knowingly into the danger, but he trusted Kane and his people, and he trusted Orlov. To a point. Their prior experience with the man hadn't been his fault, though technically it was. The man tried to do the right thing to prevent a war, and with stakes like that, Acton would never hesitate to lay down his own life to save thousands and perhaps millions.

And this situation was nothing. This was merely documents someone had come across. Yes, they might have a profound impact on history, but how could they possibly affect the present day enough for someone to threaten their lives?

Operations Center 2, CIA Headquarters
Langley, Virginia

CIA Analyst Supervisor Chris Leroux dropped back in his chair and sighed in relief as everyone in the room, in their own way—audibly and visibly—expressed the same sentiments. Dylan Kane had eliminated the target, mayhem had ensued, but he was now clear and safely on his way out of the country, a complete facial mask protecting his cover for the next time he was needed.

Kane was his best friend. They had met in high school, Leroux the brilliant dork, Kane the handsome jock who needed some tutoring to secure the football scholarship he wanted. They had become friends, Kane his protector from those who would torment the awkward Leroux. Kane had gone to college two years ahead of Leroux's graduation, and they lost touch. Leroux had been recruited out of college into the CIA, and it was a chance encounter at Langley when he discovered his friend had also been brought into the fold. The friendship had been rekindled and they were closer than ever.

And now that his friend was safe, he had another job to do—tie up a newly loosened end from a previous mission.

He brought up a secure folder on his terminal then clicked on the link that launched the encrypted messenger. He logged in and sent a short message to a long-retired agent.

Clarion 25 has made contact with Professor Acton. Intentions unknown at this time.

He sent the message then leaned back, folding his arms as he stared at the screen. Orlov wasn't under the CIA's protection. He hadn't been extracted by the Agency, and hadn't been given a new identity by them. In fact, the American government had no involvement with him whatsoever—he came under the watchful eye of the Gray Network, an organization he had been exposed to several years ago, consisting of retired spies and assets from around the world who had a desire in their old age to continue protecting what they had fought so hard for in their younger years.

It was one of theirs that had extracted Orlov, then the Gray Network had set him up with a new identity, a modest pension, and a modest home. He was their responsibility. However, that didn't mean it wasn't Leroux's moral obligation to help, especially if it involved the professors. Leroux dealt with Acton and his wife on far too many occasions, and his gut told him these two were about to get mixed up in this. If he could head off whatever it was they were about to do, he might save himself some headaches down the road.

His terminal beeped with a reply to his message.

Understood.

He was about to wash his hands of the matter when he closed his burning eyes and sighed.

"What is it?" asked his senior analyst and second-in-command, Sonya Tong.

He opened his eyes and turned his chair to face her. "Check the system. See if our troublesome professors have been flagged for anything in the past twenty-four hours."

She rolled her eyes. "Not again."

He grunted. "They keep things interesting."

The professors were good people. Too good. They never ran away from a situation if they could help those caught up in it, and far too often, they ran toward it. Yet despite their penchant for getting in trouble, when they needed help, it was rarely their fault, and quite often they were the ones helping America's assets and allies. Laura Palmer had inherited hundreds of millions of dollars when her brother died. He had been a tech entrepreneur and sold his company for a fortune. On more than one occasion, she and her new husband had used that money to help those in trouble, including members of the Delta Force's Bravo Team.

They were part of the family, a family that included Leroux, along with his CIA operative girlfriend Sherrie White, his best friend Dylan Kane, and Kane's girlfriend Lee Fang, a former Chinese Special Forces operative now in exile. They all formed a tightly knit group that often acted outside of the confines the agency he worked for was sometimes willing to get involved in. The four of them, along with Bravo Team, and the professors, worked together to do the right thing, and their little group expanded as needed. And that group, that inner circle, recently had expanded to include Tong.

He could trust her implicitly.

"Kane sent me a coded message before extraction. Apparently, Professor Orlov—"

Tong's eyes narrowed slightly. "The Russian with the Japanese imperial regalia?"

Leroux nodded. "Yeah, apparently he's broken his silence and contacted Professor Acton. Something's going down, and the sooner we know about it, the better chance we have of stopping it before it becomes a problem."

Tong turned toward her keyboard. "They're private citizens, and she's a Brit. Not much we can do about it if they want to get in trouble."

"You're probably right, but who knows? Maybe they'll exercise some good sense this time." Everyone in the operations center chuckled and Leroux smiled at them as he turned in his chair. "I know, I know. Doubtful. But one can always hope."

"And you'd be wrong," said Tong, jutting her chin toward the displays. Leroux turned to face the massive screens curving across the front of the state-of-the-art facility.

"Well, boss, you were definitely wrong on that one," laughed Randy Child, the team's wunderkind.

Leroux muttered a curse as his head shook. On the screen were three Russian visa applications for the professors and their good friend, Interpol Agent Hugh Reading, applied for only minutes ago by the professors' regular travel agent, who was far more than a simple travel agent. Leroux had checked her out after the Mongolian incident, where the professors had managed to sneak two of their friends in as crew. That wasn't something passengers could make a phone call and request, yet this woman had arranged it in a matter of hours. She appeared to have connections for everything all around the world, and he had little doubt that these Russian visas with travel dates of tomorrow would actually be granted on time.

"Maybe they're just hedging their bets," offered Tong.

He shook his head. "No. With a country like Russia, you don't make applications and then withdraw them. It brings you to their attention and they'll red flag you for the next time you want to try to get in. No, they've decided to go." He wagged a finger at the screen. "But why is Reading going with them? And how would..." He paused, his eyes narrowing as he turned toward Tong. "Where are they? Do we know?"

"Just a sec, I'll ping their phones." A few swift keystrokes later and Tong leaned back. "They're in London."

Leroux sighed. "Well, even if we wanted to try to stop them, we couldn't without stepping on toes." He chewed his cheek for a moment. "I wonder what they're up to?"

"Why don't you just call them and ask?" suggested Child.

Leroux and Tong exchanged surprised glances at the suggestion. She shrugged. "It's not a bad idea, actually."

Leroux had to agree. "It's not, but it's premature. I've already passed on the information to those who need to act on it. If we need to get involved, they'll let us know."

Child spun in his chair, staring at the ceiling. "Who's they?"

"*They* are above your security clearance."

Child dropped a foot, killing his spin. "Oh."

Leroux returned his attention to the visa applications and the flight information that Tong had added. The Actons and their friend were heading for Moscow at 7:00 AM tomorrow, London time, apparently to meet a man who had been in hiding from the Russian government with strict instructions to contact no one from his past, including his family.

Curiosity was killing him. Were the Actons heading to Moscow to help Orlov somehow? Was there some archaeological or historical discovery simply too tempting? Or was it both, like the last time they had met with the renegade professor?

He had to know.

"Can we pull their text messages?"

Tong's fingers hovered over the keyboard but didn't type. "Yes, but not legally."

"Stupid laws!" spat Child as he delivered a mock tirade. "Things would be so much easier if we were Chinese."

Tong gave him a look. "I am Chinese."

"You know what I mean. I mean, you know, not *from* China, but Chinese government."

"I'm sure that's what you meant. Just remember, there's a distinction."

"You're right, I'm sorry. I'll try to do better," replied a subdued Child.

Tong flashed a smile at the young man, winking at Leroux. "I know you will."

Leroux ignored the exchange, well aware that Tong was simply having a little fun with the whiz kid who had no filter yet. But it was perhaps a little bit of payback for an accusation hurled at her in the heat of the moment during an incident with the Chinese, questioning her loyalty. Too many people today couldn't make the distinction between someone's heritage and the government that controlled their former homeland. Just because someone was Chinese didn't mean they supported the Chinese government, and it was the Chinese government that was the enemy.

And the population of China, even if a significant proportion of them fully supported their government, did so out of ignorance. Information was strictly controlled in the communist state, and no one should ever forget that when Hollywood partnered with Chinese studios because they wanted to tap the 1.4 billion people that lived there, it meant the Communist Party and its corrupt officials were profiting. Every time you bought something manufactured in Xinjiang province, it was potentially produced by slave labor in factories packed with Uyghur Muslims held against their will. Attacking people because of their heritage or perceived heritage was nonsense, especially in a multi-cultural society. And he defied most people to tell the difference between someone from China, Korea, or Japan.

"So, what do you want me to do?"

Tong's question derailed his train of thought. "Excuse me?"

"Am I checking their text messages?"

Leroux shook his head. "No. We'll hold off for now."

Tong voiced the question that, once asked, he realized the entire team likely wanted an answer to as well. "Do you want us to stick around for this?"

Leroux shook his head. "No. Sorry, people. Our op is done. Everybody go home and get some rest. If something comes up, I'll page you, otherwise, we'll see you tomorrow morning."

The room quickly emptied out, only Tong remaining. "Are you going home?"

"Yeah. I just have a funny feeling it might not be for long."

She glanced at the clocks across the top of the displays, showing the time in various cities. The analog clocks of old were replaced with digital ones integrated into the displays' programming, allowing them to change the cities to those of importance at the moment, rather than what was important in the sixties. "Well, it's late evening in London, past midnight in Moscow. I doubt anything's going to happen at this hour."

"That flight is three in the morning our time."

Tong tapped her watch. "Exactly. You can get six or seven hours sleep then be back here if needed."

He packed up his stuff and she did the same, both of them walking to the parking garage together, and as she chit-chatted about Child's China/Chinese confusion and the discrimination she regularly faced, especially after the incident in the South China Seas, he found himself wondering what life would have been like if Sherrie had never entered the picture and Tong had asked him out instead. He was certain he would be happy with her. She was beautiful in her own way, intelligent, witty when she let herself go. And he hated to admit they had far more in common than he and Sherrie did. It had him once again doubting whether things would ultimately work out between him and his polar opposite, the vivacious, outgoing extrovert that was Sherrie White.

Tong stared up at him. "Where are you?"

His cheeks flushed at being caught not paying attention. "Sorry, just thinking about the professors." The elevator doors opened and they both stepped out into the parking garage.

She smiled at him. "I'll see you tomorrow, but if you need me to come in tonight, just call."

"If something comes up, I'm sure I can handle it by myself until the morning shift begins. You get your sleep."

She reached out and grabbed his forearm. "I mean it. Call me. I don't want you to be alone here trying to save the day by yourself."

He smiled and patted her hand. "Okay. If you want your sleep interrupted, then so be it. Good night."

"Good night," she said, and they headed in opposite directions, his thoughts once again turning to what life would be like if she had followed through on her infatuation with him.

And his stomach turned into knots of guilt as his phone rang with a call from Sherrie, no doubt to see if he would be home for dinner.

Novinsky Hotel, Room 412

Moscow, Russian Federation

Volkov sat on the edge of the lone bed in the room, Katarina beside
him as Alina took photos of the documents. After her initial shock,
they no longer scared her in the slightest, though she was shaking with
excitement. He had been reluctant at first to give her permission to take
the photos, however she had made it a condition of them staying there.
He had grudgingly agreed after she promised she wouldn't do anything
with them until they were safely out of Russia.

Unfortunately, he wasn't so certain it would be a promise kept.

She finally finished and handed the folder back to him. He tucked it
away in his bag as she wagged the phone at them. "This is incredible!
The man's responsible for the deaths of tens of millions of people, yet
three out of every four Russians thinks he's great. But what he did here,
if these documents are indeed genuine, is unforgivable to any who
worship the man. No wonder the president had this hidden away. You
said there were other boxes?"

"About twenty. I didn't count. I found what I was looking for in the first box."

She dropped into a chair in the corner. "Unbelievable! If just that first box had this in it, can you imagine what else was in there?" She paused. "Do you think you could get back in and get copies of everything else?"

"Are you insane?" cried Katarina. "Our lives are already ruined! You would have him risk it even more by going back into that place? They'd arrest him on the spot!"

Alina frowned. "You're right. I'm sorry. I'm just so excited by this. This is exactly the type of stuff we need to fight back. If we can make this public alongside experts who can verify their authenticity, it just might be enough to help turn the tide."

Katarina laughed. "I think you're reading too much into those documents. Let's assume they're genuine and you get the information out there. His people are simply going to say they're fake, even if you provide all the proof in the world. They'll believe what he says, then just claim it's another Western conspiracy to make Russia look bad."

"He might, but this might be enough to provide that crack in the dam we've been looking for. Just enough doubt. And if we keep hammering away with this information, we might get enough questioning what he's doing, questioning his message, that some of the opposition parties might be able to get enough support to meet his ridiculous restrictions and get on the ballot. If we could just get his numbers down in the next election, it would give people the confidence to vote against him."

Katarina again threw water on Alina's idea. "You could get three-quarters of the population to vote against him. He'll never cede power."

"I agree, however, then we could at least rid ourselves of this ridiculous notion that we're a democracy, and reveal to the Russian public what the world already knows—we're a dictatorship, little better than the Soviet Union. That's when those who've tasted freedom will fight back, and we can have another revolution. This time for democracy, for true freedom, not this joke we now find ourselves living in."

Volkov sat on the bed in stunned silence. He was well aware that Alina was anti-government, but he had no idea her goals were to overthrow the current regime, perhaps violently. If he had known how she truly felt, he wouldn't have associated with her or her brother. It was too dangerous. If she spouted these views to others, the government likely had a file on her, and might even have her under surveillance.

A lump formed in his throat as he stared at her. "Have you told other people this?"

"Told them what?"

"Have you talked about revolution? About overthrowing the government?"

Her eyes narrowed. "Why?"

"Because maybe somebody overheard you. You could be under surveillance. And if you are, then they might know we're here."

She shook her head. "A few of us have spoken together about such things, but never in public."

"But what if those people betrayed you to the government?"

Again, she shook her head, this time a little more vigorously. "I trust my friends completely. They would never betray me like that. I'm nobody. There's no way they're watching me. But if you don't believe me, you're free to leave and take your chances out there." She waved a hand toward the window.

Katarina took his hand, squeezing it tightly. "It's not that we're saying we don't believe you or trust you, it's that there's no way you can be certain."

His heart leaped with her use of the word "we." It was as if they were a couple again.

"But I don't think we have a choice." Katarina turned and looked at him. "I think we're safer here. If we go outside, they'll catch us for sure. Here, they'll only catch us if they've been watching her. And I think the chances of that are pretty slim, don't you?"

She could have told him rainbows were leprechaun sharts and the sky was green, and he would have said, "Yes." He managed a nod.

"Then it's settled. We'll stay here."

His stomach grumbled with hunger and he questioned if he had eaten anything today.

Katarina tilted her head toward the offender. "Any chance of getting some food?"

Alina snatched the room service menu off a nearby table and handed it over. "Tell me what you want. I'll have it billed to the room."

She smirked. "When you guys leave, you'll not only be wanted for stealing state secrets, but for skipping out on your hotel bill. Is there anything else you're going to need?"

He nodded. "Cellphones. I think they call them burners, whatever the hell that means."

"There's a kiosk around the corner. I'll get two for you, and I'll bring you up my tablet with the food. It's set up to make sure nobody knows who I am. You should be able to browse the Internet safely with it."

"Thank you so much for helping us," said Katarina. "It's truly appreciated."

Alina batted her hand. "Think nothing of it." Her phone chimed and she fished it out of her pocket. Her eyes shot wide as she read the message.

"What is it?" asked Volkov, suddenly apprehensive.

Alina leaped toward the nightstand and grabbed the television remote, turning the TV on then selecting the news channel. "It's from my brother. He says you're on the news."

And as soon as the words were out of her mouth, his picture appeared, a frame grab from the lobby of the archive, the talking head saying something about him being wanted for the theft of state secrets. A number flashed on the screen along with a ridiculously large reward. Katarina's hand gripped his even tighter as Alina turned to face them, her mouth agape.

"Until this very moment, I didn't really think this was real."

He stared up at her, noting her eyes were wide, her cheeks pale. "If you're going to change your mind, now's the time. We'll leave, then you can call and tell them everything, and that you didn't know. But whatever you do, make sure you don't mention that you saw the documents."

A debate was clearly raging in Alina's head, but it didn't last long. She firmly shook her head. "No. I'm doing the right thing. If they want you for those documents, then they're obviously genuine and they obviously fear their contents. If anything, this makes me want to help you even more. This is the chink in the armor we've been looking for, and as a patriot, I can't give up this chance to save my country." She reached out a hand to both of them, and they took them. "It does mean we're going to have to be extra careful, however. Don't contact anyone, even people you think are friends. That reward is too big for most people to pass up." She smiled at them slyly. "And don't worry, money doesn't interest me." She left the room, forgetting to take their food order, leaving Volkov to wonder whether her parting statement was indeed true. Even for a revolutionary, it was a life-altering amount of money.

"Do you think we can trust her?" he asked Katarina.

Katarina shook her head. "I don't know. But with that story out there"—she gestured toward the television report—"I think we have to take the chance."

The door flew open and they both yelped, Katarina latching on to him as he rose, placing himself between her and whatever menace was about to face them.

It was Alina.

"Sorry, I forgot to take your order. What do you two want to eat?"

They both collapsed back on of the bed, giggling with a mix of uncontrolled emotions.

Alina eyed them. "What's wrong with you two?"

Volkov sat up and exhaled loudly, raising a single finger. "We need to come up with a coded knock."

Katarina Rozhenko Residence

Moscow, Russian Federation

Nikitin stepped inside Katarina Rozhenko's small apartment. It hadn't taken long to find her once they hit Volkov's residence. The entire place was a shrine to the woman—photos, cards, saved love letters, meal and theater receipts. If it were any other investigation, he would have been concerned Volkov was a serial killer and not a traitor. A thorough search had revealed no last name, however they were already questioning his friends and family, and several had volunteered it.

His underling, Zaitsev, had come here to question her and found something that had him excited enough to call his boss in to see personally. And as Nikitin stared at the waste bin in the bathroom, he understood immediately why and placed a call.

"This is Nikitin. Tell them to start running the clean-shaven photo."

"Yes, sir."

He ended the call and turned to Zaitsev. "What else have you found?"

Zaitsev pointed at a computer sitting nearby. "Completely wiped. Government level. Whoever did it knew what they were doing." He pointed at two phones and a tablet nearby, all broken apart. "Not only did they destroy them, they made sure any memory was physically destroyed as well."

"So, we can't get anything off of anything?"

"They might be able to pull something off the flash memory, but it's going to take a lab to reconstruct. The chips have been smashed, but we might get something eventually."

Nikitin frowned. "Eventually? You mean days, not hours?"

"I mean days, hopefully not weeks."

Nikitin cursed. "All right, get the techs on it and let's start tracking down this one's friends. She's obviously in on it if she let him come here and shave his beard, then destroyed her own cellphone so she couldn't be tracked." He pointed at a photo on the mantle of a young woman smiling with what appeared to be her parents. "Show that photo to the neighbors. Confirm that it's her, then add her to the broadcast. He could be using her to venture out of wherever they're hiding. Maybe we'll get lucky and some shopkeeper will recognize her."

"Maybe."

His phone vibrated with a message and he checked it, his eyebrows shooting up. "Interesting."

Zaitsev eyed him. "Something you care to share with the group?"

Nikitin chuckled. "No, above their pay grades." He waved a hand, indicating the room. "I'll leave this to you. You know what to do?"

"Yes, sir."

Nikitin left the cramped apartment then ensconced himself inside his SUV before rereading the alert. The Japanese incident had involved three professors. Orlov, an American named Acton, and a Brit named Palmer. Orlov had handed the imperial regalia over to them, and they had escaped the country with the help of traitors. Having read the two foreign professors' files, he wouldn't be surprised if they had a hand in Orlov's escape from prison, but with the entire incident buried, they hadn't taken action against them.

But they had been put on a watchlist.

And for the first time since that international incident too many Russians had paid for with their lives, the alert had been triggered. James Acton and Laura Palmer had applied for Russian visas less than an hour ago, along with an Interpol agent named Hugh Reading. What was curious was that the approval had already been granted, triggering a second alert that had escalated it beyond his underlings and directly to his attention.

How would a visa get approved so quickly? It meant connections. He would have that looked into, but that wasn't his concern. His concern was why were two professors, involved in the Japanese incident, requesting to come to Russia at the exact same time Orlov had surfaced for the first time in years. These professors were rich, and had resources available to them that the average citizen didn't. Could Orlov have been in Russia the entire time, and they were coming to extract him now, after he found what he had been searching for? Or were they coming here to collect the documents his student had found then take them to Orlov in the West?

Normally, he would have their visas denied, but this was a golden opportunity. They could lead him directly to those he was after. He called his office and approved the visas for Acton and Palmer.

But denied Reading's.

West/Bertrand Residence

Black Forest, Germany

Alex West cursed as his phone rang on the nightstand beside him. He forced his eyes open and began the process of rolling over to grab it, made more difficult with his advanced age and the fact the love of his life, Adelle Bertrand, was draped over him. She groaned then wriggled off, and he managed to grab the phone on the fifth or sixth ring. There was no risk of it going to voicemail. It was never something used in his line of work, or at least his former line of work. He had been CIA, but that was too many years ago, his septuagenarian bones no longer spry enough for that game.

He answered the call. "Hello?"

"Are you getting slow in your old age, my friend?"

He smiled at a voice he recognized—Viktor Zorkin, a former KGB rival of his that had become a friend over the past few years, and had always been a mutually respected rival. They had never been out to kill each other, merely outwit each other. He had his victories, as did Zorkin.

And Zorkin was his age, so it was way past his bedtime, therefore waking him meant something was wrong.

West cleared his throat, making certain to do it in Zorkin's ear. "I'm an old man, and if I remember your file correctly, you're an even older bastard than me. You'd better have a good reason for waking me up at this ungodly hour."

Zorkin laughed. "I don't know who's older, all I do know is that I'm sprier."

"Who is it?" asked Adelle, now awake, rubbing her eyes.

"It's Viktor."

She flicked on the nightstand light and rolled her eyes. "He'd better be dying to call at this hour."

He grinned at her, then spoke into the receiver. "Did you hear that?"

"I did."

"Good. And she's younger than both of us, and she still thinks this is an ungodly hour."

Zorkin sighed. "I don't know how a decrepit old man like you ended up with a beautiful woman like that."

"My rugged good looks."

"Nah, it can't be that. I'm better-looking. I think she just took pity on you."

West decided he indeed was tired and put an end to the friendly banter. "Listen, buddy, if I don't get back to sleep soon, I'm going to be ruined for the next three days. So, what's so urgent you're calling me in the middle of the night?"

"Orlov has gone off the reservation, as you Americans might say."

West's eyes narrowed. "I'm not sure we would, but what do you mean? Where has he gone?"

"No idea. He might still be at home for all I know. I need you to check on him."

West rolled his eyes. "Buddy, when you say someone's gone off the reservation, that means they've left. Why do you think there's a problem?"

"Apparently, Orlov contacted Professor Acton. Acton reached out to Dylan Kane to see if it could actually be Orlov. Kane confirmed it, but also informed Chris Leroux, who contacted the Gray Network, who contacted me since I was the one who extracted him. I'm nowhere near the area, so I need you to go and check on him."

"Have you tried calling him?"

"I wasn't born yesterday."

"Hey, I had to ask. Your body might be spry, but I'm not too sure about that brain of yours."

"I'll have you know, I can still solve a Rubik's cube in no time flat."

"Bah. You and I both know that was a Communist conspiracy to drive Westerners crazy."

Zorkin roared with laughter. "And it worked, didn't it? Then we sent you Tetris and you were screwed for life."

West rolled his legs out of the bed. "Okay, he's not answering the phone, he's broken his agreement to not contact anyone from his past, and as the local representative of the Gray Network, you want me to go check on him?"

"That's about it. Maybe you're not so senile after all."

"Kiss my bony white ass."

Zorkin roared again. "How long do you think it'll take you to get that decrepit ass of yours over there?"

West glanced at the alarm clock. "I'll be there within half an hour. You put him in my neck of the woods on purpose, didn't you?" He could almost see Zorkin grinning through the phone.

"Who, me?"

"I'll contact you once I find out what's going on."

"Rub some Biofreeze on those joints and take your girlfriend with you to protect you. I know she can still handle herself if things get rough."

West glanced over at Adelle, already up and getting ready, the one side of the conversation she had heard telling her everything she needed to know—their night's restful slumber was over. "She's way ahead of you."

Zorkin chuckled. "She's a sharp one." His voice became serious. "And Alex?"

"Yes?"

"Take a weapon. Something's going on and I have a bad feeling about this. As soon as I heard what Orlov had done, I ran a quick check of his former associates. It's all over Russian state media. The police are after a former graduate student of his for theft of state

129

secrets. There's no way that's a coincidence. There's something more going on here than an old man getting lonely, so be careful."

"I always am."

"Good. Now, if something happens to you, I don't want you to worry about Adelle. I'm exactly her type, and I know I can make her happy."

West flipped the bird at the phone. "I'll call you in half an hour, asshole."

Zorkin roared as West ended the call.

Adelle sat at her make-up table, brushing the knots out of her hair. "Did the phone offend you?"

He faced east toward Moscow and threw a double bird at it.

"Ah, Zorkin offended you?"

He laughed. "The two of us have so much history together, sometimes I don't know whether to love the man or hate him."

She drew her hair back to put it in a ponytail. "Love the man, hate the game the two of you were forced to play."

"The three of us," he said as he walked over and kissed the top of her head.

"I was French intelligence. Back then we were playing both sides."

"Is there any wonder we kept you out of a lot of meetings?"

She winked at him. "That's what you think."

"Huh?"

She pointed toward the bathroom. "If we're going to be there in thirty minutes, you'd better get your butt in gear."

He glanced at the clock again and cursed. "I can't remember the last time I was voluntarily awake at this hour." He shuffled toward the bathroom, his shoulders sagging as everything that could ache did so. He flicked the light on and squinted. As his eyes adjusted, he fumbled for the club pack-sized bottle of Biofreeze, pumped a generous dollop into the palm of his hand, cursing Zorkin for knowing him so well.

Orlov better have just forgotten to pay his phone bill.

Gorki Estate

South of Moscow, Union of Soviet Socialist Republics

February 2, 1923

"The man is simply too rude for the position."

Lenin would get no argument from him. In Bazarov's opinion, Stalin was one of the rudest men he had ever encountered. An uncouth, loud bully unfit for any traditional leadership position. Yet was the General Secretary of the Communist Party a traditional leadership position? It was unlike anything that came before it. A committee of representatives who would guide the nation and its people into a future that would eventually become a global phenomenon, a worker's paradise where everyone contributed and all reaped the rewards. A global cooperative that would bring peace and tranquility to the masses that until now had been subjugated by the wealthy and powerful.

His friend was a great man, of that there was no doubt. And a strong man. He had executed countless in the past few years. It was necessary to keep order, and the best way was to remove a problem with a bullet, then let it be known why, so an example was set for anyone else who might challenge the leadership.

What Lenin seemed to have forgotten was that it was his strength, his willingness to murder and bully his way through a problem that got him to where he was today. Yes, he had become more tempered over the past few years, but he was once a revolutionary who used not only words but violence to achieve his goals.

And murder.

The Romanovs could attest to that. If any were still alive.

"Did you get an apology for the phone call with your wife?"

Lenin spat. "Yes, if you could call it that. It was one of those, 'I'm sorry, but' type of apologies."

"So, it was bullshit."

Lenin chuckled. "You have a way with words, my friend. Yes, it was bullshit. I've added an addendum to my testament on our comrade to point out how his rudeness makes him ill-suited for power."

"And it is still your intention to present this at the Congress in April?"

"Absolutely." Lenin paused, eying him. "Why? Do you have concerns?"

"Of course I have concerns, my friend. You are not well. This will cause you tremendous stress." Bazarov leaned forward, lowering his voice. "It could finish you. Mentally and physically. Not to mention the fact Comrade Stalin might unleash his hounds on you. You could find yourself and your family at the end of a gun."

"Ha! Let him kill me!" Lenin stabbed a finger at him. "But if I end up dead, I'm entrusting you to let the world know why I died, and who killed me. Let's see our dear comrade snatch power with a murder charge hanging over his head!"

Bazarov suppressed his frown. Lenin was right. If Stalin were to murder him, it was unlikely he would gain power, though it could tear the country apart and lead to another, brutal civil war, risking all they had built.

No, Stalin couldn't kill Lenin. It would destroy everything.

He looked at his friend. "The world will know who is responsible. You have my word."

Palmer Residence

London, England

Present Day

Acton was asleep the moment his head hit the pillow. At least that's how he remembered it. He had been into his third beer when Orlov had made contact. Once it was established they were going to Moscow, the alcohol had stopped and everyone headed home, Reading to his apartment, he and Laura to her apartment she kept for when she was doing business here. He pushed up on his elbows, his head pounding. He glanced over to see Laura texting. "Is something wrong?"

The glow off her screen revealed her frown. "Our visas were approved, but Hugh's was rejected."

"Did they give a reason why?"

"No. According to Mary, they usually only give a reason if there was a problem with the paperwork."

"Well, he's going to be pissed."

"That's an understatement. But the question is why?"

"Maybe because he's Interpol? The Russians don't want him there?"

"It could be." She paused, lowering the phone. "Or maybe it has nothing to do with him, and they just want us there alone."

His head pounded harder. "That's unlikely, don't you think? Orlov only contacted us a few hours ago. I doubt they'd have made any connection already. Are you having second thoughts about going?"

She reached over and turned on the nightstand lamp, then rolled over to face him. "Maybe we're being a little too hasty. Maybe Hugh's right."

"Hugh's a mother hen. If it were up to him, we'd both be sitting in a padded room back home." He held up a finger to head off a spirited defense of their friend. "Though he is right. We need to be cautious. I guess the question to ask is, what's the worst-case scenario?"

"They arrest us and shoot us?"

He chuckled. "I doubt they would do anything like that."

"All right then. Poison us."

Acton tilted his head slightly. "Yeah, that's a possibility." He grinned. "Remember, the Russians are notorious for killing their own people, no matter where they are in the world, but they rarely target foreigners, even if they're on their own soil. It could create an international incident."

"Something tells me they probably don't care too much about that these days."

"But they buried the Japanese imperial regalia story for a reason. If they touched us, Hugh would be trumpeting it to the world, and I have no doubt our friends at Langley would make sure it was trending on social media within minutes. I think either they're letting us in because they just don't care, or because they're curious. It could be that they think we're connected to Orlov and whatever he's up to, or it could merely be them asking, why would these two be stupid enough to come back to our country after what they did the last time they were here?"

Laura grunted. "Stupid, indeed."

Acton chuckled and reached out, gripping her hand. "Listen, if you don't want to go, then we don't go. We just tell Orlov, 'sorry, it's too dangerous.'"

"But what about the documents he found? If they're as important as he's implied, isn't it our duty to try and save them, to make them public?"

The academic in him screamed yes, it was their duty, though as an archaeologist, he had never sworn an oath. It wasn't his duty to rush out and protect every piece of history, yet the lack of the equivalent to a Hippocratic Oath for archaeologists had never stopped him before, and he wasn't about to stop now.

Though he probably should.

Laura rolled into a seated position, curling her legs up underneath her. "What are you thinking?"

He pursed his lips for a moment. "I'm thinking the last time he asked for our help, we ended up preventing a war. He did the right thing and paid a heavy price. Up until now, I had assumed he was dead or rotting in prison. The fact he's been in hiding and he's willing to risk his life for whatever this information is, it must be important. I just wish he'd tell us what it is."

"It makes me suspicious."

He regarded her. "In what way?"

"Well, if it's truly earth-shattering, then by telling us, he'd almost guarantee our cooperation. But by not telling us, it leaves doubt."

"But what possible reason would he have to lie? I can't believe he's trying to lure us to Moscow for some nefarious purpose."

Laura sighed. "Neither can I, but maybe this information is important to him, but not to anyone else. At least not to the extent anyone would risk their lives to protect it."

"Well, maybe there's a different way to look at this."

Her eyes narrowed. "What do you mean?"

"If it truly is an incredible discovery, something that will rewrite history, and there's a chance it could get hidden or destroyed, would you go?"

She firmly nodded. "Yes."

"So, why is it dangerous?"

She eyed him. "What do you mean?"

"Well, why is it dangerous? If we go to Moscow, retrieve these documents and we're caught with them, why is it dangerous?"

"Because the Russians don't want anybody to see them. They could arrest us, imprison us, do any number of things to us."

"Exactly, because the documents are important, right?"

"I don't see where you're going with this."

He chuckled. "If they're not important, if Orlov is lying to us or is exaggerating, and they're not at all important, then where's the risk?"

Her jaw dropped. "Ah, I see what you mean. If the documents are unimportant, then there's no risk in getting caught, so there's no point in not going. But if they are important and there is a risk in being caught, then that means it was worth going in the first place to try and save them."

He cocked a finger at her. "You got it."

She smiled. "I like that logic. I can't wait for you to explain it to Hugh."

"Yeah, something tells me he won't be so understanding, especially when he finds out he can't come with us."

"Ugh. Should I let him know now, or wait until morning?"

Acton glanced over at the clock. "We're getting up in a couple of hours regardless. I say, let the man get his sleep then disappoint him in the morning. A good rager should allow him to skip his morning coffee."

Laura giggled. "He is going to be pissed, even more so when we tell him we're still going."

Acton grabbed his phone. "I'm going to send a message to Dylan to let him know what's going on. You never know, his people might be able to help."

"It's too bad Orlov wouldn't agree to a handover. Kane could have sent somebody to the hotel to get the documents then brought them back to the embassy to be sent out in a diplomatic pouch."

Acton agreed. "He seems paranoid about trusting anyone. I guess I don't blame the guy after all he's been through."

"You're right, I don't think he'd agree to hand it over to anybody but us." Laura placed her phone on the nightstand. "We'd better get some sleep. I want to be bright-eyed and bushy-tailed if I'm going to be facing off against Russians tomorrow afternoon."

Acton finished sending the update to Kane through the secure app then lay back down, knowing full well he wasn't getting any more sleep tonight. He sighed.

"What's wrong?"

"I'm wide awake."

A hand reached out in the dark, grabbing his most favorite thing. "I know a way to help you go to sleep."

He grinned. "Oh, do tell."

Orlov Residence

Outside Schiltach, Germany

Alex West sat in the most comfortable-looking chair in Orlov's home. He and Adelle had searched it from top to bottom, confirming the man wasn't there, dead or alive. He had reported that fact to Zorkin, then they began a more thorough search, looking for any evidence of a struggle, any suggestion he had left in a hurry, but they found nothing. There were no papers to suggest anything unusual, nothing to suggest where he might have gone.

There were only two things they had found out of the ordinary. There was no luggage in the house, which suggested that he either didn't own any or he had used them to leave, and his laptop was missing.

"What now?" asked Adelle.

"The man isn't here, and everything suggests he left of his own free will."

"That means he broke the agreement, so whatever happens to him now is his own fault. I suggest we go back to bed. Things will sort themselves out, probably not in his favor."

He gave her an exaggerated wince. "You're cold."

She shrugged. "I'm French. We're practical."

"I thought the French were supposed to be romantic."

"We're practically romantic. Or romantically practical. I can't remember which."

"Uh-huh." West rose. "Let's get out of here before one of his neighbors reports us to the police. Viktor can decide what he wants to do just as easily with us at home."

He extended a hand to Adelle and she took it, rising to join him. They headed for the door when she paused. "Wait a moment." She headed for the kitchen and opened the bread box, revealing a moldy loaf of sourdough. "I'd say he hasn't been here in at least a week, maybe two."

"That means this was planned." West frowned. "Where the hell is he?"

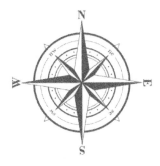

Palmer Residence

London, England

"Bollocks to that."

Acton exchanged a knowing look with Laura as their good friend heard the news.

"There's no way you two are going to Moscow alone."

Acton decided to have a little fun with Reading. "Now, now, Hugh, I'm a big boy with big boy pants. I can go wherever I want, whenever I want."

Reading growled at him. "For once in your life, would you take something seriously?"

Acton laughed then swatted his friend on the shoulder. "We'll be fine. We'll land, we'll go to the hotel, collect the documents, and leave."

"And you don't think that's suspicious? Only being on the ground in Moscow for a few hours?"

"We said we were going for three days to tour the sites."

"Then how the hell are you going to leave the same day?"

"We have an exceptional travel agent. The moment we've secured the documents, she'll have the pilot file a new flight plan to leave immediately. Laura will fake stomach cramps, and the moment they look at her scar, they won't ask twice. We'll be out of Moscow by the evening and back in London to have a nightcap with you."

"You've thought of everything, have you?"

Acton offered up a toothy grin. "Don't I always?"

Reading glared at him. "You realize I've run out of fingers and toes counting how many times you two have gotten yourselves into trouble?"

"More times than James Bond."

Reading jabbed a finger at him. "That's the problem. You think you're James Bond."

"I always thought I was Indiana Jones."

Laura rolled her eyes. "Please, Hugh, don't give him any ideas. Last year for Halloween it took me a week to get the whip and fedora off him." She pulled up a photo on her phone and held it out to Reading who glared at it for a moment then burst out laughing. Acton, now curious as to what picture she had shown, leaned over and groaned. He was buck naked with a Corona in one hand, the whip in the other, and the fedora on his man-made hat stand.

"I can't believe you kept that photo."

She gave him a look. "I can't believe you'd ever think I wouldn't. Do you want to see the video I have of him twirling the hat?"

Reading stepped back, two hands held out in defense. "Hell, no." He became serious. "I'm not stopping you two, am I?"

Acton shook his head. "No, but I promise, we'll be careful. And if anything happens to us, I've sent Tommy and Mai instructions on what to do."

Reading's eyes narrowed. "And just what are they supposed to do?"

"Set the Internet on fire about what really happened to the Imperial regalia. If the Russians really want their secret kept, they won't touch us."

Reading frowned, staring at them both. "There's one thing I think you're failing to consider."

"And what's that?"

"Whether the secret that Orlov has discovered is more important than the one you're relying upon to protect your lives."

South of France

Zorkin sat aboard the bullet train taking him from the South of France and eventually to Paris. He was pissed. He had been enjoying himself on the French Riviera, soaking up the rays that the young people were so terrified of, possible skin cancer the least of his worries. But now, Orlov's idiocy had ended the summer he had planned. If it were anyone else, he would have just let the man swing, but unfortunately, Orlov was aware of who had rescued him, and the last thing Zorkin wanted was for the Russian government to figure out his involvement.

It would prove inconvenient for his retirement.

He had managed to stay under the radar, which allowed him to travel freely to and from the motherland. He spent little time there now, as he didn't trust the current regime. His countrymen had squandered their opportunity at freedom, not having the patience to wait for the economy to recover after the collapse and, instead, turning to a strongman to lead them.

Zorkin had been KGB, one of their top operatives, and he had never met the diminutive president in all his years of service. The president had been a nobody, a cog in a massive machine that would go unnoticed if removed. How he had managed to parlay that into becoming one of the most powerful leaders in the world was impressive. But unfortunately, he was a man stuck in the past who worshipped a Soviet Union that never was, and a leader counted among the most brutal in history.

And the public loved it.

"Ignorance is bliss," as his former rival, Alex West, might have said. Unfortunately, it wasn't just ignorance. History was being rewritten, this time, ironically, by the losers. The Communists might be out, but the new political elite were no fans of democracy either, despite embracing capitalism. The country was heading more in the direction of a Chinese-style government rather than a Western one.

Zorkin doubted he would be around to see the true carnage. If something were to happen to the president, if he were to die unexpectedly, the power vacuum left behind could be disastrous for his country. But the future of his homeland wasn't what was at stake today, it was his own. He had to find Orlov and rein him back in. There was no indication he had gone to Moscow, however the professors were heading there with the understanding they would be meeting with the man.

And that had him concerned. How had they had their visas approved so quickly? And if theirs were approved, why was Agent Reading's denied? He sensed a set-up. He suspected those searching for

Orlov were hoping the professors would lead them to him, and they would be caught up in the net.

He liked them. They were good people. Courageous, though perhaps foolhardy at times, including now. They were insisting on going, a possible historical discovery blinding them—nothing out of the ordinary for them, according to Kane. It could work to his advantage, however. If they were indeed meeting with Orlov, then they were his best chance at finding the man before it was too late.

He just hoped he could get there in time to tail them to his wayward charge. Unfortunately, their money meant they could arrive hours ahead of him and he would be too late to recover Orlov.

And perhaps save the professors from themselves.

Izmaylovo Market

Moscow, USSR

March 4, 1923

"Are you Bazarov?"

Bazarov frowned at the man. "Is it wise to use names?"

The man, whose name Bazarov didn't know, shrugged. "What's important here is that you don't know mine. That way, if you're caught, you can't give them my name in exchange for leniency."

Bazarov grunted. "Comrade, if I'm caught, there won't be any room for leniency."

The man regarded him for a moment. "How did you find me?"

"Through a friend who has dealings with your, shall we say, type?"

The man chuckled. "If I cared what you thought of me, I might be insulted. But since I don't"—he shrugged—"I'm not. Now, the item you requested is tough to come by. It will cost. A lot."

"Money is not a problem."

"You say that now, but this is the new Soviet Union. Rubles don't exactly flow among the common man, and you, Comrade, appear to be most common."

Bazarov reached into his pocket and removed a wad of bills, handing them over. "A down payment."

The man's eyebrows climbed as he counted the bills. "That's a tidy sum for a man with holes in his shoes. Did you steal it?"

Bazarov frowned. "No. Where the money comes from is none of your concern. The question is, can you get it?"

"I can."

"How long?"

"Meet me here same time tomorrow with the rest of the money."

"How much?"

"Ten times this."

"Not a problem."

Bazarov turned on his heel and walked away, losing himself in the crowd and his thoughts. Ten times what he had handed over was an exorbitant amount, though he was confident he could get it—he had no choice. He needed what only this man could provide, and he needed it quickly if he were to save Lenin from himself, and the communist experiment from imploding.

Committees were a great concept, and Lenin's desire to expand the size of the current committee to reduce the power and influence of any one man was noble, but even the Round Table had King Arthur, and though his knights had a say, the final decision was always made by the king.

And Russia needed its king.

Nikitin Residence

Moscow, Russian Federation

Present Day

Nikitin yawned as he ate his breakfast, toast in one hand, his phone in the other. It had been a late night, even later for some of his team. As he reviewed the reports, his head shook. Friends and family had been interviewed, many woke in the middle of the night. Nobody had any idea where Volkov or his supposed ex-girlfriend were or where they might go. There was always a possibility someone was lying, though there wasn't much they could do about that. In the good old days, they would just take them to the basement at Lubyanka and beat them to within an inch of their life until they gave them the answers they were seeking.

Today, that only happened when there was no doubt they were being lied to, and the case was important enough to risk the potential blowback. In his time as an investigator, he noticed those pick-ups were more frequent, as were the beatings his father and grandfather described from the old days.

And the deeper he got into things, the more those old days sounded like today.

He didn't have a problem with that. Law and order had to be maintained, and if you were withholding information from law enforcement, then you were on the side of the criminals and deserved to be beaten. Crime was out of control in Russia. From the stories his parents and grandparents told, it wasn't in the Soviet Union. Yes, there were crimes of passion, but nothing could be done to prevent those. There was no drug war, little petty thievery, break-ins were rare, though his grandfather joked that it was because nobody had anything worth stealing.

The biggest thing that Soviet law enforcement had to deal with was espionage and the black market. Now, there were drugs, smuggling, human trafficking, prostitution, extortion. The gangs were brutal, and law enforcement seemed unable to get things under control. In the old days, and perhaps again soon, every suspected gang member would have just been rounded up and shot. China didn't have problems like this—you dealt drugs, you got a bullet to the head. As it should be. What a wonderful world that must be where criminals got what they deserved.

No second chances.

Deal in poison, you die. You're a member of a gang, you die. You associate with them, you die. It would clean things up quite quickly. Yes, a lot of innocent people would die along with the guilty, but ultimately the state would be stronger and the resources wasted combating criminals could be used to improve the lot of their victims—the average citizen.

He loved his country and would do anything to keep it strong, which was why he was such an admirer of the president. He had taken over the country when it was collapsing, when it couldn't afford to pay its soldiers, when its military was crumbling, when it was no longer feared by its enemies. The president had turned it all around, and now Russia was once again respected, once again feared. Its military was reequipping and developing weapons that terrified even the Americans.

He didn't want war. No sane person would. He merely wanted his country to be strong enough to never worry about the Americans interfering in its affairs. And anyone who would do anything that threatened his country's future or its reputation had to be tracked down and imprisoned or executed.

That included Professor Orlov.

And now it would appear his protege Volkov and the girlfriend Katarina.

She had him concerned. The file on her indicated she worked in information technology and was familiar with computers. It explained the government-level wipe they found, and the careful destruction of all the flash memory. She knew what she was doing. According to the interviews, she had broken up with Volkov over a month ago, yet he had still gone to her and she felt it was necessary to wipe her own equipment. It suggested to him she either had been involved from the beginning, or when he had arrived on her doorstep, she had helped him in some way.

He opened up the latest message and cursed. It was a report from her Internet provider showing a very large upload taking place last night, and the destination couldn't be determined beyond the fact it went to the Dark Web. The investigator that had sent the report indicated it was his belief that a single compressed file had been uploaded containing a large volume of data, and that data was likely images or video due to the size.

Since a scanner was found at the scene, he believed whatever documents had been stolen had been scanned then uploaded. It meant whatever secrets had been stolen were now out there, though without the originals, they might as well be digital forgeries. It made the need to find Volkov even more urgent.

He finished his breakfast, drained his coffee, then wiped his mouth. He looked across the table at his wife, doom scrolling through her tablet, a frown etched on her face since they had woken. "Are you still not talking to me?"

She glanced at him for a moment then returned her attention to the tablet, saying nothing.

"I guess not. Well, this may interest you. The case I'm working on directly involves the president. If I can solve it, who knows what might happen?"

She looked up from her tablet, her eyes slightly wider. "Really?"

He smiled slightly. The woman was a gold digger. He wasn't certain what the equivalent would be to describe him, but he was no better.

They both wanted to live better lives than they were now, to associate with better people, to be the snobs that now stared down on them with disdain. He was well on his way. He had climbed a good number of rungs on the ladder to power, though there was a long way to go, and if he could please the president by preserving the man's secrets, he just might get closer to the top of that ladder.

"I'm supposed to brief his chief of staff in a couple of hours. That means my words will be repeated directly to the man himself." Just thinking about it was exhilarating. Walking in the halls of power, rubbing shoulders with the elite of society was what he had always dreamed of. And though he rarely got to speak to them, this was an opportunity to perhaps join them.

He suddenly felt nervous, and she noticed.

"What's wrong?"

He shivered. "Just a case of the jitters, I guess. It's an important meeting and, unfortunately, there's no good news."

"But that's not your fault."

"No, of course not. However, if they look for someone to blame, it's going to be me."

She rose from her chair and rounded the table. She put her arms around his neck and leaned in, pressing her forehead against his. "Then you'll just have to go in there with confidence and make bad news sound like progress."

He drew in a deep breath. "I guess you're right."

She extended a hand and he took it. She tugged at it and he rose. "I know how to settle your nerves."

He checked his watch. "I don't have time."

She pressed a finger against his lips. "Don't worry about me. This is for you and our future."

He grinned as he followed her to the bedroom. She might be a gold digger, but she was his gold digger.

Novinsky Hotel, Fourth Floor
Moscow, Russian Federation

Sofia pushed the cart with the room service order, her heart pounding with excitement. When Alina had handed over to the day manager, the overheard conversation indicated VIP guests had checked in overnight. They weren't to be disturbed as they wished to remain anonymous. Alina had said she would return to handle their lunch order and would start her evening shift early to deal with dinner.

It was a little unusual. Typically, VIPs who wished to remain anonymous had their own assistants who would take care of food orders and whatnot. Perhaps these people were so well-known that even their assistants might be recognizable, or they had traveled with no entourage whatsoever to maintain a low profile. She was leaning toward the latter, as the room they were in wasn't very impressive, nor was this hotel. It wasn't a dump by any means, though it was certainly not a five-star establishment. Yet if one wanted to remain anonymous, avoiding the flashiest of hotels was probably a good idea.

It had her so incredibly curious, she was doing something stupid—delivering a breakfast order that had never been placed in the hope she could catch a glimpse of who it was that Alina had stashed away overnight. It wasn't fair that Alina got to deal with all the interesting people, though she supposed Alina had earned the right, having put in her dues to become the night manager. Sofia couldn't imagine working nights. What kind of life was that? How could you ever have a boyfriend or any type of social life for that matter? 8:00 PM to 6:00 AM? Horrible.

She reached the VIPs' door and inhaled deeply, steeling herself for what could be an awkward encounter. She rapped twice. "Room service!" She heard movement on the other side of the door but no one said anything. She knocked on the door again and repeated her call, this time adding English to the mix as most foreign stars, no matter where they were from, spoke the language. To her delight, this garnered a response.

"We didn't order anything." It was a man's voice in heavily accented English, and unfortunately, the accent sounded Russian. Not as exciting as catching Chris Hemsworth or Drake, though there were plenty of Russian stars that she would die to get a picture with, or an autograph.

She pressed her luck even further. "Alina thought you might enjoy some breakfast. I'll just leave it out here for you."

"That's fine, thank you," called the voice through the door. She positioned the cart so it was just far enough from the door that he would have to step out into the hallway to retrieve it, then headed down the hall, fishing her phone out for the money shot. She turned the corner then peered out from behind it, the video recording. The door opened, sending her pulse racing. A man stepped out, checking both ways before grabbing the handle of the cart and dragging it into the room, the door closing behind him. She stopped the recording and played it back, zooming in then pausing it at a good shot of his face. He was young, around her age, maybe a few years older, the unkempt hair suggesting he was in the entertainment business, though his face was clean-shaven.

But it was the eyes that caught her attention. They were filled with fear and fatigue, saddled with sallow, black circles. Her shoulders slumped with disappointment. She had no idea who he was. If he were famous, he should at least tweak a memory, but he didn't. He might not be in the entertainment business after all, but the treatment he was receiving meant he had to have money. He could be the son of some billionaire oligarch hiding from his father or his father's rivals. A slight smile cracked her disappointment, and she wondered whether the video might be worth something to someone, perhaps a paparazzi outlet that might give her some money.

But she needed to know who the man was. She posted the video with a message.

Does anybody recognize him?

She headed for the elevators, wondering what kind of pay day she might be in for if this man were indeed somebody of interest.

Novinsky Hotel, Room 412

Moscow, Russian Federation

Volkov attacked his food. He was starving. He hadn't expected to get any more food until lunch when Alina returned, so this was a pleasant surprise.

Katarina eyed him, not partaking. "How can you be hungry at a time like this?"

He shrugged, continuing to shovel. "I have no idea when I'm going to get a chance to eat next. For all we know, Professor Orlov could be here any minute and then who knows what's going to happen."

Katarina shook her head. "I think you're dreaming. He's a wanted man. He has no way of getting in the country."

He wagged a finger at her. "You're assuming he left."

"You really think he's been in the country this entire time?"

He shrugged. "No idea, but if he intends to meet us, he would have to be, wouldn't he? They would be watching for him at the airports, and with facial recognition software, they'd spot him in an instant."

"I agree, just like they'd spot us in an instant, too."

Volkov pushed his plate away, resisting the urge to lick it clean. He wiped his mouth with the cloth napkin, then drained his orange juice. "Well, if that's the case, and he is here, how does he expect to get us out?"

"If he's here, then that means he hasn't been able to get *himself* out in all this time, so there's no way in hell he's going to be able to get *us* out." She burst into tears. "We're screwed! You realize that, don't you? Our faces are all over the news and everybody in Russia is looking for us. Even our own friends and family would be fools not to turn us in for the amount of money they're offering as a reward. We have to start thinking about saving ourselves."

He rubbed his tongue along his teeth, frowning, for she was right. It was clear to him since last night's fiasco had begun that Orlov had no plan. The documents were supposed to be public, therefore taking them shouldn't have been a criminal act. Stealing them had never been in the cards.

He didn't believe Orlov was in Russia. If he had indeed escaped from prison, he had help doing so. And if that help could break the man out of a prison cell in Russia, then those connections also had a way of getting him out of the country. There was no way they would break Orlov out and leave him here. Katarina was right. There was no way he would have any hope of coming back to Russia to retrieve them and the documents.

He exhaled heavily, his lips vibrating. "He's not coming for us, is he?"

"No shit."

"Then what are we going to do?"

"What can we do? Eventually, we'll be tracked here, then we'll be arrested. End of story."

"Then what are we going to do? We can't go out on the streets. There are too many cameras, and if we stay here, you're right, they'll eventually track us down."

Katarina dropped into the second chair at the small table. "We need to stop panicking and think logically."

He sniffed loudly and held his breath for a moment, struggling to control his nerves. He finally let out a burst of air and nodded. "All right, logically. What is our problem?"

"The government's after us."

"Right. And why are they after us?"

"Because you stole information they don't want made public."

"Right. So how do we make it so that they don't want to arrest us? Give it back to them?"

She shook her head. "No, they'll still arrest you for having stolen it, and both of us for having seen it. Remember, this is a secret that they don't want to get out to the public."

He chewed his cheek then his eyes shot wide. "What if it weren't a secret?"

She eyed him. "What do you mean?"

"I mean, if everybody knew the secret, then it wouldn't matter if we had it. Catching us would be pointless."

Her jaw dropped. "You mean release it to the public?"

163

"Exactly."

"They might kill us for that."

He shrugged. "Better dead than being tortured and put in prison."

She grunted. "I suppose, though I don't like any of the options." She gestured toward his bag containing the stolen documents. "Isn't it all worthless without the proof? We can't just go and put the scanned images up on the Internet. The government will just say they're fake and still come after us to get their hands on the originals. The only way any of this works is if we get the originals into the hands of someone who will do something with them, who can spread the word that they are real. Only then does catching us become pointless."

"Maybe we can contact a reporter."

She laughed. "I hope you don't mean a Russian reporter. The only ones who would take us seriously are the same ones that almost nobody takes seriously. We have to get the originals into the hands of an American reporter, or a Western European reporter."

"Which means we need to get out of Russia." He threw up his hands. "How the hell are we supposed to do that?"

She shook her head. "You're forgetting that there are foreign reporters here."

He tossed his head back and groaned. "You're right, but how do we find one of them?"

"We need to find out what reporters are stationed here in Moscow, then send them a copy of the files and see if they're interested."

"You really think they would be? This is sort of an 'important to Russia' story, not important to anyone else."

"Well, if we're to believe our glorious president, everyone in the West is out to embarrass us, and what better way to embarrass us than to shame one of its greatest heroes."

He spat. "Not my hero."

"Nor mine, but he is our president's hero."

Volkov glanced over at the tablet Alina had provided them. "Do we dare?"

Katarina shrugged. "I don't see that we have much choice."

He rose. "If we're going to do this, we have work to do. That file is way too big to be emailed. I'm going to pick out half a dozen of the most incriminating pages, then we'll pick out the biggest reporters stationed here in Moscow and try to reach out to them. Hopefully, before we're ready to do that, we'll have heard from the professor."

She rolled her eyes. "With his gloriously clever plan to save us, I'm sure."

Izmaylovo Market
Moscow, USSR
March 5, 1923

Bazarov had it. In his pocket. The exchange had been smooth, the money handed over, the package inspected. Unfortunately, he had no idea what to look for, and had no way to confirm what had been delivered worked.

Bazarov had eyed the tiny glass vial. "How do I know this is what you say it is?"

"When your victim keels over and dies, you'll know you got your money's worth."

He frowned. "How quickly does it work?"

"If he takes the full dose, he'll be dead in minutes."

"And if he doesn't?"

The man shrugged. "I don't know. Force it down his damned throat if you don't think he'll take it."

"And is it traceable?"

"Only if they're looking for it, which they won't be, I assume."

Bazarov was certain they wouldn't be. Not with his friend's health history. Most expected the man to be dead within the year, and if it weren't for the Congress in April, waiting for nature to take its course would have been enough.

But it wasn't.

The future of the great socialist experiment was at stake, and its fate couldn't be left to chance. Lenin must die, and soon, before he delivered his testament to the Congress and tore asunder what so much spilled blood had created.

The man eyed him as he folded up the package and placed it in his pocket. "Just so you know, I'm leaving Moscow, so if you need anything else, you won't be able to reach me."

Bazarov's eyes narrowed. "Why?"

"Because with the amount of money you paid me without even haggling, whoever you're planning on killing must be important."

Bazarov leaned closer to the man. "I suggest you take that money, and that tongue, and get as far away from Moscow as you can, because if this doesn't work the way you say it will, they will tear this country apart looking for you."

The man paled. "Won't they be looking for you as well?"

Bazarov smiled slightly. "I'm prepared to die for my country. Are you?"

The man jabbed a finger at him as he backed away. "You're insane."

Bazarov chuckled at the memory. He wasn't insane. What he was about to do might be considered by some to be the act of an insane man, but sometimes it took an insane act to make certain sanity prevailed.

And next week, when he made his usual visit to his old friend, the insane act would be committed, and his patriotic duty complete.

He would poison his best friend to save what they had all fought so hard for.

Vnukovo International Airport

Moscow, Russian Federation

Present Day

Acton followed Laura down the steps of their lease-share private jet. It was a beautiful summer day in Moscow, and the flight here had been uneventful. Laura's trick for helping get them both to sleep had worked, though, unfortunately, there were too few hours left in the night for it to have made enough of a difference. Fortunately, he never had trouble sleeping on an airplane, especially a Gulfstream G5. He was well-rested, and hopefully prepared for whatever was about to be thrown at them. The fact they hadn't been greeted by half a dozen machine gun-toting security personnel suggested they might actually make it off the airport grounds.

A buxom young blonde greeted them with a Hollywood-white smile. "Professor Acton, Professor Palmer, my name is Natalya, and I'll be facilitating your entrance today."

After exchanging pleasantries, she escorted them into the charter terminal reserved for the well-heeled, chattering away the entire time. They both remained politely engaged, though his focus was on their surroundings, keeping an eye out for extra security, for men whispering into their wrists, for a newspaper positioned just low enough to see over.

But he saw nothing.

And he saw everything. If he weren't careful, he would become paranoid and cause the regular security to take an interest in him, when, for the moment, they had none. Customs clearance was a formality with apologies made for the limited inconvenience. In less than 15 minutes, they were in their SUV rental, heading into the city.

"Why don't you set up the GPS so we know where we're going?" suggested Laura, handling the driving duties.

Acton fished out his phone now that they were mixed in anonymously with the heavy Moscow traffic. "I've got a message from Hugh."

"Of course you do."

Acton chuckled and fired an innocent message, just in case the authorities were monitoring somehow.

Picked up our rental, heading for our hotel. Talk to you soon.

He sent a hugs and kisses emoji just to toy with the man and a flipped bird was returned. "I think Hugh's starting to get the hang of this texting stuff."

"I wouldn't tell him that. He's liable to be insulted. You better contact Arseny."

He sent a message to Orlov.

We arrived and are heading to the hotel now. Would you like to meet for drinks?

The reply was instantaneous.

Delighted to. I'm in room 412.

Excellent. See you within the hour.

Acton wagged the phone. "So that was him. He'll meet us in his room." He pulled up the hotel address on his phone then input it in the vehicle's GPS, the computer indicating 40 minutes to their destination.

Laura changed lanes. "I still don't understand what's going on. I thought he wasn't supposed to be in Russia. He has to be wanted by the authorities, so flying in wouldn't be an option unless he had one of those Ethan Hunt masks."

"Anything's possible if Dylan's involved, but at least we know he's here and we'll soon know what the hell this is all about."

Laura agreed. "I just hope it was all worth it. What do you think he's found?"

Acton chewed his cheek. "It has to be something that the Russian government would be interested in, otherwise he could've just stuffed it in a FedEx envelope and couriered it out of the country. He has to think they're actively searching for it, and it has to be smuggled out by hand."

"But if the government's after it, then doesn't that mean it's stolen?"

"Possibly, or it's just embarrassing." He sighed heavily, shaking his head. "I just have no idea. All I do know is the last time he was this

171

excited, we almost went to war. If we had ignored him then, we probably would have. I think we owe him enough to see what it is he thinks is so important that it could rewrite history."

A police car blasted past in the opposite direction, causing them both to flinch. Acton exhaled, exchanging a glance with Laura. "We're going to have to do a lot better than that if we don't want to draw attention to ourselves."

"No kidding." She splayed her fingers on the steering wheel, relaxing her grip. "So, let's review our plan and try to take our mind off things."

Acton leaned his head back and closed his eyes for a moment. "We arrive at the hotel, check in, then go to our room."

Laura raised a single finger from the steering wheel. "Wait. Are we parking or are we valeting?"

Acton pulled up the hotel on his phone. "There's no indication here whether they valet or not, but maybe it's a good idea to park on the street in case we have to leave in a hurry. We don't want to be waiting for a valet to bring our car around."

Laura's head slowly bobbed. "But if we're leaving in a hurry, doesn't that mean it's all gone wrong?"

"Perhaps. Or perhaps it means if we don't leave quickly, things *will* go wrong. Have you seen any indication we're being followed?"

Laura rechecked the rearview mirror. "No, but the traffic's so heavy, there's no way to be sure. And they could be using a drone or a helicopter, and we'd never know. I think we have to go under the assumption that we are being watched, and they're looking for us to do something out of the ordinary."

Acton grunted. "Like meet with a wanted man in a hotel room?"

"Exactly." Laura growled. "I swear, if these documents don't force them to rewrite all the textbooks on Russia, I'm going to be pissed."

Acton laughed. "I remember when I was in elementary school, our science textbook talked about the moon and how it was created, and the summary stated that maybe one day, if man goes to the moon, we'll be able to answer these questions."

Laura cocked an eyebrow. "Have you been lying about your age?"

He laughed. "No. That's just how out-of-date the textbooks were in my public school."

"Good thing your school district didn't teach that the science on the moon was settled."

Acton chuckled. "Yeah, I always get a kick out of that. Whenever I hear someone say, the science is settled, I assume I'm either listening to a politician or an idiot. Don't get me started on agenda-driven science." He held up a hand, stopping himself. "So, back to planning. We park as close as we can to the hotel, we check in and go to our room, then meet with Arseny, get the papers, go back to our room, order some room service, call Mary to have her reschedule the flight for an early departure, call down to the front desk to tell them we're going to have to check out early, head for the airport, get on the plane, and we're back in London before midnight. As long as we remain calm and don't draw any attention to ourselves, we shouldn't have any problems."

"From your lips to God's ears."

Acton laughed. "I don't think I've ever heard you say that before. You better not let Hugh hear you talk like that, or he'll insist you remain in London." He paused for a moment, thinking of their friend. "He is right, though."

"About what?"

"We don't get together enough."

"And I don't get back enough."

Acton turned to face his wife, their current concerns forgotten. "Are you unhappy in the States?"

She shook her head vigorously, reaching out and grabbing his forearm with one hand, giving it a squeeze. "No, not at all. That's not what I'm saying. I'm very happy, but London is home, or at least it was for almost my entire life. It's natural to miss it."

"Of course it is. Maybe we could split our time. I could talk to Greg and see about teaching only one term, and you could talk to your old school to see about teaching a term there."

She thought for a moment, a frown rapidly creasing her face. "No, I really don't have any family in the UK that I'm close to, and I was always so engrossed in my work that I didn't have many friends. But back home, our home, we've got Greg and Sandra, Tommy and Mai, your father. We should, though, try to see Hugh more often. I think he's lonely now that Martin's gone."

"Maybe we should get a bigger place," suggested Acton. "I'm not talking some palatial estate, but just something with an in-law suite or something like that, where he could come over and stay with us for a few weeks and have a little independence."

"But that would mean giving up your home."

"That's not my home. That's my house. I bought it because my parents kept harping that I shouldn't be paying rent, I should be building equity. Home is wherever my head hits the pillow, preferably with you beside me."

"Then it's settled. When we get back home, we'll look for a bigger place."

He reached out and squeezed her thigh. "I think it's a fantastic idea. And besides, with all the people who've been trying to kill us, a change of address might not be a bad idea."

Novinsky Hotel, Room 412

Moscow, Russian Federation

Volkov's finger hovered over Alina's tablet as his heart hammered and his pulse pounded in his ears. Once he tapped the screen, there was no going back, yet if he didn't, they might have no future.

"What are you waiting for?" asked Katarina. "Are you having second thoughts?"

He stared at her. "Aren't you?"

She sighed. "I suppose, but what choice do we have? The only way we can take away their reason for chasing us is to make that reason public. And the only way we can make it public in a meaningful way is through the press."

He tapped the screen, the "Send" icon briefly flashing before the message addressed to a dozen foreign reporters based in Moscow disappeared from the screen.

"What do we do now?"

He shrugged. "We wait, I guess."

"How long do you think it'll take for them to respond?"

"My guess is none of them will. They'll think we're crazy. But you never know. We could get lucky. They should at least be curious as to whether the copies of the documents we sent them are genuine."

"In the meantime, what do you want to do?"

"Alina should be here in about an hour."

Katarina leaned back and stretched, and he couldn't help but stare at her chest. "What could we do that takes about an hour?" she asked as she groaned. She came out of her stretch but he didn't notice. "And just what are you staring at?"

"Huh?" he asked, still staring. His head jerked up, his cheeks flushing as his eyes met hers. "Umm, sorry."

She smirked at him. "Well, it *is* one way to kill an hour."

He gulped, his eyes widening. "Are you serious?"

She held up a finger. "It's just sex. It doesn't mean we're back together."

He didn't care. He was so horny and desperate for a distraction, she could have lumped on any conditions, no matter how outrageous, and he would have agreed. "Just sex," he repeated.

She rose and took his hand. He stood and followed her to the bed, then spun her around, wrapping his arms around her. She moaned as he squeezed her tight, and as he leaned in to give her the kiss he had so desperately wanted to give her for so long, the tablet beeped, indicating a message from Orlov.

They both groaned.

He let her go and sat back at the table, bringing up the secure app Katarina had installed on Alina's tablet.

Be ready to leave within the next half-hour.

He turned to face Katarina, excited. "He's coming in the next thirty minutes!" He checked his watch and glanced over at the bed. "Thirty minutes." He rose and grabbed her, his eyebrows bobbing. "We've done it before."

She gave him a look. "If we're going by your previous record, we've got time enough for ten goes at it."

He turned away sheepishly. "Hey, sometimes I get excited."

A hand on his cheek redirected his gaze forward. She smiled at him. "Who could blame you?" He chuckled as she gently slapped his cheek. "But, no, that message said 'within.' That means he could be here any minute. Besides, I want to have a good time too."

He sighed. "I suppose."

She squeezed his chin tight between her fingers. "But if we make it out of this alive, you and I have a date with the sheets."

He flashed her a toothy grin as someone down below looked to sign the agreement. There was a quick rap at the door and they both gasped as it flew open and Alina burst in.

"What happened to the coded knock?" cried Volkov.

Katarina turned her head slightly toward him, her voice a whisper. "Good thing the professor interrupted us or who knows what she would have walked in on."

"No time for knocks. We've gotta go now!" said Alina, the urgency in her voice putting an end to any thoughts of a joy ride, fear once again gripping them both.

Approaching the Novinsky Hotel

Moscow, Russian Federation

Acton pointed ahead at an empty parking spot just vacated as a tow truck removed a notorious British sportscar, likely broken down rather than tardy on the meter. "There."

Laura gunned the engine, determined to get the spot, already having lost out on two others to Muscovite drivers who had no concept of etiquette. She forced her nose in before another car, crossing the two lanes from the opposite direction, could, and she flashed the driver a grin as they shook a fist. The spot claimed, she parked properly and Acton took a photo of the floor, marking their GPS location should anything go wrong and they lost their bearings. Laura did the same as she climbed out.

Acton grabbed his satchel from the back seat, filled with a couple of hundred printed pages from various academic works in English and Russian that they had printed off at her apartment last night as they formulated their plan of escape. The intention was to mix the documents among those they had brought with them with the hopes no one would know what was what. He unloaded their two carry-ons, handing one to Laura, then took her hand. They walked calmly toward the hotel just up the street and were greeted by the doorman who bowed slightly as he smiled broadly. Acton returned the smile and followed Laura inside. They quickly checked in and were escorted to their room. Amenities were pointed out and a tip was handed over, then a few minutes later they were headed for the elevators and their rendezvous.

Acton spotted a camera out of the corner of his eye and decided small-talk could prove beneficial should things go south. "I'm looking forward to seeing Arseny. It's been so long."

Laura caught on immediately. "Me too. I haven't heard from him in so long, I was concerned maybe something had happened to him. I guess he was just too busy with his work to respond to emails."

He chuckled. "We all know what that's like, though I think he took it to the extreme."

The doors opened and they stepped out, his heart drumming for a mix of reasons—fear, anticipation, excitement. He was excited to see that Orlov was well, but he was even more so to see the documents the man had referred to. What was so important that he was willing to risk his life? What had he discovered that he was convinced could rewrite history?

"This is it," said Laura, pointing at a door ahead. A raised woman's voice had her pausing before knocking.

"Why did you open the door? I told you not to!"

"But she said you sent her with breakfast."

"I already brought you breakfast before I left."

Laura turned to Acton, puzzled. "Neither of them sounds like Arseny."

"Is it the right room?" But he already knew the answer. It was, unless Orlov had sent the wrong room number. "What do you want to do?" he whispered.

"I didn't come all the way to Moscow to just turn around now." She reached out and rapped on the door, silencing the argument on the other side. "Arseny, it's us."

An excited utterance from the other side of the door, cut off with a hiss, convinced Acton they were indeed at the right room. But something was wrong. They could turn around now, perhaps walk away without involving themselves further, but if the police were inside waiting for them, why wouldn't they just open the door and arrest them now? No, something else was going on.

He leaned closer to the door. "Arseny, it's us. James Acton and Laura Palmer. We came all this way at your request. At least do us the courtesy of opening the door."

"James Acton? As in Professor James Acton?" It was a young man's voice, trembling with terror.

"Yes, Professors James Acton and Laura Palmer. Professor Arseny Orlov requested we meet him here."

A whispered exchange erupted on the other side of the door, then there was a click. The door opened and a woman wearing the hotel's uniform stared at them. Laura smiled at her and extended a hand.

"I'm Laura."

The woman grabbed her hand and yanked her inside, then reached out for Acton, pulling him in as well. She shoved the door closed, straining the pneumatic closer. "Identification," demanded the woman.

"Now, look here," began Acton before he was cut off.

"Identification or leave."

He frowned but handed over his wallet as Laura retrieved hers from her purse. The woman read the two IDs then handed them back. "Satisfied?" asked Acton.

"No, but I don't really have a choice. If you were the authorities, then you've already found them."

Laura's eyes narrowed. "Them?"

Acton ignored that part, focusing more on the mention of the authorities. It meant something illegal was going on. She led them into the room and they found a young couple sitting on the bed, holding each other, both trembling, their eyes wide. Acton made a cursory check of the room to make sure they were alone before facing the man. "Do I know you?"

The young man shook his head. "No. My name is Dmitri Volkov. I was a graduate student of Professor Orlov's before he was imprisoned. He mentioned your name on several occasions, and as a student of archaeology, I, of course, know it."

"Then perhaps you know my wife, Professor Laura Palmer?"

The man's face brightened. "The former head of archaeology at the British Museum?"

"Yes." Laura smiled at the young woman. "And you are?"

"Katarina Rozhenko."

Laura turned to the staff member who had let them in. "And you are?"

"None of your concern."

"Her name is Alina," muttered Katarina.

Alina glared at her. "Our bigger concern is that." She jabbed a finger toward a room service cart.

Acton glanced at it. "Why are we concerned about that?"

"Because I didn't deliver it. One of my colleagues did, against orders. She has a habit of doing things like this, trying to get photos of celebrities." Alina held out her phone, a video playing on it, showing Volkov stepping out of his room then pulling the cart inside. "This is on the Internet."

Volkov paled and Katarina visibly tightened her grip on his arm. "Why would she post it on the Internet?" whispered Volkov.

"Because she wanted to know who you were, so she posted it to her friends. It's been up there for hours. "

Acton held out his hand. "May I?"

Alina handed him her phone. He ignored the video and instead quickly scrolled through the comments, all in Russian, several dozen replies visible. He scrolled back to the top and brought up the profile of the woman who had posted the video and flipped through some more of her feed and cursed. She had scores of photos of her at the hotel, so if anyone saw this, they would know where she was working. "Okay, we have to get out of here now," he said as he handed the phone back.

Volkov looked up at him. "But she said nobody knew who we are."

Alina threw her hands up. "Idiot! There's a ten million ruble reward out for you. They're not going to post who you are if they recognize you, otherwise they might have to share the reward."

"She's right," said Laura. "We have to get out of here now."

Acton held up a finger. "We came here for some papers that were supposed to be handed to us by Arseny." He cursed. "And where the hell is he?"

Volkov shrugged. "I have no idea. None of this was supposed to happen. The papers were supposed to be in the public archive, but they weren't."

"And where were they?"

"They were in a secret archive in the basement of the building. I broke into it and stole what the professor wanted."

"Bloody hell," muttered Laura. "So that's what this reward is for? They're after you because you stole the papers?"

Volkov nodded.

Acton turned to Laura. "If they're already after him because he stole the papers..." He paused, his head whipping toward Volkov. "Do they know your name?"

"Yes."

Acton cursed again. "If they know who you are, then they know you used to be a grad student of Orlov's. And they know our association with him." His voice drifted as his eyes widened slightly.

It was Laura's turn to curse. "How long have they known your identity?"

Volkov shrugged. "I don't know. I saw the first report on the news last night."

Laura's jaw dropped slightly as she faced Acton. "That's before our visas were issued."

Acton tossed his head back and growled. "That means they probably knew we were involved from the get-go. They probably followed us from the airport."

"Then why haven't they hit us yet?"

Acton stepped over to the window and peered down at the street below, seeing nothing out of the ordinary. "Maybe they're just getting in position. Whatever the hell is going on here, we're now up to our necks in it." He shook his head as his jaw clenched. "The next time I see Arseny, I'm beating the shit out of him."

"Me too," agreed Katarina. "He's ruined all our lives."

Volkov's shoulders slumped and his head drooped. "This is all my fault," he murmured. "I'm so sorry."

Acton regarded the young man for a moment then made eye contact with Laura. They could leave now, simply head to the hotel room, feign ignorance if they were questioned, and follow through with their original plan, leaving these people to their own fate. They were strangers. He had no responsibility toward them. His responsibility was to protect Laura, though she would reject that notion and likely claim her responsibility was to protect him.

He thought back to the conversation they had had the previous evening with Reading. Was their duty to protect themselves, or to help these people? To him, there was no question. They had to help, or at least get help.

He pulled out his phone and quickly sent a message with their situation to Kane, praying he could send that help.

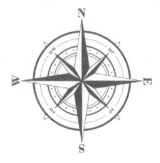

Outside the Kremlin

Moscow, Russian Federation

Nikitin sat in his SUV, scrolling through his messages. Thousands of tips were pouring into the hotline, and he was beginning to believe it had been a mistake to offer a reward. Every greedy bastard out there was phoning in that his neighbor with the noisy stereo was the man they were looking for. They were running down every lead, but it was taxing all their resources with little progress made. His briefing of the chief of staff had gone well. He was due to give another one in a few hours, and unfortunately, he had nothing new to report beyond the fact the professors had arrived and had checked into their hotel. Other than that, no progress had been made.

His phone rang over the vehicle's Bluetooth, and he took the call from his partner. "Tell me you've got news."

"I might have something, I just sent you a link. You're going to want to see it."

Nikitin brought up the message and tapped on the link. "What am I looking at?"

"Somebody sent this into the hotline earlier today. Who does that look like to you?"

He watched the video, a smile spreading as there was little doubt that this was Volkov. "Where was this recorded?"

"I don't know. Apparently, the tipster said they want their money before they give us that detail."

"Nuts to that. For all we know, this video was taken a year ago. Have our people look over it, see if there's any metadata embedded in it. The GPS location might actually be in the file."

"I already sent it over. We should know shortly."

He squinted at the video. "And see if they can isolate that food cart. The cloth on it has a crest. They might be able to identify the hotel."

Zaitsev cursed. "I didn't even see that."

Nikitin chuckled. "That's why they pay me the big bucks. And contact the tipster. Tell them we'll give them half the money up front. I want to know who the hell recorded this video, and I want to know now."

Magnaura Palace Hotel
Istanbul, Turkey

Kane sat on the balcony of his hotel room in Istanbul. The sun was baking down on the streets below, but his room was opposite the sun, leaving him in the shade. He sipped on his ice-cold bottle of Turkey's own Efes Pilsen. He was due to meet his handler in a couple of hours for a debrief. The mission had gone well, his target eliminated, the man brokering intellectual property stolen from one of America's biggest defense contractors, now dead.

A message had been sent, and the secrets were safe.

At least for today.

Tomorrow, they could be stolen again. The Chinese had built their economy on the backs of the free world's brains, and now they were reequipping their military with technology that should be beyond their capabilities. But with a relentless campaign to steal foreign technology, they were progressing to the point where they would soon exceed America's capabilities, or at least be able to neutralize them.

Hacking was out of control, with cyberattacks initiated by Chinese and Russian proxies not taken seriously enough. They had to be treated as acts of war. That didn't necessarily mean if the Chinese hacked you, that you bombed Beijing. It had to be more subtle, similar to how the Cold War was treated. If the Chinese hacked us, then seize assets, block their companies from doing business in America, kick the children of the Chinese elite out of the Western universities and colleges. Why were we educating the enemy? It was insane.

As long as China went unchallenged, it would continue to test the boundaries of what it could get away with. Hong Kong had been a test, and the West had failed. What would be next? The Chinese now arguably had the capability to take Taiwan. The only thing holding them back was what America would do. Would Americans be willing to shed blood again after twenty failed years in Afghanistan?

And this was an entirely different situation, an entirely different enemy, an enemy with nuclear capabilities and unlimited manpower. The Chinese wanted Taiwan. As far as they were concerned, it was a renegade province. The only reason it wasn't part of the communist state was because it was an island and the Chinese didn't have a blue-water navy. But they had been building it rapidly over the past few years, and it now included aircraft carriers. If the world didn't stand up to Chinese aggression now, they could very well be facing a China emboldened enough to invade Taiwan, and then the question was would America intervene, and would others join in, leading to a wider war?

Actions like he had taken yesterday were designed to send subtle signals to Beijing that America wouldn't be putting up with its nonsense anymore. But sometimes subtlety wasn't enough.

His watch gave him a jolt and he brought up the message indicating another update from Acton. He picked his phone up off his chest and logged into the secure messaging app, slowly shaking his head as he read the latest on the situation. He had told the man to be careful. There had been no point in telling him not to go. He was going regardless of anything he said.

He wasn't surprised Orlov wasn't there. There was no way the man was getting into the country without help. Not from where he was hiding. But the question was, where *was* he hiding? West had reported Orlov's house had been abandoned at least a week earlier. What was the man playing at? What was so important that he had involved a former student of his in something that had the Russian government apparently going apeshit, offering a ten-million-ruble reward? Why had he tricked Acton and his wife into meeting him in Moscow with no actual intent to meet?

The man had clearly gone off the deep end. He wouldn't be the first, nor would he be the last. Exile was never fun, especially his type. His wasn't an exile in a foreign land with a fat pension paid for by a grateful government. It was a privately funded exile equivalent to a meager pension in a foreign country. They should have extracted the family as well, but the Gray Network hadn't approved it. The son had been exonerated of any involvement, and the wife had never been a suspect. Bringing them out would be risky and expensive, and with the son a fully grown man in the prime of his life, he could have proved difficult to control. And if his father's recent activities were any indication, it appeared the assessment had been correct.

Now the question was, what to do about the current situation? Yes, the professors had gotten themselves into it, but he couldn't exactly leave them twisting in the wind, especially with all they had done in the past to help him and his friends. He forwarded the message to Leroux along with his own.

Ask the Chief how involved we can get.

He had a feeling Director Morrison was going to say, "Not at all." Extracting Orlov hadn't been a CIA operation. It was Zorkin, a former KGB operative, going rogue on the Gray Network, then dropping a problem into their lap. And while the Gray Network was mostly retired CIA, they weren't CIA. The best he could expect would be Morrison approving Leroux's team for support functions only. Yet that could be incredibly helpful, though access to CIA boots on the ground would be more so. If sanctioned, he could simply have someone collect them and pull them into the underground railroad. They would be out of the country within 24 hours.

But the only way he was ever getting that type of authorization was if he knew what the hell this was all about. All he knew was they were in trouble, but he didn't know why, and he wasn't even certain Acton knew why. He sent the man a message.

I need to know what these documents contain.

He forwarded the message from Acton to Reading with his own note.

Don't you dare go to Moscow and create another problem for me.

Then he sent one final message to the only person he could think of that also operated in the area, and might have some free time on his hands.

McDonald's Restaurant

Minsk, Belarus

Jack—just Jack—sighed with relief as he took advantage of a McDonald's bathroom. He had pissed in some godawful hell holes around the world, but wherever there was a McDonald's, he could be assured there was a relatively clean bathroom in it. It was a taste of civilization that went far beyond their sandwiches and fries.

His current assignment had him in Minsk. Langley had him extract an opposition party leader they feared was about to be handed over to Moscow, the Belarusian dictator a good friend of his Russian counterpart. The extraction had gone well, but the handover to the assets that would get him out of the country had been delayed. The pickup had occurred less than half an hour ago, after which the toilet was sought.

He had spotted the Golden Arches on his way to the parking garage where the exchange had occurred, and decided a few extra minutes were worth not encountering shit-stained walls and sticky floors.

And it meant a quarter pounder with cheese, fries, and a Diet Coke.

His CIA-customized Casio sent an electric pulse through his wrist. It was subtle but surprised him nonetheless, and he momentarily lost his aim. He cursed and regained control, finishing his business. He flushed the toilet, washed his hands, then got in line for his indulgence. He brought his food out to his car and shoved some fries in his mouth, groaning in pleasure and patting the bright red container they came in.

Oh, how I've missed you.

He pressed the buttons along the side of his cheap watch, his cover not warranting a $5,000 TAG Heuer like some agents he knew. The technology Langley had packed into it was worth tens of thousands, but it would never impress the ladies. His eyebrows shot up. The message was from the man himself, which was rare. They barely knew each other, but they trusted each other, and something must be up for Kane to have contacted him outside of channels.

He brought up the secure app on his phone and read the message. The professors were in trouble again, this time in Moscow, and Kane wanted to know if he could help. Jack's op was over. He was to report to Berlin Station in three days. What he did between now and then was his business. He typed a quick reply.

I'm in Minsk. Will try to get to Moscow ASAP. Will let you know when I'm on the ground.

He sent the message, then another to the office that handled all of his travel bookings.

Change of plans. Need ticket for Moscow leaving on next flight, return flight to Minsk tomorrow afternoon. Current cover.

He hit *Send* and leaned back in his seat, savoring every chew of his end-of-mission reward, and opened the secure file Kane had sent, hoping for an explanation as to what the hell two archaeology professors could have done to piss off the Russian government.

West/Bertrand Residence

Black Forest, Germany

West woke to find Adelle lying beside him, staring with a smile. "It's about time you woke up."

He stretched and groaned then glanced over at the alarm clock. "You let me sleep in." He pushed up on his elbows. "We should have been up two hours ago."

She shook her head. "No, you would've been dragging your butt all over the place. An extra couple hours of sleep means I should be able to get a full day out of you."

He gave her the stink eye. "When haven't you been able to get a full day out of me?"

"Oh, I don't know, every afternoon around three, when someone has to have their nap."

He grunted as he rolled his legs out of bed. "No one ever said that getting a nap in the afternoon wasn't part of a full day, especially at my age."

She hopped out of bed and he shook his head with envy. "To be ten years younger."

She stared at herself in the dresser mirror. "To be fifty years younger." She lifted her boobs. "These used to be much perkier."

He laughed as he joined her naked in front of the mirror. He pointed at his boys. "And these didn't used to reach my knees." She giggled and threw her arms around him as they both stared at their reflections. "Youth is wasted on the young."

She patted his chest. "You won't get any argument from me."

He kissed the top of her head. "If you could do it all over, would you change anything?"

She nodded. "Just one thing."

"What's that?"

"I would have told you about Alexis. I never would have wasted all those years."

He wrapped both arms around her and held her tight, his eyes glistening at the mention of their daughter. "And if I had to change one thing, I never would have let you go."

She sighed heavily. "Well, there's no point dwelling on what can't be."

He patted her back and pushed away. "We better get cracking. Any word from Viktor while I was asleep?"

She shook her head as he made for the bathroom. "He got on his flight and it should be arriving in Moscow any minute. Other than that, nothing."

"And the Gray Network?"

She gave him a look. "I figured you didn't want me prying your eye open for the retinal scan while you were trying to sleep."

He positioned himself in front of the toilet and began the battle with his prostate. "While I was getting my beauty sleep, did you think of any way we might track Orlov down?"

"We could talk to his neighbors, but I think that would be a waste of time. Every indication from our previous encounters with him was that he hadn't made any friends where he was."

"So then, where do you think he is?"

"I'm thinking he must be at a hotel. If he doesn't have any friends, he doesn't have a lot of choices. He either went into a hotel or he rented another apartment." Adelle entered the bathroom. "Or he's living out of his car."

West threw a victory fist in the air as the dribbles turned into a stream. "Maybe that's how we track him."

"What?"

"Well, his car wasn't there, so he must have taken it to wherever he was going."

"Do we have his plate number?"

He nodded. "It's on my phone. As soon as I'm done here, I'll have the Network put out an alert for it."

She left the bathroom and reappeared a moment later with his phone. She held it up to his eye and the phone scanned it.

"Impatient, are we?"

She gestured toward the weak stream. "Every minute counts, and you could be there until lunch."

Novinsky Hotel, Room 412

Moscow, Russian Federation

Acton gestured at the young couple still sitting on the bed. "Get up, grab only the necessities, and don't forget whatever the hell it was that has the government after you."

Volkov pointed at a nearby bag. "All the papers are in there."

Acton spotted a thick file folder sitting on top of the bag and was desperate to know what this was all about, but they didn't have time. "Grab it and let's get the hell out of here." He turned to Alina. "They're going to be after you now, too."

"Are you sure?"

"Yes. They're going to figure out that that video was taken at this hotel. Someone's going to look at the cameras and is going to realize you were in this room, so you knew they were here. You're in this just as deep as the rest of us."

Her chest swelled and her jaw squared. "I don't care."

Laura placed a hand on the woman's shoulder. "What you did to help them was very brave, but bravery only gets you so far. If this is as serious as it appears to be, then they'll arrest you and interrogate you. This is Russia. You know you don't want that."

Katarina joined in. "She's right. You know what those papers show. There's no way they'll let you free if they think you've seen them. They might even kill you."

If just seeing the documents might kill someone, then Acton had to see them for himself. What could possibly rewrite history and have the Russian government willing to offer a massive reward for the capture of those involved? What history were they talking about? To him, history wasn't what happened in the past couple of decades, though so much had changed in Russia in the past 30 years, it was possible. He had just assumed it had something to do with the Soviet Union, and maybe he was wrong.

He put an end to the debate. "Listen, come with us now, and you can change your mind later. If you want, you can turn yourself in, tell them that you were helping your friends to what you thought was a romantic getaway, you had no idea they were in trouble, and when you found out after your shift, you came back here to confront them and we forced you to come with us. You convinced us to let you go and you turned yourself in. There's no guarantee it'll work, but it'll work a lot better than you just continuing your shift at the hotel."

Alina regarded him for a moment then nodded. "I think that's a good idea."

"So do I," agreed Volkov.

Acton slapped his hands together. "Good. We're agreed. Now, let's get the hell out of here."

"Where are we going to go?" asked Katarina.

Laura headed for the door. "First we have to go to our room to get our luggage and passports. Alina, you stay between us. That way, it'll look like we were forcing you to go with us."

Volkov grabbed the bag with the documents and zipped it up before taking Katarina's hand. Acton herded everyone toward the door. "Let's get the hell out of here before Vlad himself comes knocking on the door."

Washington Post Moscow Bureau

Moscow, Russian Federation

Kaye Dempsey's head still pounded from the previous night's activities. For some reason, vodka just didn't agree with her, yet in Russia, it seemed to be all her domestic counterparts wanted to drink. Shot after shot. It was ridiculous. They had grown up on the stuff. She was certain that when the doctor smacked a Russian baby's ass and it cried out, shot glasses were handed around the room to everyone involved, including the newborn. She, on the other hand, had her first drink on her 21st birthday, having been a bookworm with no social life until and beyond that point.

Her fellow bookworms in college had insisted they all go out on her 21st. It was a local Mexican restaurant, and margaritas and tequila were on the menu. She remembered the homemade tortilla chips with fresh guac. And that was it. The next thing she remembered was waking up on the bathroom floor of her girlfriend's apartment.

And she swore she would never drink again.

Of course, it was an oath she broke, though she still maintained control as best she could. But last night had been stupid. Her colleagues at the Moscow foreign press pool had insisted on taking her out. It was her last official day on this beat. She was heading home, back to America, back to her country that had changed so much since she had been gone. She wasn't certain she would recognize it anymore. If it were as bad as some of her colleagues made it out to be, she just might be talking to the producers about getting another foreign assignment. Beijing intrigued her, and she had started taking Chinese lessons a year ago hoping it might put her on the radar should an assignment come up.

The writing had been on the wall for weeks now—the Kremlin was no longer taking her interview requests. She had asked too many difficult questions and was now on their blacklist. To her, it meant she was doing her job. Management agreed—that she had done it a little too well.

She checked her email one last time before starting the gauntlet of goodbyes that awaited her beyond her office door. Most were well-wishes, a few spam, and some updates from the various news wires. One with an attachment indicator caught her eye, the subject line causing her to be at once skeptical and intrigued.

We require your assistance. Russian government is after us because of attached information.

She opened the email and quickly read the plea for help. She was about to delete it when her brain registered what the next paragraph said.

The government is offering a 10-million-ruble reward for our capture.

Her jaw dropped as she experienced a flashback from the night before, the TVs in the bar playing the news report about the manhunt.

She finished reading the email and opened the first of half a dozen attachments. It was a document written in Russian that appeared quite old. She could speak Russian well enough to exchange pleasantries and navigate the supermarket, but reading something this old, handwritten in Cyrillic, was beyond her. She pushed the intercom button. "Inessa, can you come in here for a moment?"

"Right away."

Inessa was Russian, born and raised, a local hire invaluable in situations like this. She entered with a smile. "Please tell me you're not working."

Dempsey shrugged. "You know me." She pushed back from her desk. "I want you to tell me what this says."

Inessa leaned over the keyboard, staring at the monitor. Her jaw slackened and she muttered a curse as she jerked away from the screen.

"What is it? What's it say?"

What Inessa told her had her firing back a reply to the sender.

Gorki Estate

South of Moscow, USSR

March 10, 1923

Bazarov stepped into Lenin's dacha a bundle of nerves. He was here to kill his best friend, to save the future of the workers of the world. This was his moment to be a hero, and if everything went right, no one would ever know. He would leave an anonymous hero, taking no credit for what he had done.

The truest of heroes.

A selfless hero.

His eyes narrowed at the bustle of activity inside. Often, his friend's convalescence was busy due to the nature of his work, but it was always controlled chaos. This was panic.

He flagged a servant. "What's going on?"

"Comrade Lenin has had another stroke!" The man rushed off, the anguish on his face genuine.

Bazarov's heart ached for his friend. It would be his third stroke in less than a year, and if fortune saw fit, it might be his last, negating the need to poison the man, and ending his suffering.

Yet he had survived two, so why not three?

Bazarov rushed up the stairs toward his friend's bedchambers, and found a gaggle of staff outside his door. "Is he inside?" he asked as he approached the group.

The estate's head butler turned to face him. "Yes, sir. He is with his wife and his physicians."

"And his status?"

"I have not been made privy yet, sir."

Bazarov grabbed his forehead, squeezing tight. "Do we know if he's alive?"

"I believe so, sir, though I cannot affirm that his status hasn't changed."

"Who found him?"

A young woman curtsied. "I did, sir."

"What can you tell me?"

"I found him at his desk, sir, slumped in his chair. He couldn't speak. He just…he just made odd noises."

Bazarov cursed then paced in front of the door for several minutes before it finally opened and Lenin's wife, Nadezhda, stepped out and rushed into his arms at the sight of him.

"Oh, Anatoly, thank goodness you're here! It's awful! Just awful!"

"Is he…"

She shook her head. "He's alive, though for how long, the doctors cannot say. He's lost the ability to speak." She stared at him, her eyes red, her cheeks stained. "Of all the people to lose the power of speech! Such an eloquent man, such a commanding presence! To be silenced like this!"

He guided her to the side, away from the others, and lowered his voice. "Forgive me for this, however it is gravely important. The Congress is in a month. Do the doctors believe he'll recover by then?"

"I asked that very question. He so wished to deliver his Testament to the others, but I don't see how he can."

Bazarov suppressed his sigh of relief. "May I make a suggestion, one you may need to convince him is best for all?"

"Of course, Anatoly. He trusts you more than anyone."

"I suggest no mention be made of the Testament to anyone. If our dear comrade has any chance of delivering it in person, he must be given that opportunity."

"But that could mean waiting another year!"

"Yes, I realize that, but imagine the impact. Comrade Lenin battles back from a brutal stroke to reclaim his place at the head of our great nation, then delivers in person the words that will save our future from tyranny and ultimate failure."

She drew a long, deep breath, her head slowly bobbing. "You are right, of course. But what if he dies?"

"Then you as his wife will petition to present it posthumously, and it will have an even greater impact, as our dear leader will be guiding us forward from the grave."

She smiled and gripped his arm. "You have always been such a good friend to my husband. To us both. We shall make it so."

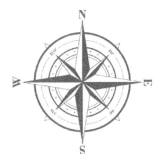

Sheremetyevo International Airport

Moscow, Russian Federation

Present Day

Zorkin handed his Russian passport over, the bored customs official scanning it. His entire body ached. He was getting too old for this shit. An emergency train ride from the south of France to Paris, three hours waiting at the airport for a three-and-a-half hour flight in coach, then an hour-long line-up. Security was heavier than usual, and it had him wondering why. If it were related to Orlov, then things had escalated.

And it could prove unfortunate.

"Stay here."

Zorkin flicked a wrist as if there were no point in arguing, as there wasn't. The man walked away, then returned with someone more senior who examined the passport and the computer screen.

"You purchased your ticket last-minute."

"Yes."

"Why?"

Zorkin shrugged. "I had the urge to return home."

"In the middle of the night?"

Again, Zorkin shrugged. "When you get to be my age, you don't necessarily follow the same schedule as a youngster like you. I'm always up in the middle of the night."

The man frowned. "According to this, you come and go quite frequently, usually just for a day or two."

"I'm enjoying my retirement in the south of France, but you just can't get good Russian food outside the motherland."

The man chuckled. "No, I suppose not." He beckoned two armed guards over. "Please follow them for further questioning."

Zorkin tensed slightly though he hid it. "Did I do something wrong?"

The man shook his head. "I'm sure you didn't, but we have orders to question anyone who purchased last-minute tickets."

Zorkin feigned interest, leaning in and lowering his voice. "Are you guys after somebody?"

The man gave him a look. "A man your age should know better than to ask a question like that."

Zorkin pushed away from the glass, raising his hands. "Sorry, you're right. Sometimes I forget things aren't so different than they used to be." He was led through a security door then directed toward a chair. He cursed. At least a dozen people were already waiting and. Minutes were critical, and this looked like it could take hours.

There was no way in hell he would be helping the Actons.

Departing the Kremlin

Moscow, Russian Federation

"It's the Novinsky Hotel."

Nikitin nearly hit the brakes. He instinctively leaned closer to the radio. "Did you say Novinsky Hotel?"

"Yes, sir. They positively identified the crest. It's definitely the Novinsky Hotel."

Nikitin pulled into an empty parking spot so he could focus on the conversation without rear-ending someone. "Isn't that the same hotel that those professors checked into?"

Zaitsev cursed. "I think it is. Just a second." Sounds of fingers tapping on a keyboard replaced his underling's voice for a moment. "Yes, sir. Our tail from the airport has them parking near the hotel, then entering with their luggage. Why wouldn't they have had their car valeted? They're rich, aren't they?"

Nikitin ignored the question. It was unimportant. What was important was the fact his suspicions were correct. The professors were at the same hotel as Volkov was. There was no way that was a coincidence. They were obviously there to meet. The question was whether Orlov was there as well. "Send the address of that hotel to my phone."

"Done."

His phone beeped and he tapped on the address, the navigation system automatically bringing it up with directions. "I'll be there in fifteen minutes," he said as he pulled out from the curb. "Send two teams. I want all the exits covered. Nobody goes in until I get there. Start checking any camera footage we have of the area. We know the professors are in there, but we need to confirm that Volkov is still there, and more importantly, Orlov. I don't want to hit them if he's not. This might be our only chance to get him."

"Yes, sir. Oh, and sir, we've identified who originally posted the video. Once our guys identified the hotel, I had them run the registered employees and it just came in while we were talking. Her name is Sofia Sidorov. She posted the video on social media this morning, asking if anyone knew who it was."

"Ping her phone. See if you can find out where she is. If she's not at the hotel, have her picked up for questioning. She might know whether Volkov is still there." He checked the time and cursed. "And let the president's Chief of Staff know that I'll be late for the meeting, but we'll hopefully have good news for him and the president shortly."

There was a pause at the other end. "Are you sure you want to say that, sir? What if something goes wrong?"

Nikitin frowned. Zaitsev was right. If there was one thing you didn't do in today's Russia, it was making promises you couldn't keep. It could kill careers. "You're right. Just tell them I'll be late for the meeting because we're conducting an operation. I'll provide them with an update as soon as I have one."

"Very wise, sir."

Nikitin chuckled. "I didn't get where I was by being stupid."

"No, sir. Most have family connections, and your parents, like mine, are nobody's."

Nikitin roared with laughter. "Be careful, my friend. You never know who's listening on the other end."

Zaitsev grunted. "Well, if they are listening, let's hope they're either too stupid to understand what I said, or they're one of the smart ones that agree."

Nikitin grinned. "I'm ending this call before we're both sent on assignment to Siberia." He pressed the button on his steering wheel, ending the call, then checked the navigation system. Ten minutes to his destination. Ten minutes to perhaps recovering the stolen files and arresting the traitor Orlov.

Ten minutes to an even higher career trajectory.

Agent Hugh Reading's Office, Interpol

London, England

Reading stared at the clock. They should already be at the hotel, and if they followed the plan, they should have already met up with Orlov. If he were running things, it would have been a quick exchange. They should have returned to their room, ordered their room service, feigned Laura's illness, and had their flight rebooked for immediate departure.

And they should have sent him an update.

He had none, yet he did have a message from Kane indicating he was to head to Moscow under no circumstances. That meant something had gone wrong. It had to. Unfortunately, or fortunately, depending on how it was looked at, his denied visa prevented him from even boarding an airplane destined to the Russian capital.

His partner, Michelle Humphrey, leaned into his office. "You look like shit, Hugh. Somebody shoot your dog?"

He looked up at her. "Huh? Shoot my dog?"

She shrugged. "I've been broadening my horizons and watching more American programming on Netflix rather than the BBC."

He eyed her. "I don't even know if an American would say that."

"I'll do better." She grinned then became concerned again. "Seriously though, what's bothering you?"

"Jim and Laura are off doing something stupid again."

She shook her head as she leaned against the doorframe. "How about you just tell me when they're not doing something stupid?"

He chuckled half-heartedly. "Yeah, I suppose."

"What are they up to this time?"

"They're in Moscow, meeting up with a known Russian fugitive. He's supposed to hand over some documents that have been discovered that rewrite history, apparently."

Michelle whistled then stepped inside, closing the door. She dropped into a chair in front of his desk. "Are you doing anything about it?"

"I tried to go with them, but my visa was denied, and they're overdue for a check-in." He glanced at his phone again to make certain that was still true. It was.

"What about your 'friends?'" she asked, air quotes delivered.

"They're involved, but I don't know to what extent."

"Then all you can do is wait. If everything's fine, you'll hear from your friends shortly, and if not, your other friends are better equipped to help."

Reading sighed heavily, leaning back. "You know me. I'm not one to sit idly by."

"Then you definitely picked the wrong job. Interpol is mostly sitting idly by while everyone else takes the glory."

"I never should have taken this job, though the Yard would have stuck me behind a desk after my face was all over the news."

Her jaw slowly dropped. "That's right, I forgot all about that. You were questioned by a parliamentary committee about your involvement with that Apache on the motorway."

He rolled his eyes. "Ugh! Please don't remind me. I've been trying to forget that since it happened."

"But isn't that how you met them?"

He nodded. "Yes, it is."

"Then perhaps that's what you should focus on. Sometimes good things can come out of bad situations."

He grunted. "I can't see what good can possibly come out of this. They're risking themselves for pieces of paper."

She held up a finger with a smirk. "Pieces of paper that could rewrite history."

"Bollocks! I like my history just the way it is."

She laughed. "It was never my best subject. I'm terrible at memorizing dates, so I'm with you on that one. Do we at least know what history is being rewritten?"

He shrugged. "I assume something to do with Russia, other than that, who the Devil knows?"

"Well, it has to be something that makes them look bad if the Russian government is after them."

His shoulders slumped. "That's just it. As far as I know, the Russian government *isn't* after them. At the moment, it's all in my head, all because they missed a check-in." He regarded her. "Well, that and the fact that in the years I've known them, they're always in trouble with someone."

"I could say the same about you."

His phone vibrated with a message.

Stood up by our friend. Laura's not feeling well. Hopefully home tonight. James.

Michelle leaned in. "News?"

"Yeah. The person they were supposed to meet didn't show up, but they're still going ahead with their plan."

"Plan?"

"Laura fakes an illness, they rebook their flight for tonight, and come home directly."

"If they're sticking to the plan, then that's good, right?"

"Yes, but something's gone wrong."

"Why would you say that?"

"Because he signed the text message, 'James.'"

Michelle chuckled. "I can't remember the last time somebody signed a text message. Just how old-school is this guy?"

Reading shook his head. "He never signs them, and he never calls himself James. Something's definitely wrong."

Novinsky Hotel, Penthouse Suite 2

Moscow, Russian Federation

Acton scanned the room, searching for anything they had missed. Satisfied, he turned to the others. "Okay, time to go."

Alina jerked away from the window she had been peering out the entire time.

"What's wrong?" asked Laura.

"A black SUV just double-parked on the street below. One man in a suit got out of the back seat."

Acton stepped over to the window and peered out between the curtain and the glass. He spotted the SUV in question, still double-parked. It could be innocent, though he had learned that in some countries, being suspicious of everything was just being smart.

And this was one of those countries.

He stepped back. "Okay, we have to assume they're here for either us or you two," he said, nodding toward Volkov and Katarina.

"What do we do now?" asked Katarina.

He leaned against the dresser. "I'm not sure. If only one of them got out, he probably went to the back to cover any rear exits, and the rest are watching the front." He cursed as something occurred to him. He rushed back to the window and peered out once again. "You've got to be kidding me."

"What is it?" asked Laura.

"They're double-parked right beside our rental."

"Bloody hell! That can't be a coincidence."

"No. And it means they know we're here."

"Which means they're probably after us."

Volkov brightened at this. "If they're here for you, then doesn't that mean they're not here for us?"

Acton shook his head. "No, if they're here for us, then it's because they think we're meeting with Arseny, and with that video going around, they've probably figured out you're here too. We have to assume they're here for all of us."

"Then how the hell are we going to get out of here?" cried Katarina.

"I have no clue." He pulled out his phone and quickly sent an update to Kane.

Trapped in our hotel room. Authorities likely outside blocking our vehicle. Anticipate arrest any minute now.

It wouldn't help, but at least somebody back home might start looking into things if they disappeared.

Operations Center 2, CIA Headquarters
Langley, Virginia

Leroux's terminal beeped and he brought up a newly arrived message from Kane.

Nothing I can do. I'm being reassigned. I've requested Jack's assistance, and no one's heard from Zorkin since he took off. Try to get the Chief's blessing.

Leroux frowned. He had already tried, and the Chief had said no. Actually, he had said, "CIA assets aren't to be used as bodyguards for the professors' stupidity." Morrison had indicated he was willing to revisit the decision should things go south, but until then, the answer was no. The question was, were things about to head south? Acton's latest update, attached to Kane's last message, certainly suggested they were.

He picked up his phone and dialed the Chief's extension, the call picked up immediately. "This is Leroux. Is he in?"

"No, he isn't. As a matter of fact—"

The door opened and Director Leif Morrison entered the room.

"Never mind. He just walked in."

"No problem."

He ended the call and rose as Morrison climbed the steps to Leroux's station at the center of the state-of-the-art facility. He examined the screens arcing across the front of the room showing various satellite feeds and updates on the extraction of a Belarusian activist who had been targeted.

"Good, I see you're following my orders, unless you guys have a boss key set up."

Leroux stared at him blankly and Morrison chuckled.

"Am I really that old?"

Leroux shrugged. "I'm not touching that one, sir, but I guarantee you, I'm Googling it after you leave the room."

"Don't! That's an order. I don't want you getting any ideas." Morrison flashed him a grin.

"Fortuitous timing, sir. I was just coming to see you about our friends in Moscow."

"Yeah, that's why I'm here too. I just received word from some *old* friends."

The emphasis on the word "old" had Leroux assuming the Gray Network was implied.

"They've lost touch with one of their assets. He apparently landed in Moscow, but they haven't heard from him since. They think security might have picked him up as part of the net they've thrown down because of those papers that kid stole."

Leroux jerked his head toward his terminal. "I just received an update from Dylan. He forwarded me a message from Professor Acton. He says they're trapped in their hotel room and they believe the authorities are outside. They expect to be arrested any minute now. Does this mean they're in deep enough for us to get involved?"

Morrison gave a curt nod. "We're already involved. I had Kane reassigned, but he beat me to the punch. Jack's headed to Moscow and might already be on the ground. But he's there unofficially."

"Are we making it official?"

Morrison pursed his lips for a moment. "Yes, let him know, but observer only. I don't want him shooting any Russians unless it becomes absolutely necessary."

"Let's hope it doesn't come to that, sir."

"Okay, your number one priority is that Belarus extraction, but you now have my permission to use our resources to monitor the professors' situation."

"Yes, sir. Thank you, sir."

Morrison headed for the exit. "Keep me in the loop."

"Will do."

Morrison left and Leroux dropped in his seat. "You heard the man."

Tong tapped a couple of keys and everything currently displayed shrank to the left side. The right was replaced with satellite images and camera footage of the hotel inside and out that the Actons were staying at.

Child spun in his chair behind them, laughing. "His generation might have invented the boss key, but our generation perfected it."

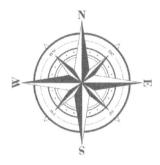

Novinsky Hotel, Penthouse Suite 2

Moscow, Russian Federation

Volkov flinched as Alina's tablet beeped in his bag. They were in the professors' suite, discussing what they should do now that they were surrounded, and he was already on edge—beeping devices were the last thing his frayed nerves needed. He unzipped the bag and grabbed the tablet, checking the message. "It's from one of the reporters!"

Acton's eyes narrowed. "Reporters?"

"We were desperate. We didn't know what to do, so we sent an email to a bunch of different foreign reporters based in Moscow to see if they wanted the story. We figured if the world knew the secret, then our government would have no reason to come after us."

Acton's head bobbed in approval. "Smart thinking. They might still want you out of revenge, though."

"But the reporters might be able to protect them," said Laura. "What does the message say?"

"She wants proof before they meet," said Volkov.

225

Acton chewed his cheek for a moment. "Laura and I should be all the proof they need, but we need to know what the hell this is all about. Arseny told us nothing except that it would rewrite history. Will it?"

The three Russians' eyes widened and they nodded vigorously. "Absolutely!" said Volkov.

"Completely," agreed Alina. "If you knew what those documents showed, you'd understand why our glorious president is so desperate to get them back in his hands."

Acton threw his own hands up. "*If* I knew! I need to know! That's what I'm trying to tell you people! Show me the damn papers!"

Laura placed a calming hand on his shoulder. "Do we really have time for this, James?"

"We're going to have to make the time. Watch the window. The fact they haven't busted in here yet tells me they're waiting for someone or something." He stuck out his hand. "Now, give me those papers."

Volkov retrieved the folder and handed it over as Laura exchanged positions with Alina at the window so she could see them as well. Acton eagerly flipped it open then cursed at the sight of the first page, handwritten in Russian. He flipped through them carefully, the pages quite old. "There are no translations?"

Volkov shook his head. "No, I guess Professor Orlov assumed you would have them translated for yourself when there was time to do so."

"Are these the only copy?"

"I scanned them and sent the files to the professor last night."

"Any other copies?"

"Just the half-dozen pages that I sent to the reporters."

"And the ones I took," added Alina.

Acton carefully closed the folder and handed it back. "Be careful with those, they're old."

Volkov's eyes shot wide as he took the folder. "So, they're real?"

Acton shook his head. "I can't speak to that because I don't know what they say, but the papers themselves appear to be about a century old, give or take twenty years. It's tough to tell because I don't know how they were stored. But again, context. What the hell do these papers say?"

"Some are notes made of conversations between Lenin and his trusted friend, Anatoly Bazarov, in which he expresses his fears about Stalin succeeding him."

Acton tilted his head to the side and frowned. "That's hardly news. Pretty much any historian worth his salt is aware of the problems those two had."

Laura shook her head. "Why would Arseny put our lives at risk over something like that? He said this would rewrite history."

Volkov leaped to his former professor's defense. "No, no, no, you don't understand, there are more papers in there. They show that Bazarov betrayed Lenin and was feeding Stalin everything that Lenin was saying about him."

Acton exchanged a glance with Laura. "With someone as paranoid as Stalin, and possibly mentally ill like many historians believe he was, that would have played straight into his paranoia. But still, hardly earth-shattering stuff."

"No, you don't understand." Volkov flipped to the rear of the folder, pulling out a page near the back. He held it up and translated it.

"Comrade, I have acquired the poison as you instructed and I'm ready to proceed as soon as you give me the word." He fished out another page. "Comrade, it is with a heavy heart that I must instruct you to proceed. Our mutual friend has lost his way, and those he has surrounded himself with are too weak to continue the revolution. Our friend must die so that our future is secure." The young man shook the page as he stared at Acton who winced, fearing it would crumble. "Signed by Stalin himself. And there's more! There are papers in here that document not only the lead-up and justification of the assassination, including diary entries from Stalin and Bazarov, but also the aftermath and what happened to him after he had successfully poisoned Lenin. It's all in here. It proves that Stalin assassinated Lenin by having him poisoned by someone Lenin thought was a trusted friend, all because Lenin was concerned that Stalin would be too brutal a leader."

"Well, he was right about that," muttered Laura.

Acton stood in stunned silence. Orlov was right. This did rewrite an important piece of history. If these pages were indeed genuine, it meant Lenin hadn't died from a hemorrhagic stroke as the world thought. He had been murdered by his successor who then ruled Lenin's creation with an iron fist for decades, murdering millions to maintain his paranoid grip on power.

Yet it should merely be a curiosity, and 20 years ago it might have been, perhaps even 10, but today it was more than that. The Russian leader was rewriting history. Stalin was now portrayed as not being responsible for the deaths he had ordered, and instead as having put an end to the murders, the act of a strong, uncontested leader.

And exactly what Russia needed today.

He was the Russian president's posterchild for a bygone era he was desperate to recreate. Recent polling showed that the rewriting of the history was successful, with nearly three-quarters of the Russian population having a favorable opinion of Stalin.

But there were no statues of Stalin anywhere.

Yet Lenin's tomb still stood, the leader's embalmed body still on public display, for Russians loved Lenin even more than Stalin. But like Stalin, the current Russian leader believed Lenin was too weak to lead his country into the future. Iron-fisted rule, uncompromising, no consultation with others. One man, one rule, no questions. That was how the Russian president thought his country should be led. But if the man he idolized, if the man he had been pushing as an example of what Russia needed, were to have murdered one of the people's heroes, it would shatter the image and might just have people questioning whether a man who modeled himself after the brutal dictator was the right one to lead their country into the future.

Those papers might not only rewrite history, but they might very well rewrite Russia's future. He understood now why Orlov was so desperate to get them safely out of the country. He eyed the folders still gripped too tightly in Volkov's hands. "Perhaps we should take those." The folder was handed over without hesitation.

"Done," said Volkov.

Acton suppressed a smile as he took the folder and placed it in his satchel. "Now at least I know what we're risking our lives for."

"Now we need to figure a way out of this hotel," said Laura.

Alina raised a finger. "I might have an idea on that."

Washington Post Moscow Bureau

Moscow, Russian Federation

Dempsey stared at her screen, impatiently waiting for a reply from Volkov, or at least who she was assuming was Volkov. It could all be a trick, but as her assistant, Inessa, continued to send her the translated pages, she prayed to God this wasn't a hoax. She couldn't stand the Russian president. He was more arrogant than any man she had ever encountered, and his machismo belonged in another era, though that was perhaps her Western values tainting her opinion.

Russia didn't have Western values. It was still stuck decades in the past when it came to things most of the civilized world accepted as normal now—equal rights for all sexes, creeds, and colors. In Russia, one of the most powerful countries in the world, sexist, masochist behavior was applauded like it once had been back home. Homosexuals were still beaten in the streets, and minorities, along with anyone perceived as different, discriminated against in all aspects of their lives. It might not be the Soviet Union anymore, but it wasn't a good country.

And where there had been rapid progress after the collapse, they were just as rapidly receding back toward that totalitarian state. She had come here with an open mind, willing to believe that many of the reports she had read were biased. But after living here, she realized they weren't. This was a once promising country turning into a true danger to the world, and with democracy abandoned, she feared what might happen when the Russian president died.

And that thought had her staring at the translations in a different light. Could history repeat itself? Could someone kill the Russian president, perhaps for the opposite reason, perhaps because he was too much of a hardliner? Stalin's actions had resulted in what he desired— himself coming to power, and he achieved that because he was willing to kill anyone who would oppose him. They were terrified of him. But if someone were to kill the current Russian president because he was *too* strong, it would imply that someone didn't wish to rely on fear and violence to take control.

It would probably be someone who desired free and fair elections, and that might be well and good, but Russia was filled with hardliners, and if the president died, especially if he were murdered, someone worse could step in, or the country could break apart into factions supporting one new hardliner over another.

If that happened in a country like Brazil, the world might watch on in horror but not fear. In Russia, with its massive nuclear arsenal and arguably the second or third most powerful military in the world, the world would watch on in horror and fear. It was a terrifying notion, though she doubted it was something in Russia's immediate future. It merely lent context to what happened a century ago, if these pages were indeed the truth.

While the papers were fascinating, and she was quite certain there were reporters back home who would go nuts over them for their academic value, she was more interested in the here and now. The Russian government must obviously believe the papers were genuine, otherwise they wouldn't be so eager to get their hands on Volkov and his friend, both of whose images had been playing on Russian television in a continuous cycle. A 10-million-ruble reward was massive as well. It was worth a little over $100,000, huge by anyone's standards, even back home. But here, it was even more than that. The buying power of $100,000 went far beyond what it did in America. It could change lives, which meant friends and family might turn in the poor man just for a chance at it.

It had been a smart move to reach out to the press, and as she stared at her inbox, eager for a reply, she questioned her motives. Why was she so keen to get this story? Was it for the scoop to beat out all her fellow reporters one last time, or was it to help this young man who could face imprisonment or worse? He had chosen her for a reason. He obviously wanted her to tell the story, her to help him, her to… She paused then reopened the message, staring at the header then kicking herself at her arrogance. That inflated opinion that had gotten her in trouble and reassigned, had her assuming the message was sent directly to her, but it wasn't. There was nobody in the "To" field. It meant she had been blind CC'd on the email. There was no salutation addressed to her. In fact, there was no salutation at all. This could have been sent to dozens of people, and perhaps one of them had replied back before she did and was getting that scoop. It likely meant there was no scoop at all to be had, at least by her.

She stared at the message, her fingers drumming on the desk as she debated what to do. She had been taught that the press were supposed to report on the facts. They were supposed to report on the story, not become the story. She was supposed to be a dispassionate observer of events, but that wasn't the press anymore. That had been destroyed by the likes of CNN, Fox, and countless other cable news networks. Reporters were now activists. It was wrong and it sometimes made her ashamed of her profession.

When her grandfather had been in the business, reporters were reporters and editorialists were editorialists. Opinion was reserved for the opinion pages. But no longer. And with the majority of people getting their news from social media, where the algorithms intentionally slanted the stories they saw to their detected biases, her profession was further doomed. It sometimes had her wondering, 30 years from now, when the next generation should be reporting on the news of the day, would they even exist? Would there be reporters, or would people simply go to the trending section of their favorite social media platform and watch the most popular video of the day taken out of context with some moron's interpretation spliced in of what they thought they had just seen?

She shuddered at the prospect. Democracy relied upon an informed populace, and a free press was designed to fulfill that requirement. It was one of the pillars of a free, democratic society, and it was disappearing, or at the very least, failing in its function. People could no longer make informed decisions because the opinion-makers in the press had already made their own and were foisting it upon an ignorant public.

A friend of hers from a British newspaper had told her of spending two weeks in New York last year where every day she alternated between CNN and Fox, and her conclusion was that there were two different countries being reported on. The stories were so polarly opposite, it was stunning, and what was equally appalling was that both stations were equally guilty. She was forced to agree with her friend, though the CNN and Fox reporters at the table that night, drinking themselves into oblivion, had vehemently denied their own guilt then walked away.

And today, she had a choice to make. Be a reporter, or become part of the story. She leaned back and folded her arms. Perhaps she was oversimplifying things. Perhaps she could do both. She continued to stare at the screen, then cursed as she noticed a little error icon on the bottom right, indicating a problem connecting to the mail server. "Inessa, is your email working?" she yelled through the walls.

"Yes."

"Well, mine isn't."

"Check the time. You're not supposed to be here, so they probably shut down your account's Internet access."

She cursed and pulled out her phone. Her email address was for the paper, not for the Moscow office. She had it since the day she had been hired. She squeed as she spotted the reply she had been waiting for. She tapped on it then her heart raced at the mention that Professors James Acton and Laura Palmer were now involved.

This was a real story.

Outside the Novinsky Hotel
Moscow, Russian Federation

Nikitin parked behind one of his team's SUVs and was joined by Zaitsev a moment later. "Is everyone in position?"

"Yes, sir."

"And there's been no activity?"

"Negative."

"Good. Let's go."

Zaitsev hesitated. "What about Orlov? We haven't been able to confirm he's here."

"If he's not here yet, then I don't think he's coming. If he did try to come to Moscow, they've got him at the airport, and if they don't, they'll get him on the way out. I'm more concerned with digital copies of those documents being transmitted, and those papers perhaps being handed over to someone else. I think we have to assume that those professors now have the papers. And while copies are just that when sent by a grad student, copies where the originals have been seen by professionals who are well respected in their field are an entirely different matter. They're given gravitas."

"So, we're going to arrest them?"

"Absolutely."

"What if they've already talked to someone?"

"Then I'll beat his wife in front of him until he recants. There's no way those two are leaving this country until nobody believes the papers are real."

"And if we then let them go, and they recant the recantation?"

"We'll have the originals and they can claim whatever they want. It doesn't matter what the world thinks. It only matters what our people think, and they'll think what our president tells them to think."

Nikitin stepped out of his vehicle and headed for the hotel entrance with Zaitsev on his heels. The SUV he had parked behind emptied, six men with submachine guns joining them. The smile on the doorman disappeared as the young man's face slackened, all color draining from it, his job momentarily forgotten before he hurriedly grabbed the handle and held the door open. "W-welcome to the Novinsky Hotel."

Nikitin flashed a smile. "Thank you." He pointed at both sides of the entrance and two men dropped back to cover it. He marched over to the front desk and held up his identification. "Deputy Director Nikitin, Presidential Executive Office. Tell me what room number Professor James Acton and Professor Laura Palmer are in."

The young woman behind the counter gulped, her eyes wide, and moments later had his answer. "Penthouse level, suite two."

"And the names of the occupants of room four-one-two?"

She checked then shook her head. "That room is vacant, sir."

He pursed his lips. Could they be wrong about the hotel? The video showed Volkov was in room 412. Could they have incorrectly identified the crest from the room service cart? It didn't matter. There was no time to waste second-guessing themselves. "Where are your stairwells?"

"There's a set of stairs over there, sir." She pointed to his right.

"Is that the only set?"

"No." She pointed to his left. "There's another set there."

"And those are the only stairs?"

"Yes, sir."

He pointed toward the four elevators. "And those are the only elevators?"

"Yes, sir. Oh, wait. There's the service elevator."

"And where is that?"

She pointed and he indicated to three men to cover the possible exits as four men from the second team stationed at the rear of the hotel entered the lobby area. He stabbed a finger toward an open elevator. "Hold that." One of the new arrivals jogged over and stuck a hand in before the doors could close. Nikitin reached the elevator and found a family inside. He jerked a thumb over his shoulder. "Everybody out." The man was about to protest when two of the assault team appeared, weapons on display. The man picked up his daughter then hustled his wife out of the elevator. Nikitin stepped in and pressed the button for the fourth floor as Zaitsev and the others joined him.

They rode up in silence. There was no need to brief anyone. These men had trained for operations like this for years. They would breach the room, secure it, and shoot anyone that aimed a weapon at them. He wasn't expecting much opposition, if any. These were academics.

The doors opened and he stepped out. He directed an arm toward the room and the team sprang into action as he and Zaitsev hung back. The door was kicked open, shouts erupted, and less than 60 seconds later the team lead stepped out, shaking his head. "Nobody here, but somebody was. There's a room service cart."

"Leave one man behind to secure the room. We're heading to the penthouse." He stepped back on the elevator held by Zaitsev, not pleased. He had maintained some faint hope that these fugitives hadn't yet met with the professors, but it was clear now they had. It meant they had seen the stolen documents, so they now knew more than he did. He still had no idea what was in the files. He couldn't even be certain they had anything to do with Stalin. All he knew was that they were state secrets the president didn't want revealed.

The doors opened to the penthouse level and he stepped out to find there were four rooms. He suppressed an envious sigh. This was the life he wanted. Penthouse suites and five-star luxury, though this was definitely not that. It was further proof that the professors being here was no coincidence. He had read their files. They were ridiculously wealthy. Well, she was, and he got lucky. They would never stay at a hotel like this unless it were necessary. Taking one of the luxury suites was merely a lame attempt to keep up appearances.

He wanted power, and the respect that came with it, as well as the opportunities senior positions provided to increase one's wealth. But there was something else he craved that his current position had given him a taste of. He had been surprised at how much he relished it at first, but every time someone's eyes bulged, every time someone gulped, every time cheeks paled as the blood drained from them, a surge of hormones rushed through his system as if he had injected a potent drug.

Fear.

When those before him cowered in it, it was like nothing else in life. It was better than sex, though he did wonder what sex might be like with a terrified partner. He would have to try it someday, though not with his wife. While she didn't mind the occasional smack on the ass during their lovemaking, pain and terror were two different things. Terrifying her would mean the end of his marriage, a messy divorce, and a hit to his social standing. The men whose respect he clamored for admired counterparts with pretty wives they controlled, and true control meant a mistress or two on the side, absolute control shown when the wife was aware yet did nothing about it.

He snapped out of his fantasy state as the door was kicked open and his team surged inside. This time, he didn't wait for the all-clear. He rushed in after them, suppressing a smile as his future success was about to be cemented.

Under the Novinsky Hotel

Moscow, Russian Federation

"Not a lot of people know about this tunnel because it's in the basement and you need a manager's key to get into the access room. Nobody really gives it a second thought. Years ago, when the hotel was first built, the laundry and kitchen were across the street, and this tunnel was used to move things back and forth so that nothing would be out in public or a Moscow winter."

"Where does it come out now?" asked Acton as the small band of fugitives made their escape.

"In a shopping plaza."

"Won't they have an alarm on the door?"

"They do, but we have an arrangement with them for our VIP guests."

Laura eyed her. "Really? A shopping plaza has an arrangement like that?"

Alina laughed. "Not the management, I can assure you, but the security team. They're the same company that does our security, so I know them all. Don't worry, it won't be a problem."

They reached the end of the short corridor and Alina opened the door then stepped into a dark room. She reached out and the room was bathed in light as she flicked a switch. "Come on, everyone inside."

They followed her and she closed the door then stepped over to another on the opposite wall, waving at a camera mounted in the corner. There was a buzzing sound and she pushed the door open, flashing a grin at whoever was watching. They stepped out into a dimly lit corridor and followed her to a stairwell. Moments later, they were in a brightly lit corridor that led to an impressive lobby.

"Now where do we go?" asked Acton.

Alina shook her head. "I have no clue. I'm just stunned we got out of the hotel."

"Is there a food court?"

"One floor up."

"Then let's go there. We're too conspicuous standing here."

Alina led them to an escalator that carried them to the next floor and into a busy food court. He spotted two tables near the far wall where a small nook would keep them partially out of sight. He walked toward it with purpose then indicated for Volkov and Katarina to sit in the two chairs with their backs facing the other patrons, since theirs were the only photos broadcast to all of Moscow. He and Laura sat opposite them as Alina pulled up a chair from the second table, angling slightly toward him and Laura.

"What are we going to do now?" asked Laura.

Acton had no idea. They had to put some distance between themselves and the hotel, and without a vehicle, that could prove difficult. Even with one, the authorities were after them all now. They couldn't exactly head to the airport and get on their plane. They would be arrested the moment their passports were scanned.

The situation had quickly spiraled out of control.

He nodded toward Volkov's bag. "Check that computer of yours. See if the reporter replied back."

Volkov's jaw dropped for a moment and snapped shut as he grabbed at the zipper. Acton fired a message off to Kane, giving him their new location and a status update, then leaned back, gripping the phone.

And cursed as a two-man security team appeared.

"We can't stay here."

Novinsky Hotel, Penthouse Suite 2

Moscow, Russian Federation

Nikitin punched the door to the bathroom, sending it slamming against the doorstop. The room was empty, and it appeared that if anybody had been in it, it had been for only minutes. He spun toward Zaitsev. "Seal off this hotel. Search it top to bottom. I want to know where the hell they went. And get someone in the security booth. They have to have cameras here." He paused for a moment, turning to face the room as Zaitsev barked orders over the radio, calling for more personnel. Yet it was a wasted effort. They had been one step behind the entire time. His suspects were already gone. There was a remote chance they were hiding in another room, but he doubted it.

They had help.

Room 412 was officially vacant, yet there was a room service cart inside. The professors were here, which meant this was the correct hotel. Volkov had been here, he had no doubt.

Someone in the hotel was obviously helping them.

It was the only way room service would have delivered to a vacant room. It meant hotel staff. And if there were a secret way out of this place, staff would know. He pointed at the team lead. "Have one of your men secure the room." He headed for the elevators and was soon in the lobby, confronting the young woman he had spoken to earlier. "There's another way out of this hotel. Tell me about it now, or I'll have this place shut down and you tossed in a cold, dark cell somewhere no one will ever find you."

The girl swooned and he reached out, grabbing the front of her shirt before she dropped to the floor. "Breathe," he ordered, and she sucked in a breath, a hint of color returning to her cheeks. But her reaction had told him everything he needed to know.

There *was* another way out of this hotel.

He hauled her closer. "Where is it?"

A shaky finger pointed to the left and he let her go.

"Show me."

Operations Center 2, CIA Headquarters

Langley, Virginia

Leroux read the latest message from Acton. Now that Kane's reassignment took him out of the picture, his friend had set up his secure messenger app to automatically forward him anything from the professors, Jack, Reading, or the Gray Network. Leroux stared at the camera feeds they had tapped, that moments before had shown Russian security forces entering the hotel from the front and rear, feeds they had fully expected would soon show the professors and the two Russians they had found in the room instead of Orlov, led out in handcuffs.

He turned to Tong. "Acton just sent an update. Apparently, they've managed to escape the hotel and are in the cafeteria of a shopping plaza directly across the street."

Tong's eyebrows rose slightly. "How'd they manage that?"

Leroux shrugged. "You can ask them when you see them, but right now, we're watching the wrong place. Let's see if we can find some eyes in that building. Any word from Jack?"

"Nothing. The Russians are pulling aside anyone who booked a last-minute ticket for further questioning. He could be tied up for hours."

Leroux cursed. "If that's the case, then he's useless to us. This is going to be over long before that, and not in a good way. We need to bring in more sanctioned assets."

"I thought the Chief said we're allowed to observe only."

"Just a second." He fired back a message to Acton.

Need to know what this is about.

The reply came back immediately.

Proof that Stalin murdered Lenin.

"Holy shit," muttered Leroux. He collapsed back in his chair.

"What?" asked Tong, concerned.

"They found proof that Stalin murdered Lenin."

The entire room came to a halt as everyone stared at him. Child shrugged. "So? Some dude from a century ago killed another dude. Who cares?"

Tong rolled her eyes. "It would be like finding proof that Johnson killed Kennedy. It might have happened sixty years ago, but people would still care here, while other countries might not give a shit. The impact of this in Russia could be even bigger. Here in America, people don't give a second thought to LBJ anymore, but in Russia, Stalin has been set up as a hero that the current president modeled himself after. If it came out that he murdered Lenin, a man Russians still admire greatly, perhaps even more so than Stalin, it would shatter the image that the Russian administration has been building of the man, and perhaps make the citizenry question whether having another strongman leader was wise."

Child chewed his cheek for a moment. "Huh. So, I guess that's why they're all horny to get their hands on these papers."

"Crudely put, but yes." Tong's fingers drummed on the armrest of her chair. "I guess the question is, does America care?"

Leroux's eyes narrowed. "What do you mean?"

"I mean, it's not exactly a national security issue. If these papers make it out of Russia or don't, does it really change anything for America? It could, for Russia, I suppose. Is the Chief going to get us involved over a century-old murder plot?"

"I think he might. What you're forgetting is that we're in the middle of a second Cold War, and just like in the first one, anything that tarnishes a nation's reputation is welcome. Part of the new Cold War is attacking our cultural institutions. It was shown that Russian hackers flooded review sites, panning movies like Solo before the movie was even released. There was so much negative press out because of those fake reviews, that the movie didn't do well, and the whole Star Wars franchise was rethought."

Child eyed him skeptically. "They actually care about Star Wars?"

"Star Wars is a cultural institution for many in the West, and to interfere with that is a victory for our enemies. While I'm sure Russia has its own movie and television franchises, they are nothing compared to what we have here in America that have a worldwide reach. Internally, they have their own heroes, like Stalin. Remember, they believe he's the man who won the Great Patriotic War."

"Huh?"

"World War Two."

"Oh."

"You have to remember that until the early nineties, these people had no free press whatsoever, and now they barely have it again. They believe what's being churned out by the Kremlin because every news source they have access to that they think is legitimate doesn't question the story. So, when the government decides that Stalin didn't murder millions, that it was local officials who did it against his orders, they believe the story. Anything that contradicts it is Western propaganda designed to embarrass Russia. And that's exactly what Washington would want to do with this type of information, is make sure everyone knows that the man the Russian leadership worships, murdered the man who started it all. The potential to embarrass the Russian president might just be enough to get us fully involved."

"Let's hope so," said Tong as she nodded toward the screens. "I think our Russian adversaries just figured out the professors' Houdini trick."

Leroux turned to see the increased security presence around the hotel leaving their posts and rushing across the street. He fired a message to Acton.

They know where you are. Leave now.

Lotte Plaza Cafeteria

Moscow, Russian Federation

Alina waved at the two guards, flashing them a smile. Acton wanted to punch her in the throat for drawing attention to them, but the men waved back, a joke in Russian exchanged before they moved on. His phone vibrated with another message and he tensed at the urgent update from Leroux.

"They know we're here. We have to leave now." He rose, not allowing anyone to question the urgency. If the authorities knew where they were, then they would be switching their attention from the hotel to here. It meant the majority of the forces would be at the front. "We need to go out the back of this building. Now."

Alina pointed toward the escalator. "Back downstairs then turn right. There's a set of doors that lead to the outside."

"Okay, let's go, as casual as possible. You two stay behind us," he said to the young Russians. "And don't try to make it too obvious that you're hiding your faces."

The table rose and they all headed toward the escalators. No one appeared to pay them any mind, and he exhaled audibly as he placed a foot on the first step. Moments later, they were in the lobby and soon out the rear doors.

"Left or right," asked Acton, his voice low.

"Left," replied Alina immediately, the uncertainty tainting her murmured response not filling Acton with any sense of confidence. As they reached the sidewalk, he turned left, and at the next crossroads sirens wailed behind them.

"Nobody look," he said, the tires screeching behind them indicating the new arrivals were coming to a halt far enough back to suggest they were covering the entrance they had just used to escape. The light changed and they crossed the street, taking them out of the direct line of sight of where they had been. "Where are we going?"

Alina shrugged. "My apartment is the only place I can think of to go."

Acton suppressed a groan. "They know you're involved now. And if they don't, they'll know the moment they realize you're not at the hotel where you're supposed to be. It's the first place they'll look."

"You have a better idea?"

"We need some place that we can hole up in for potentially a couple of hours, out of the public eye." He examined their surroundings as they continued to walk at a brisk pace, putting as much distance between them and the authorities as they could. A smile broke out as he pointed across the street. "Is that a movie theater?"

"Yes. Not a great one, though. Mostly second or third run movies."

"Even better. Do you have enough cash on you to buy us all tickets?"

She nodded.

"Good, go get us five tickets and we'll meet you in the lobby."

"What movie?"

He gave her a look. "Do you think it really matters?" He paused, realizing her question wasn't that stupid. "Something unpopular. The fewer the people, the better."

"All right." She looked both ways then bolted across the street. Acton led the group to the traffic lights so no one would have an excuse to pay them any mind for jaywalking. Minutes later, they were in the dimly lit lobby of the multiplex that had seen better times. Alina held up five tickets then led them toward their screen. She handed the tickets over to the bored, pimply-faced teenager who tore off the theater's portion of the stub before returning what remained. They entered the darkened theater and Acton smiled. There was one couple sitting in the back corner making out, and no one else. He indicated a row halfway up and they all took their seats.

He leaned closer to Alina. "This is perfect. Good job."

"This place is never really busy, especially at this hour."

"What movie did you pick?"

"Cats."

Acton chuckled, wondering if it were as unpopular here as it was at home. He adjusted the brightness on his phone to the bare minimum, then took a photo of their ticket stub with the theater name on it and sent it to Leroux. He glanced over his shoulder to see if the amorous couple in the rear had noticed his poor theater etiquette, and found the

252

girl no longer in sight. It had him concerned for a moment until he noticed the facial expression of the man.

Well, they won't be a problem.

He turned to Volkov. "Get that tablet out and see if there's anything from that reporter. She could be our ticket out of here. See if she can pick us up in a vehicle that will carry the five of us."

Volkov pulled the tablet out of his bag, turning it on and wisely reducing the brightness as well. "There's a message here from her. She says she wants to meet."

"Good, tell her what we need for transportation and where we are. Tell her to get here as soon as possible."

Volkov's thumbs flew over the virtual keyboard. The movie started, and as Acton watched the box office bomb with Russian subtitles, he prayed the reporter would be here soon to end what he feared would be prolonged suffering.

Washington Post Moscow Bureau
Moscow, Russian Federation

Dempsey read the latest message. "Inessa!" she cried, her assistant rushing in. "Please tell me you drove in today."

Inessa shook her head. "No, my husband dropped me off."

Dempsey cursed. "I need a vehicle that can seat six adults."

Inessa's eyes shot wide. "Six? I thought we were dealing with two Russian students?"

"What can I say? Six people. I guess two of them are Professors Acton and Palmer, and I don't know who the other one is."

"Well, what about one of the pool vehicles?"

Dempsey smiled. "Yes! That's right!" She cursed again. "I lost all my authorizations." She leaned toward the door. "Jerry!"

Jerry Doyle poked his head into the office. "What the hell are you still doing here? My pounding head assures me we said goodbye to you last night."

"Last-second story. I need you to sign out a big SUV or a van for me, something that'll seat six adults at least semi-comfortably."

He stepped all the way in, closing the door. "You've got something big going on?"

"Could be. I don't know yet, but the only way I'm going to find out is if I can get my hands on a vehicle. And right now, I don't even have access to the network." He wasn't moving, so she gave him the stink eye. "Jerry, don't be a pain in the ass. Just sign out the vehicle, will you?"

"Listen, you're leaving. You're not even officially a reporter anymore. I'll sign out a vehicle, but I'm coming with you. You know as well as I do that if this turns into a story, it's going to get reassigned."

Dempsey growled in frustration. "Fine, you can come with me."

He grinned. "Good. Now that I'm coming with you, is this dangerous?"

She jabbed a finger at the television mounted on the wall in her office, yet another report playing about the fugitives and the massive reward on offer.

His eyes bulged. "Holy shit! You mean that email was real?"

She had to admit the fact he was on the blind CC list cut a little.

"Okay, I'll get us a vehicle, but you should know I just got a tip from a Moscow Police source. He says they're conducting a major operation at the Novinsky Hotel that involves this investigation. They might already be arrested by the time I sign it out."

She shook her head. "They're not there anymore."

"And you know where they are?"

"They'll be in that damn vehicle if you stop asking me questions."

He gave her a thumbs-up. "I'm on it."

He disappeared and she returned her attention to Inessa. "Have you finished those translations?"

Inessa shook her head.

"Then hurry up. I'm leaving here in five minutes."

"Yes, ma'am."

Dempsey sank back in her chair, collecting her thoughts. Her press ID expired yesterday, so she didn't have the protections she normally would from the Russian authorities. Perhaps having Doyle along might prove useful.

She just prayed there was a vehicle available and they would get there in time.

Novinsky Hotel, Basement

Moscow, Russian Federation

Nikitin rushed through the underground corridor, Zaitsev and several of the team on his heels. He yanked open a door and stepped into a dark room, the only light the dim glow from the corridor he had just left. Cellphones were pulled out and flashlights activated, including his own. He found a light switch and flicked it on. He tried the door on the opposite wall, but it was locked.

"Sir, there's a camera," said Zaitsev, pointing to the corner.

Nikitin's head swiveled toward it, and he pulled out his ID, holding it up to the camera. The door buzzed and Zaitsev pushed it open. Nikitin pointed at the camera then at the floor, indicating someone should meet them. The door buzzed three times in acknowledgment. He stepped out into a dim corridor, devoid of any human activity. If security had to buzz people through, then somebody in this building had helped his suspects escape.

257

He spotted a sign for the stairwell and headed for it. An elevator chimed behind him and he spun on his heel to see a security guard step out. Nikitin pointed. "Hold that elevator!" The man stepped back inside as Nikitin rushed toward him, the elevator quickly filling up. "You let some people through that door a few minutes ago."

The young man paled slightly. "Sir?"

Nikitin grabbed him by the tie and yanked. It snapped off, the cheap clip-on worn for that exact reason. Someone snickered behind him. Nikitin's hand darted out, gripping the guard by the throat, squeezing it tight. "Every second counts, and every one of them you waste is another hour that my men beat you, so start talking."

The man nodded and Nikitin released his grip. "It was Alina from the hotel across the street. They use the corridor when they have VIP guests who don't want to be seen in the lobby."

"And this happens often?"

The guard shrugged. "Not really. It's not the greatest hotel. Most VIPs stay at a lot nicer."

"Did you recognize who was with her?

"No."

"How many were there?"

"Four people with her, two men, two women."

Volkov, his ex-girlfriend, and the two professors.

"Where did they go?"

"I don't know. Last time I saw them on the camera was in the cafeteria."

"Take us there."

258

The guard hit the button and the doors closed. Moments later they reopened and the elevator emptied out into the cafeteria, kiosk restaurants lining the edges with hundreds of chairs and tables filling the floor. "Where did you see them?"

The guard pointed to a table to their right.

"Last I saw, they were sitting there."

The table was empty and he didn't have time to waste. He put his fingers to his mouth and blew, an ear-piercing whistle bringing the chatter from those gathered to a halt, everyone turning to face the intrusion. Nikitin pointed at the table. "Five people were sitting there a few minutes ago. Where did they go?"

Nobody said anything. He flipped open his ID. "Nikitin. Presidential Executive Office. Those people are wanted for theft of government secrets. Where are they?"

A hand rose with a finger pointing toward the escalators, then several more pointed in the same direction. Nikitin made a beeline for the escalators and tossed the question over his shoulder. "How long ago?"

"Twenty minutes, maybe thirty," shouted someone.

Nikitin cursed. It was too big a gap. They could be anywhere by now. And any hope of finding them could be lost.

Approaching Karo Theater
Moscow, Russian Federation

Dempsey gripped the dashboard with one hand and braced herself against the passenger window with the other as Doyle had them careening around a corner before straightening out the top-heavy camera van that wobbled precariously for several moments. "Are you trying to get us killed?"

"Hey, you're the one who said we had to get there fast."

"Sorry, I guess I should have said 'fast and alive.' We're no good to them if we get in a car accident or pulled over by the police."

"Don't worry about it. We're almost there. And besides, the police never pull over camera vans."

"I don't know if that's true."

"You'd have to hit a police vehicle for them to care. In all my years of driving in Moscow in one of these, they've never pulled me over."

"You mean you drive like this on a regular basis?"

He grinned. "More than a few times, let me tell you." He patted the dash as she pried her fingernails out of it. "This old girl's been my go-to for years. Never given me a day of trouble, never given me a single ticket, which is exactly why I chose her instead of an SUV like you wanted." He jerked a thumb over his shoulder at the rear. "It'll be cramped back there, but they'll be safer. Have you figured out what you're going to do with them yet?"

She shook her head. "Beyond getting the story out, I don't think there's much else I can do. But this whole Stalin murdering Lenin thing? Without the original paperwork, it's just their word against history. They claim to have the originals, but I don't know if that's enough."

"Well, unless those originals are made public, it's still he said, she said."

"You're right. We need to get those papers out of the country."

He tapped the GPS. "Two minutes."

She grabbed her phone squeezed between her knees and sent a message. Her heart hammered as Doyle made the final corner, easing off on the gas as not to draw any attention as the GPS announced their destination was ahead. She wondered to what lengths the Russian government might go to preserve the secret that had been discovered. A wave of goosebumps rushed over her body at the thought of who she was dealing with, and part of her was tempted to tell Doyle to keep driving on.

She resisted the urge. She was a reporter and this was a story. But what was the story? Was it that Stalin had murdered Lenin? Or was it the extent to which the Russians were going to keep that fact secret? She had a sense it was the latter, and if that were the case, she was about to become part of the story.

Doyle brought them to a halt then cursed. "Where the hell are they?"

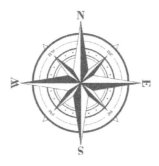

Karo Theater

Moscow, Russian Federation

Volkov held up the tablet. "Two minutes."

Acton rolled his eyes in relief as too many people who had no business being musical pranced around the screen. "Okay, let's go. If anyone asks why we're leaving, it's because the movie sucks."

"You won't get any argument from me," said Laura as they rose then slid down the row of seats and into the aisle. They left the cinema and were out into the corridor, the pimply-faced ticket checker smiling at them, saying something in Russian. Alina laughed and said something, then offered up a thumbs-down. They continued past then out the front doors. Acton spotted a news van parked ten yards away—it had to be the reporter they were waiting for. A woman stepped out of the passenger side, beckoning at them, then slid open the side door.

"Let's go, nice and orderly-like," urged Acton as everyone headed for their escape vehicle. Alina climbed in, followed by Katarina and Volkov, and finally Laura then himself. The door slammed shut behind him as they all struggled to find a place to get comfortable. The passenger door closed and the engine gunned, sending them all tumbling backward onto the unforgiving metal floor. He cursed, then an apology was tossed over the driver's shoulder.

"Just hang on for a couple of minutes until I can put some distance between that theater and us."

Acton struggled into a seated position. "Slow down or you're going to draw attention to us. If they knew we were in the theater, it would already be too late."

The man glanced in the rearview mirror at him then nodded, the rev of the engine easing as he put some distance between the pedal and the metal. They turned a corner and the $64,000 question was asked. "So, where are we going?"

Acton grunted. "I was hoping you could tell us."

The reporter, Kaye Dempsey, whom he recognized from the news, twisted around in her seat. "You have the papers with you?"

Acton patted his satchel. "Yes."

"And you're willing to testify that they're genuine?"

"No."

She cursed. "Haven't we gotten past this yet? Without you authenticating those papers, there's no story here."

"Yes, there is," he said. "Once I get these safely out of the country, I can have them properly analyzed and confirm whether they're genuine. But that's not the story here, is it? We know they're genuine simply because the Russian government is doing everything it can to recover them. If they were fake, then they wouldn't care. But that doesn't matter.

This"—he swirled a finger at their surroundings—"is the story. Two young kids, an American professor, a British professor, and a hotel employee all being pursued by the Russian authorities because of stolen documents a century old. What are they going to do with us if they capture us? That's the story, and now you're part of it. Whatever they do to us, they're going to do to you too, because they're going to assume you've seen the papers. So, how would you save yourself, because that's what we're talking about now."

Her eyes flared, though only for a moment. "I can't allow myself to become the story."

Laura flicked her wrist as she positioned herself across from Acton. "I don't think you can avoid that now."

The driver adjusted his mirror for a better view of his passengers, now all seated on the floor behind him. "I don't care one way or the other if I'm part of the story. I just need to know where the hell I'm driving everyone."

"Just keep putting some distance between that theater and us," said Acton.

"What about one of our embassies?" suggested Laura.

"That'd be good for us, but not them." Acton pulled out his phone and sent another update to Kane and another request for help. There were now seven people involved.

The driver spun excitedly in his seat, staring back at them. "I have an idea!"

Dempsey reached out and spun the man's head back toward the road. "Like I said before, getting there alive is of critical importance."

"Yeah, yeah. Didn't I tell you I've got eyes at the back of my head?"

Alina gave him the finger.

"I saw that."

Dempsey flashed the young woman a grin. "What's your idea?"

"You've got a flight that's leaving shortly."

"So?"

"Get on it with the papers. They don't know you're involved yet. You could be out of the country before anyone knows. I'm sure one of the professors has a contact there that could authenticate those papers, and then you could go live with the report. Then it's too late for the Russians to try to hide the secret. That should mean they lose interest in everyone else."

"This flight, when does it leave?" asked Acton.

Dempsey checked her watch. "In two hours."

"How far are we from the airport?"

"Not even fifteen minutes," replied the driver.

"Then let's head there now and get her on a flight. Then I want everyone thinking of some place where we can lie low for possibly a day or two, because things are going to get worse before they get better."

Operations Center 2, CIA Headquarters

Langley, Virginia

Leroux read the latest update from Acton as security camera footage that they had tapped was replayed, showing their escape from the theater. "What do we know about this reporter?"

"Washington Post, stationed in Moscow for three years as their chief correspondent."

"Anything that gives her some pull with Washington?"

Tong continued reading the file then smiled. "Her grandfather is apparently quite well known. He was involved in the Pentagon Papers story."

"Is he still alive?"

"Yes."

"Good. That means he has the connections to raise a stink if Washington doesn't agree to help." He dialed Morrison's office, the Chief's assistant answering. "This is Leroux. I need to speak to him at once."

"One moment."

Morrison picked up. "What is it, Chris?"

"New information that Washington might want to know about. The professors and the Russians have just been picked up by a Washington Post reporter named Kaye Dempsey. Her grandfather is Chester Dempsey. He was involved—"

"Yes, I know who he is. Pretty much every one of my generation knows. What of it?"

"Well, sir, if Washington doesn't want to commit and he finds out, something tells me they're in for a world of hurt with the press."

There was a pause on the other end. "That just might be what we need. I'll get back to you. And in the meantime, keep tracking them and arrange for a safe house. We'll have to have some assets ready to extract them. Get everybody in place so that when we get approval from DC, we can act immediately. Don't let the professors know yet, because I don't want to make promises we can't keep."

"Understood." The call ended and Leroux turned to Tong. "Your little discovery might just pay off. Let Moscow Station know we're going to need a safe house and personnel ready to get them off the streets."

"Yes, sir." Tong got on the line with Moscow as Leroux turned his attention back to the screens. He glanced over his shoulder at Child. "Any luck tracking that van?"

"I've got them on camera a few times."

"Can you extrapolate where they might be heading?"

"My best guess is the airport."

Leroux spun his chair to face their whiz kid. "The airport? They're not that stupid. There's no way they could think they can get on an airplane."

Child shrugged. "Hey, I'm just guessing. Maybe their favorite Pizza Hut is just up the road from where I last spotted them and they're jonesing for a stuffed crust meat lovers."

Leroux chuckled. "Okay, keep tracking them." He raised his voice. "And somebody tell me they've been able to reach Jack. They could be heading straight toward him."

J. ROBERT KENNEDY

Sheremetyevo International Airport
Moscow, Russian Federation

Jack—just Jack—patiently sat, at least outwardly, in the jam-packed waiting area for those flagged for secondary reviews, doom scrolling his news feed. He had switched to the Russian news to not blow his cover in the event someone was playing Jimmy Stewart over his shoulder. He had traveled on a Russian passport and spoke the language fluently. And it was educational. The anti-Western slant on the feed was as obvious as the news back home was slanted to either side of the political spectrum. The difference here was no one was getting the truth, they were only getting the government's truth. Back home, both sides were receiving partial truths.

The world over, the news was no longer the news. It was somebody with an agenda delivering it. He didn't blame people for claiming that the news was fake, for it too often was. Unfortunately, those who love to say it the most didn't get their news from the mainstream media. They instead got it from social media where fake news thrived. It was laughable, abandoning the mainstream media due to your belief it was fake news, then turning to social media to be assured of getting it.

It was asinine.

The proper thing to do was to reclaim the media, to demand the sources, whether they be TV, radio, or newspapers, whether in digital or print, return to their core values and report the news and the news only— shelve the intermingled commentary. Force them to make it crystal clear when something was opinion by separating it in an obvious manner, clearly labeled with the participants not the same people reporting on the news.

Unfortunately, in today's busy lifestyle, few had the time to eloquently complain. Thanks to social media, society had degenerated into hurling anonymous insults. While researching a cover last year, he had stumbled upon a plumbing-related question that even he knew the solution to— use a washer. Twenty years ago, someone would have answered that question saying, "Use a washer. That should fix your problem." Today, the response would be, and in this case indeed was, "Use a washer. What are you, a moron?" And more piled onto this poor person's request. They didn't know who that person was. It could have been someone's grandmother. How would they like it if their grandmother was spoken to that way for asking an innocent question?

The violent vitriol that now permeated throughout society today had to stop. Eliminating anonymity from the Internet would be a good first step that he was in favor of—then you could implement the Purge for 12 hours and hunt down those who didn't get the message.

He chuckled to himself, and an elderly man sitting across from him smiled. "Something funny?" he asked in Russian.

"Yeah, this whole situation. Why are we Russians being treated like this? I can understand the foreigners, but why us? This is our country. We can come home whenever we want, for whatever reason we want. Who the hell says we have to plan it days or weeks in advance?"

The man nodded. "I agree wholeheartedly." He turned toward one of the guards standing at the far end of the narrow room. "Hey, how about you put the Russians at the front of the line?"

Jack added his two kopecks. "Yeah, listen to the old man. Why are you wasting our time? Make the Americans wait, not us."

More chimed in, including some of the foreigners who he was speaking against, ignorant as to what he was saying but hopeful that whatever was being said would get them out of there quicker. Little did they know. A more senior officer stepped out from behind a glass-enclosed office, whispering to the guard who singled out Jack and the old man.

The new arrival jabbed a finger at both of them. "You two troublemakers, get up here now."

Jack and the old man exchanged grins and rose, Jack ceding the front of the line to his elder despite the fact he was on a deadline, his watch electrocuting him non-stop for the past 15 minutes, the coded pattern indicating Langley was desperate to get in touch with him. It meant something was wrong. They were either warning him about something, or activating him, but there was no privacy here. He couldn't risk activating the watch nor could he bring up the secure messenger on his

272

phone. He had to get out of this room, and being the squeaky wheel might be the only way.

"So, why are you two in such a hurry?"

The old man grunted. "When you get to be my age, you start to count how much time you think you've got left in months, not years. And when years become months, then weeks become days and days become hours. And I don't have days to waste in your lineup. I'm an old man. I'm Russian. This is my country. I was born here, probably around the same time your granddaddy was born. I've seen it all, and this is bureaucratic bullshit. You're looking for someone, that's fine. But why the hell are you looking for Russian citizens coming here?"

"We're looking for people who booked last-minute tickets." The guard held out his hand. "Show me your ticket." The old man fished the folded-up itinerary from his pocket and handed it over. "It says here you bought your ticket late last night, why?"

"Like I said, when years become months and days become hours, well, it works the opposite way too. Hours become days. Last night, I decided I wanted to come home and get some real Russian food, not the shit they call Russian in the south of France. I want real blini and kasha, real borscht and pelmeni, made the right way, so when I'm dead in my grave, I'm still repeating. Not the toned-down bland versions of things they serve in France at restaurants not meant for Russians but for Frenchmen too accustomed to eating croissants and cream on everything. So, are you going to let me get my fill, or am I going to drop dead right here right now out of boredom?"

Both guards were chuckling at the tirade and the itinerary was handed back, the senior guard holding his hand out again. "Passport. If it's clean when I run it, you can go."

The old man handed it over. "Thank you."

The guard disappeared and returned a moment later, handing the passport back. "You're good to go, Mr. Zorkin."

Zorkin extended a hand as Jack suppressed his surprise, as this was the man Kane had informed him was also on his way to help as part of the Gray Network. He extended his index finger and tapped Zorkin's inner wrist twice. "Pleasure to meet you, old man. Let's hope they treat me as well as you."

"Let's hope." Zorkin didn't return the impromptu coded signal, which was unfortunate. It would have been easier if they teamed up.

"Now, why are *you* in such a hurry?" asked the supervisor.

Jack was already prepared with a cover. He tapped his phone screen, holding it up to his face, then brought up a photo of a ridiculously endowed blonde. "Her."

Both men's eyes shot wide. "What about her?"

"She's been dating an asshole friend of mine for three years."

"If he's a friend of yours, why is he an asshole?"

"Because he's dating her. They broke up yesterday and she sent me a message saying she had to see me. You realize how many years I've been waiting for a shot at her?" He continued to hold the phone in their faces so there was no avoiding the ample assets.

"You think you've got a chance?" asked the younger one.

"All I do know is I have none if I'm stuck in here much longer. I'm supposed to meet her in half an hour for lunch. At her apartment." Jack's eyebrows bobbed.

The younger one grinned and held up a fist. Jack bumped it. "Come on, boss, you have to let him go. Look at her."

The older one sighed. "If I knew then what I know now." He shook his head. "Fine. Passport."

Jack handed it over and the man disappeared, returning a few moments later, handing it back. "You're free to go. Good luck."

Jack grinned, patting his stomach. "With abs like these, I don't need luck."

The man laughed and patted his rotund stomach. "With abs like these, even luck can't help me."

Jack waved the passport at them. "Thank you very much. You two have a great day."

The guard buzzed him through the exit as the older one shouted to the room. "Anyone else here have a hot date that they're late for?"

The crowd erupted, apparently everyone about to meet a long-lost love.

Jack walked down a corridor and emerged into the arrivals area of the terminal. He stepped to the side and pressed the coded sequence on the edge of the watch face.

Urgent you make contact now.

"I always wanted one of those."

Jack had learned long ago to never flinch, no matter how surprised he might be. By maintaining control, it made the other person think you had been fully aware the entire time they were there, and might have already had a chance to ready a weapon while your back was to them. The voice was in English, not Russian, like when he had first heard it. "Mr. Zorkin," he said as he smiled, turning around to face the old man. "I see you got my signal."

"A little too obvious, young man, using a modified Freemason's handshake."

Jack shrugged. "Well, I couldn't exactly say I was here to meet you since you didn't match the photo I used."

"Photo?"

Jack shook his head. "Never mind." He extended a hand. "My name's Jack."

"Jack, what?"

"Just Jack. You want me to call you Viktor or Mr. Zorkin?"

"Call me whatever the hell you want." He nodded toward the watch. "You could have skipped the secret handshake. I already knew what you were."

"Because of my watch? Bullshit. It looks like any other cheap-ass Casio."

"Yes, but every time it zaps your wrist, your eyes narrow slightly at the edges, then you scratch your forearm."

"Really?"

"Yeah. You better work on that."

Jack logged in to the secure messenger, skipping to the last message. He cursed.

"What is it?" asked Zorkin.

"The professors are on the way to the airport with three Russian nationals and two American reporters."

Zorkin's nostrils flared. "What the hell is going on? When I got on the airplane, I was coming here to collect Orlov. Now there are seven people involved?"

Jack rolled his eyes. "You obviously haven't worked with these professors before. They're like victim magnets."

"What do they want us to do?"

"The reporter's getting on a plane with some documents that the Russians are after. Langley wants me to intercept them and get the documents because they don't trust that the plane won't be turned around. They just got approval for a safe house, so they want me to get them there if I can intercept them, since I'm a familiar face."

"Then what are we waiting for?"

"You to finish asking me questions."

Zorkin chuckled and held a hand out, directing him toward the doors at the front of the terminal. "Please, don't let me hold you up. I'll get us a car."

Jack fished an AirPod from his pocket and shoved it in his ear. It paired with his phone as he tapped an icon to connect to a Moscow Station relay. There was a double beep. "Hey, it's me Jack."

"Voice identity confirmed," came the computerized reply, followed by another double beep then a click.

"I see you got my message," came Leroux's voice over the lone earbud.

"Which one? There's been so many."

Leroux laughed. "I assume you got caught up in the security sweep?"

"Yes. So did an old friend of ours."

"He's with you now?"

"He's getting us a car."

"Good. We need you to do an intercept. They're about three minutes away."

"Do they know?"

"No, we haven't told them yet because we weren't able to make contact with you. Can you make the arrival's drop-off within three minutes?"

"I'm staring at it now."

"Good. I'm sending you a photo of the vehicle. It's a news van, you can't miss it."

His phone vibrated and he tapped the message, a picture of the news van embedded. He walked through the front doors and headed left. "Got it."

"They're entering the airport now," said Leroux in his ear.

"Does that mean you have eyes on me as well?"

"Negative, we're using a satellite. We don't want to risk hacking any airport cameras. The Russians can't know what we're doing."

"Copy that. I'm twenty meters left of the entrance."

"Then you should be able to see them now. Blue van, some transmitters on the roof."

Jack peered ahead then caught sight of it. "I see them." The arrivals area was bustling, and there were no available parking spots between him and them, which meant they would be passing him at any moment. He squeezed between two taxis then held out a hand before stepping in front of the van. Tires screeched as it came to an abrupt halt, the driver shouting a string of colorful metaphors that would have a sailor blushing. Jack glared at them then walked over to the passenger side window.

The woman rolled it down, her eyes filled with horror, a smile forced. "Are you all right?"

He maintained the angry face, but his voice was calm. "Perfectly fine. Pretend you're scared of me and that we're having an argument. Professor Acton, it's Jack."

"Jack!" cried Acton from the back, out of sight. "Thank God!"

"I understand you have some papers for me."

"She's taking them on a plane."

"No, she isn't. The plan has changed."

"Am I not getting on the plane?" asked the woman.

"I don't care what you do. However, if you've got a chance to get out of the country, I suggest you take it." He activated his comms. "Control, I need that safe house address." Jack looked at the driver. "Pen and paper." The man reached into the center console, grabbing both. "Write this down." He fed him the address as Leroux repeated it in his ear.

"Tell them when they get there, the garage door will open automatically, and to pull in," said Leroux.

Jack repeated the instructions as a file folder appeared. He held out a hand, stopping the pass. "That's everything they've gone apeshit crazy over?"

"Yes," said Acton, wisely remaining out of sight in the back. "Will we see you at the safe house?"

"I don't know. I have to get these files safely out of the country. If you don't see me, I have no doubt someone will be helping you now that the Agency is involved." He reached forward and angrily grabbed the folder from the woman's hands then stepped back, shaking a fist. "Watch where you're driving next time, asshole," he shouted in Russian.

The van jerked forward and Jack shook another fist at it, spitting.

"I thought you were going to go with them," said Leroux in his ear.

"Hell no. I don't want to get arrested. My understanding is the Russians want these papers, and if our people are caught with them, we may never see them again. As long as they don't have them, they're safe. Let me get these out of the country, and you get them out of the country."

"And have you got a plan for that?"

A car horn honked and Jack glanced over to see Zorkin behind the wheel of a sedan, beckoning to him. "I do now."

Acton repositioned as Doyle jerked the wheel to the right, sending him tumbling into Volkov. The young man helped him to his feet and he caught a glimpse of the too-small parking spot Doyle had jammed the nose of the van into.

"Go! Now!" ordered Doyle. "There's no time for goodbyes. Remember, your luggage has already been sent ahead, but you have to claim it here first. You've got your ID and passport, and your itinerary is on your phone."

Dempsey stared at Doyle, tears in her eyes. "I'm worried about you."

"Don't worry about me. I've been through hell and back in Afghanistan and Iraq. These Russians don't scare me."

"They should."

"And you should know when I'm lying. Now, just get the hell out of here." He reached over and gave her a hug then yanked the handle, opening the door.

She turned back to Acton and the others. "Good luck to you. If you—I mean, *when* you get out, contact me. I won't rest until I know you're safe."

"We'll be fine," said Acton. "Now get out of here and save yourself so you can tell our story."

She flashed a weak smile then reached out one last time and gave Doyle's hand a squeeze. She stepped out of the van then closed the door. Doyle backed up then pulled away, giving her a final wave. Acton held on to a drawer handle as Doyle surged into traffic. Everyone remained silent, and Acton was certain he wasn't the only one praying that not only did she safely make it out of the country so their story could be shared with the world, but that Jack somehow got the documents out as well.

They were the only leverage over the Russians they had.

"We've just left the airport grounds," announced Doyle. He handed back the piece of paper he had written on earlier. "Somebody read this to me."

Laura leaned forward and took the paper, reading the address for the safe house as Doyle operated the navigation system.

"Eighteen minutes to safety," he announced.

"Then what?" asked Volkov.

It was a legitimate question. Dempsey's flight was leaving in 90 minutes. It would take her about three-and-a-half hours to reach her stopover in London after she was in the air. Her plan was to stay there so she could work the story in safety. Once landed, she would send them a message indicating she was safely out of the country. But until then, they wouldn't know whether she had been arrested the moment she attempted to clear security in Moscow, or if she had made it back home unscathed.

Yet that wasn't necessarily true. If they were going to a CIA safe house, then there had to be some way for them to communicate with Langley. Langley should know whether she made it on the plane, or at least find out.

Laura leaned closer, her voice low. "Penny for your thoughts, as you Americans like to say."

Acton flashed her a smile. "I don't know if I've ever actually said that in my life. My mother, God rest her soul, said it all the time. She always knew when something was troubling me."

She wiped a tear from the corner of his eye, the mere mention of his recently departed mother still painful.

"I'm just thinking about what's next."

She sighed. "We've only got ourselves to blame for this one."

He chuckled. "True, though this one isn't so bad, is it?"

"Not yet, no. Nobody's been shooting at us, but I have no desire to spend any time in a Russian jail, even if I know I'll eventually be released."

He nodded toward the other three, young enough to be his children. "It's them I'm really worried about. I doubt the CIA is going to want to extract them along with us. In fact, I'm not sure if there'll be any extraction at all. I think everything will be negotiated behind the scenes, and they'll be a mere afterthought."

"I'm sure Dylan will figure out something."

"I hope so. All I know is one thing is for sure."

"What's that?"

"That if anyone ever asks me to come to Russia again, I'm going to say, nyet."

She smiled broadly at him. "I don't believe that for a second."

Entering Central Moscow, Russian Federation

Zorkin guided them deeper into Moscow then toward an apartment no one knew about, the name on the rental agreement not remotely related to him. He jerked his chin toward the file folder on Jack's lap. "So, is that what they're all after?"

Jack opened the folder, quickly skimming through the pages. "Yeah, looks like notes and correspondence from Lenin, Stalin, and some others. Lenin looks like he's growing more concerned about Stalin, and Stalin looks like he's becoming more paranoid about Lenin." He closed the folder. "I'm sure if I had time to get to the end of the book, it would have proof that Stalin killed Lenin."

Zorkin whistled. "That would be big news in Mother Russia."

Jack shrugged. "Would it? It would be like saying, Truman killed Roosevelt. It would be of mild interest to the bespectacled crowd, but other than that, I don't think it would even make the evening news."

"Yes, but do you worship Truman?"

Jack laughed. "I'm willing to bet half of Americans don't even know who the hell he is."

"Exactly. You have to think bigger, like Johnson killed Kennedy. You need to take two heroes from your past, then discover one killed the other for his job, and that everything you've been told about him was a lie. Then couple that with the fact the victim was an even bigger hero, think Thomas Jefferson murdering George Washington but only a century ago, where there are people still alive today who would remember living under Jefferson. That's what it would mean to Russia, one hero killing a greater hero. When this gets out, if it's believed, Russia will be talking about nothing other than this for some time, and then hopefully begin questioning why their current leader, if he knew the truth, speaks so fondly of the man and a bygone era that never existed. And if they begin to question our dear leader, the opposition might just have a chance in the next election."

Jack eyed him. "Ignoring the fact you forgot John Adams was president between Washington and Jefferson, do you honestly believe that your president would ever let anyone beat him in an election?"

"Absolutely not. And I'm not even suggesting that the opposition would get a majority. What I'm saying, is that if all of your friends swear up and down that they voted for the opposition, and all *their* friends do the same, are you really going to believe they only got five or ten percent of the vote? You see, the problem here is that the conspiracies some of your people claim are happening in your country, are actually happening here, but the state-controlled media never report on it, because the vast majority support the president. They would write it off as fake news, much like your people, but if suddenly instead of five to ten percent of the population, thirty or forty oppose the president, that's a significant enough number to begin asking questions when the poll numbers don't match with reality. Remember, the victor never questions the results. Shake the core belief system of enough of his supporters, and it just might change the tide, and even if it doesn't, if it at least gets him off the course of following in Stalin's footsteps, that can only be a good thing. The world should never have another Stalin, just like it should never have another Hitler. The technology we have today could mean the end of us all."

Jack patted the folder. "Well then, I guess we have to make sure these become public. I have a plan for getting this out of the country, but the fact you haven't asked me for any thoughts on the matter, I assume you have a plan as well?"

"Yes, I do, and I'm willing to hear your plan, but let me ask you this."

"What?"

"Does your plan involve handing the papers over to your government?"

"Of course."

"Then I must respectfully reject your plan."

"But you haven't even heard it. It's an excellent plan."

"I have no doubt, but it doesn't serve my purposes."

"Your purposes? I thought you said these plans could save your country from a possibly dangerous future, not to mention the fact they could be key in saving seven people from the wrath of the Russian government."

"Oh, don't get me wrong, all of those things are important and are still true, and my plan doesn't change those facts. But you're forgetting one thing, the one thing that triggered all of this."

Jack stared at him, his eyes narrowing. "And that is?"

"Orlov. We have to find him. I no longer give a damn whether he's safe, but he's the one who broke the agreement and made contact with his past life. I need to find him so that I can deliver the message to him personally that he's out of the program. And besides, if anyone gets killed because of his actions, I want to personally lay down his final beating."

Jack tapped the folder. "You plan to use this as bait?"

"Exactly. Those documents were so irresistible to him that he put everything on the line to get his hands on them. Once I get them safely out of the country, all I have to do is send him a message, and he'll be there in no time. Then we can truly put an end to this."

Jack chewed his cheek for a moment, eying him. "Fine, we'll go with your plan, old man. But when you have Orlov, I get the documents."

"Agreed."

Deputy Director Nikitin's Office, The Kremlin

Moscow, Russian Federation

Nikitin yawned and tore his eyes away from the screen. They were burning after staring at so much footage for so long. They had tracked the news van to the airport and had footage of a woman exiting the van and entering the terminal. They had managed to identify her as a Washington Post reporter named Kaye Dempsey. What was odd was that the ticket had been purchased two weeks ago by her company—this was not some last-minute escape.

There was no doubt those they were after had been picked up in front of the theater by her news van. What was going on, he had no idea, but it didn't matter. She was a reporter, she was on a plane leaving the country, and there was no way in hell his targets hadn't taken the opportunity to hand the documents over to her, documents he still had no clue as to their nature, but with each hour, it appeared more and more did.

He had passed the bad news on to his superiors—the documents were now on an airplane and out of their reach. It was now up to the Kremlin to decide how far they wanted to take this, but unless that plane turned around and landed again in Moscow, his involvement was over. He had failed. Now, the only way he had to redeem himself was to catch Orlov, and to do that, he had to catch his targets. Interrogating them would lead him to the professor, and if he could hand a wanted fugitive over, he just might save his career. If he were truly lucky, perhaps they could use them as leverage over the reporter to not release the documents.

All was not lost. There was still time to turn this around.

"Sir, you need to see this."

Nikitin opened his burning eyes and he glanced over at Zaitsev. "What is it?"

Zaitsev pointed at the screen in front of him as his underling manipulated the video image. "Remember we saw the van stop at the airport, and there was an altercation with someone before they moved on. Well, I found a better angle so we could see the passenger side, and look at this."

Nikitin watched as the man leaned in the passenger window, gesturing animatedly in what appeared to be a fairly one-sided argument, though with the glare off the windshield, he couldn't see what was happening inside. "Yes, I'm aware of this. Why are you wasting—"

"Just a second. Watch."

The man reached in, and when his hand came back in sight, it held a thick folder. He shouted one more time, shaking his fist as the van rushed off, then calmly walked away before stepping back into traffic and climbing into a white sedan.

Zaitsev looked up from his chair at him. "What do you think is in that folder?"

Nikitin smiled. "I think it's the documents we've been looking for."

"They never got on the plane!"

Nikitin shook his head, tempering Zaitsev's enthusiasm. "We can't be sure, but I'm willing to bet drinks tonight that we haven't lost this yet." He stabbed a finger toward the car the stranger had climbed into. "We need to find that car. That was a staged handover, which means they have a plan for getting the papers out."

Zaitsev folded his arms, leaning back. "That means we don't have much time."

"No, we don't. Leave one man working on the van. I want everyone else focusing on that car and its occupants. We need to know who they are, where they came from, and most importantly, where they went."

"Yes, sir."

"Now, I have to brief the Chief of Staff so the president knows the reporter might not have the stolen documents on that plane.

Over Russian Airspace

"American Airlines Flight 6968, this is Moscow Control, come in, over."

Captain Adam Powell cocked an eyebrow at his copilot, Kim Dunbar. "I wonder what they want?"

Dunbar shrugged. "We're not due for a handover, so there must be some emergency, maybe with one of the passenger's families."

Powell activated his mic. "Moscow Control, this is American Airlines Flight 6968. Go ahead, over."

"Flight 6968, you are ordered to immediately return to Sierra-Victor-Oscar, over."

This had Powell's other eyebrow joining its partner as his chest tightened. Russia wasn't the Soviet Union, but it wasn't far enough away from the stories he had heard of the old days for him to not be nervous. "How far are we from leaving Russian airspace?"

"Less than a hundred-fifty klicks. We'll be in Latvian airspace in under ten minutes."

Powell cursed then checked his airspeed indicator. With what had recently happened in Belarus, there was no way in hell he wanted to risk any of his passengers being hauled off by the Russian regime for some offense that would simply be free speech in the civilized world. But ten minutes was an eternity. He increased his speed gently to the maximum allowed, though the increase would shave less than a minute off their time.

"Are you going to respond?" asked Dunbar.

"Get the head office on the line. I want instructions from Fort Worth before I turn a planeload of mostly foreign nationals around."

Dunbar's eyes bulged at the prospect of disobeying the orders from Moscow Air Traffic Center, but made the call.

Powell activated his mic. "Moscow Control, this is American Airlines 6968. Can you please repeat your last transmission, over?"

"American Airlines Flight 6968, you are ordered to return immediately to Sierra-Victor-Oscar, over."

"Yeah, that's what I thought you said," he muttered. "ETA to the border?"

"Eight minutes."

"Moscow Control, can you please let us know why you're ordering us to return, over?"

"Negative, Flight 6968. You are ordered to return immediately. No explanation is required while in Russian airspace, over."

"What's our closest airport?" he asked.

Dunbar responded immediately. "Riga International. We can be there in twenty minutes."

Powell pushed forward on the throttle, exceeding their legal speed limitations, though not the plane's capabilities. "Moscow Control, we can be at Riga International in less than twenty minutes. If there's a mechanical or medical emergency we're not aware of, then we need to land as quickly as possible. There's no time to return to Sierra-Victor-Oscar. I am increasing speed to reduce flight time, over."

"Negative, Flight 6968, you will reduce your speed and immediately change your heading to zero-nine-zero for an immediate return to Sierra-Victor-Oscar."

Dunbar frowned. "He doesn't sound happy."

Powell had to agree. "No, he doesn't. Have you got through to Fort Worth yet?"

Dunbar tapped the phone pressed against her ear. "I've just been transferred."

"Flight 6968, respond immediately."

He eased back on the throttle, resetting them to the legal limit their flight plan allowed. "Stand by, Moscow Control, reducing speed now."

"I've got headquarters."

Powell switched channels. "This is Captain Adam Powell, flight 6968 out of Moscow. Are you aware of the situation?"

"Yeah, Adam, your copilot brought me up to speed."

Powell breathed a sigh of relief at the friendly voice on the other end. Mike Broughton was a man he had known for years, and a man he trusted. "Recommendations?"

"How far are you from leaving their airspace?"

"Distance to border?" he asked Dunbar.

"One hundred klicks," replied Dunbar, still on the call.

"So, about seven minutes," said Broughton.

"Yeah. I already tried pushing my luck by increasing our airspeed, but they're demanding we change course immediately. What should we do?"

"As you know, you're in command of the aircraft, so I'll support whatever decision you make and back you all the way."

Powell rolled his eyes. "Come on, Mike, you can do better than that. I need advice, not rehearsed corporate garbage."

"There are three possibilities that I see here, Adam. One is you turn around, you land, they arrest somebody on the plane, and then you refuel and resume the flight. Two is that you ignore them, leave their airspace, they raise a stink, perhaps revoke our landing license, and three, they blow you out of the sky."

Powell chuckled. "I hardly think they're going to do that."

And as if to make him out to be a liar, his collision avoidance alarm went off and a fighter jet buzzed their cockpit, a new voice entering the conversation.

"American Airlines Flight 6968, this is Flight Leader Zero-One, you will immediately alter course as instructed by Moscow Control, over."

Tracer fire flashed in front of the cockpit, quickly followed by a second fighter passing far too close.

"What the hell was that?" asked Broughton.

"We just got buzzed by two MiGs. They fired warning shots across our nose!"

"Holy shit, Adam, you better do what they say!"

Powell gripped the controls, his knuckles white as he squeezed tightly. "If they're willing to go this far, then whoever they want on board is a dead man."

"You're right. And maybe he deserves it. It could be a murderer for all you know."

Powell grabbed the throttle. "If this were some regular criminal, they would have told us. The fact they're refusing and the fact they already had planes in the air to intercept us means they're after somebody either for political or national security reasons. One of our covert ops guys might be on board, or an opposition leader, or even a member of the press that's pissed them off."

"What are you saying? Please tell me you're not thinking of ignoring them."

"Maybe in times like these, it's best not to think and to just act." He switched channels then flicked a switch on his panel. "Mayday! Mayday! Mayday! This is American Airlines Flight 6968! We have been struck by bullets fired from a Russian fighter jet and we have lost cabin pressurization! Beginning emergency descent!"

He shoved forward on the throttle then put them into a rapid dive to gain even more airspeed in what just might be his final act on this earth.

Dempsey yelped as did half the plane, the other half screaming as the engines whined and the aircraft tilted forward at an angle she had never before experienced in flight. The shock momentarily had her forgetting the sight of the fighter jets that had just opened fire on them moments ago. She tightened her lap belt and pulled out her phone, the plane's WiFi still operating. She began sending messages describing what was happening, Hootsuite automatically posting them on her various social media feeds. The world had to know that this was happening and why. It was because of her. Obviously, the Russians believed she had the documents they were after.

Sweat broke out all over her body as her heart pounded. She had never been so frightened in her life, yet she had a job to do, a job more important than giving in to her fears. She was a reporter, and unfortunately, she was not only in the story, she *was* the story. It was impossible this was merely a coincidence. By getting her story out for the world to see, live, as it happened, someone might be able to let the Russians know she didn't have the papers, that there was no reason to kill everyone on board to preserve a century-old secret.

How insane was the Russian president? That was the question the world should be asking, and she put it out there to her followers. Then she made a decision that could either kill them or save them, and livestreamed their plight, staring into the phone, creating a visual record that would resonate more with those accustomed to no longer reading.

"The reason the Russian government is attempting to shoot us down is because the government has been keeping secret the fact that Stalin murdered Lenin. I have seen the documents. They appear genuine. This is why the Russian president wants us dead, but now the world knows and the proof will be in your hands soon enough, even if I die here today, because I don't have the documents with me. Share these messages, spread the word, so that the world knows that whatever story the Russian government tells about what is happening, is a lie. We were attacked to preserve a secret that is a century old, all because it might embarrass the current Russian president."

She switched over to her email and crafted a final message for her parents, her shoulders shaking as she sobbed at the thought they would outlive her, a lost child something no one should ever suffer.

Then her eyes shot wide. "Grandpa!"

Operations Center 2, CIA Headquarters

Langley, Virginia

Leroux stood in the aisle, his hands on his hips as they watched on radar two Russian MiGs engaging the civilian airliner with Dempsey on board, while on the right of the screen, Child had her various social media feeds streaming along with trending statistics showing how fast the story was spreading.

The door hissed then was swept aside as Morrison charged into the room, his eyes already glued to the displays as he joined Leroux. "Status?"

"They're toying with them at the moment. Warning shots only. Buzzing them. But they're almost at the border. If the Russians are going to commit, they're going to commit any moment now."

"And I assume we haven't intercepted any chatter?"

"The pilot just broadcast that he was hit and they've depressurized. He's begun an emergency descent."

Morrison frowned. "Is it true, or is he playing for time?"

"Moscow's not buying it."

"Didn't think they would, but they're pretty damned close to leaving Russian airspace, and his little stunt will increase his airspeed." Morrison nodded toward the social media feeds. "What's she saying about all this?"

Leroux snapped his fingers over his shoulder and Child reported. "She's revealed that the reason they're being attacked is because of the Stalin murdering Lenin thing. She's saying she doesn't have the documents. Other than that, it's mostly pleas to share the stories so the world knows what's happening."

"And is the story spreading?"

"Like wildfire, sir. She has a lot of followers. She's got over a million interactions across the platforms already and it is growing exponentially. I'm also finding live streams from other people on board. The story is out there, and the Russian government is going to be embarrassed, but something tells me they don't give a shit." Child's eyes shot wide. "Sorry, sir."

Morrison chuckled. "Don't worry about it, son. My wife tells me I must have been a sailor in a previous life."

"Is there anything we can do to help, sir?" asked Tong. "Is DC aware of what's going on?"

Morrison turned toward her. "Oh, they know. And I have no doubt the red phone is ringing, but there's no way it'll be answered until that plane is either shot down or crosses the border. What's the status on the professors and their new Russian friends?"

"They arrived at the transfer location safely, and they've been moved to the safe house. That press van stuck out like a sore thumb, so they would have been easily traced. They're secure for the moment, sir."

"And Jack?"

"We're waiting for him to report in. The last update was that Zorkin had a plan that he wasn't sharing."

Morrison cursed. "Those papers were supposed to be handed over to us. That's why we committed assets. We should have Jack just take the damn papers. To hell with what Zorkin wants."

Leroux smiled slightly. "He did offer to punch the man in the throat a few times and do just that, but I declined his offer. Zorkin has assured him that eventually the documents will be passed over. He wants to use them as bait for Orlov."

Morrison growled. "Don't get me started—"

A voice cut in on the overhead speakers, drowning out the occasional shouts between Moscow Control and the American Airlines flight. "We have confirmation of missile launch."

Everyone spun toward the displays, no breaths un-held, as hundreds of innocent souls were about to die to protect one man's ego and a mass murderer's rewritten legacy.

National Control Defense Center

Moscow, Russian Federation

Nikitin's pulse pounded, not only from the excitement of the situation, but the fact he was standing here in what was nicknamed the War Room, the president himself not ten paces away, staring at the massive displays monitoring the situation in the air. Zaitsev was back at headquarters, feeding him updates on the ground situation through his earpiece in case the president had any questions. So far, the president had ignored him, much to his chagrin and relief. While he would love to speak directly to the man, the very notion terrified him. Nikitin towered over him by at least half a foot, yet the confidence the man exuded, the power—it was awe-inspiring. He couldn't imagine what it must be like, and he never would. Few had this kind of power, and it was awesome in its scope.

He both feared and revered him.

Somebody shouted excitedly from the front of the room. "Sir! Zero-Two has just launched a missile!"

Shouts erupted and Nikitin's eyes bulged as a cockpit feed showed a missile streaking toward the airliner.

"Abort the missile, immediately." The president's order was calm yet firm, and sliced through everything.

"Abort the missile! Abort the missile!" shouted someone in a panic, and Nikitin stepped closer to the displays, praying the abort signal got through in time, for if it didn't, the blood of those people was on his hands. He was the one who had tracked down the reporter and passed on the intel about what flight she was on. Hundreds were about to die because he had failed in his pursuit and let her escape.

And if that plane were destroyed, all of his dreams would go down with it.

Over Russian Airspace

Dempsey gripped the rear of the seat in front of her as she prayed aloud for the first time since she was a child, yet she kept forgetting the words.

"Our Father, who art in Heaven…"

"Brace! Brace! Brace! Heads down! Stay down!" shouted the flight attendants in unison, all now strapped into their jump seats. Every time they reached the end of their refrain and began it once again, she would be forced to restart her final plea to God to save those who surrounded her, their screams and sobs heartbreaking. Nobody's final moments should be filled with terror like this.

Her phone pinged with a message and she brought it up, gasping out a cry as it was from her mother. An explosion erupted, the entire sky lighting from a fireball behind them. The plane jerked, even the most stoic screaming. Her thumbs flew.

Goodbye. I love you all.

She hit *Send* and prayed it made it out before they were torn apart, for this was the end, as even the flight attendants had stopped chanting their instructions.

Even they knew all hope was now lost.

"Are we hit?" cried Dunbar.

It was a reasonable question, but Powell had no time to answer it, his eyes instead scanning all the indicators his copilot had access to as well as he struggled to regain control. There was no doubt there had been an explosion, but nothing suggested any damage to the plane, the only indicators screaming for attention warning him that what he was doing wasn't wise. He managed to level the wings, though maintained the steep dive.

"ETA to border?"

"Thirty seconds!"

Powell pulled back slightly on the stick, deciding pancaking on the ground wasn't an acceptable alternative to being blown out of the sky. He rechecked the indicators. "I don't think we've been hit."

"Then what the hell was it?"

"It had to be a missile."

"Are you saying they missed?"

Powell shook his head. "There's no way in hell they missed from this range."

"Then what just happened?"

"They must have aborted the missile."

"What do you think that means?"

"It means either someone made a mistake, or someone changed their mind. Either way, they're letting us go." Powell eased up on the throttle and pulled back harder on the stick.

"Ten seconds," said Dunbar, the excitement in her voice shared.

Powell slowly leveled out the rattling airframe, the roaring engines settling. The two fighter jets pursuing them crisscrossed in front of the cockpit before banking back home. He re-engaged the autopilot, instructing the computer to return to cruising altitude as he switched his mic over to the cabin speakers.

"Ladies and gentlemen, this is your captain speaking. As I'm sure you're aware, we just had an altercation with the Russian Air Force. We are now in Latvian airspace, and those planes have broken off. We believe a missile was fired and then aborted, which is the explosion you felt. We have no indication up here that we sustained any damage. We're now returning to cruising altitude, and are awaiting instructions on what to do next. Please remain calm and take it easy on our flight crew, as they know no more than you do. Oh, and drinks are on American Airlines."

Dunbar chuckled. "You know those cheap bastards are liable to take that out of your paycheck."

Powell laughed. "Nothing would surprise me after the day we've had. Now, get me Fort Worth again so we can give them an update and request instructions. We need to land so that the plane can be inspected. I don't think it was ever designed to survive a near missile strike."

"Yes, sir."

Powell removed his headset. "I'm going to go check on the passengers."

Dunbar shifted uncomfortably. "Do you mind if I take a couple of minutes before you?"

Powell's eyes narrowed inquisitively and Dunbar lowered her voice, knowing full well the cockpit recorder was catching everything being said.

"I think I might have had a bit of an accident."

Powell couldn't help but roar with laughter at the revelation, and decided to have a little fun with her, the tension breaker desperately needed. He reached forward to activate the cabin speakers. "I'm sure somebody back there has a pair of Depends that you can have."

Dunbar gave him a look.

"Or someone with a baby can lend you some wipes."

A finger was extended. Powell roared again as he reached for his oxygen mask. "Fine, fine. You go first."

Dunbar rose, shaking her head at him. "If you hadn't just saved my life, I'd kick your ass."

"You mean my clean ass?"

Two fingers.

Powell grinned. "Stick one of those where the sun don't shine next time, and you might not have an accident."

Dunbar's shoulders slumped and she laughed. "I hope I'm there the next time something like this happens and you shit your pants."

Powell eyed her with a smirk. "Yes, the next time the Russians try to shoot me out of the sky, I hope you're there with me too, but there's no way you're going to catch me filling my drawers."

"Oh yeah? Why's that?"

"Because I'm never flying again without wearing adult diapers." He jerked a thumb toward the bathrooms. "Now go and make it snappy. I have to change my own shorts."

National Control Defense Center

Moscow, Russian Federation

The entire room let out a collective sigh of relief as they watched the planes break off and the American passenger jet continue safely into Latvian airspace. Though not everyone was pleased. The president turned on his heel and marched out of the room, saying nothing, his entourage following.

Zaitsev, ignorant to what had just happened, interrupted his train of thought. "Sir, we've been able to trace where the men who took the handoff went. Do you want me to send a team?"

Nikitin said nothing for a moment as his mind continued to race.

"Sir, are you there?"

"Yes. Send a team, but have them stand by."

"What about Volkov and the professors? I've been told we might have a location for them shortly. A review of satellite footage found a vehicle leaving the site where we found the news van almost immediately after it arrived. We're tracking it now through traffic cameras. We'll hopefully know within a few minutes."

"Excellent work. As soon as you find them, send a team, then we'll hit both places at once."

"Yes, sir."

Now, to save my career.

He raised a hand. "Mr. President!"

The president turned, making eye contact, his face cold, his eyes piercing as if boring into his soul as they took a measure of what kind of man Nikitin was. Then he turned and continued out of the room, but something was whispered and a wrist flicked over his shoulder. The Chief of Staff dropped back then beckoned Nikitin over. Nikitin scrambled to join the man.

"What is it?"

Nikitin drew a quick breath. "We've found the location for those who were handed the documents. And we're about to find the people who stole them."

"It's a little late for that now, don't you think? If this was as professional an operation as it appeared to be, then even if you find those the papers were handed over to, it's already too late."

"No, sir. I have an idea on how we can turn this all around and still save our nation from any embarrassment, and bring a traitor to justice."

The man eyed him then delivered a curt nod. "Walk with me, and if I like your plan, you'll present it to the president himself."

Zorkin Safe House

Moscow, Russian Federation

Jack sat in an apartment that was either a safe house owned by Zorkin, or one available to him, likely through the fabled Gray Network. There were personal touches throughout that made it appear to be a home, though there were no pictures. Knick-knacks were strategically placed where one would expect, each of which a skilled spy could produce a backstory for. It could be that this was an Airbnb for spies, though it could also be that a man like Zorkin, doing the job he did, never had a chance to settle down to have a family, to make friends. Perhaps this was the end result of the profession he was now in, and what he had to look forward to in retirement.

Zorkin's phone chirped and he logged in to read the secure message. Then cursed.

"What is it?"

Zorkin ignored the question, instead tapping at his keyboard until he cursed again, holding up the phone for Jack to see. It was a video of the street below.

"What the hell am I looking at?"

Zorkin pointed at a window to his left. "I've got cameras on all the windows looking at the streets below. My contacts tell me we've been located and they're sitting on the apartment. Black SUV just down the street."

Jack leaned closer, peering at the image. "Does that mean they're not going to do the pick-up?"

There was a knock at the door, coded.

"Nope, they just thought we should know." Zorkin grabbed the folder that had caused so much trouble and headed for the door. He opened it and a woman in her sixties smiled. She handed over a pizza box and Zorkin placed the file folder on top. The woman flipped it open, removed the pages, slipped them into the delivery bag, and placed a different set of papers in the folder.

"Enjoy!"

"We will."

She stepped back into the hall as Zorkin closed the door and flipped the file folder shut. He brought the pizza over to the table they had been sitting around then placed the folder still sitting on top of the box aside. He opened the box, revealing a reasonable-looking pizza, though nothing like back home. But Jack was hungry, and didn't particularly care. He grabbed a slice then took a bite. It was over-sauced with a bland paste that undoubtedly came out of a can, leaving the thin crust soggy.

Zorkin took his own piece and bit into it, sighing. "Nothing like the taste of home."

Jack shrugged and took another bite. "To each his own, I guess."

Zorkin swallowed. "What? You don't like it?"

"It's edible."

Zorkin chuckled. "I said there was nothing like the taste of home. I didn't say home tasted good."

Jack snorted. "No, I suppose you didn't."

Zorkin wiped his mouth and hands with a napkin then opened the folder, flipping through the photocopies of papers from the archive, all of them public.

"Do you think they'll buy it?"

Zorkin shrugged then shut the folder. "I doubt it. By now, I'm sure they've identified which papers were taken by young Mr. Volkov, but"— he tapped the folder before grabbing another slice of pizza—"this gives them an acceptable alternative should they choose a different narrative."

"I hope you're right. I've managed to steer clear of Russian prison cells so far. I'd hate to ruin my record over some hundred-year-old secret."

The door burst open, half a dozen heavily armed suits rushing in, barking orders. Jack ignored them, instead continuing to stomach his slice of pizza, uncertain when he would get his next chance to eat. Zorkin did the same as they were covered by four men, the other two clearing the rest of the apartment. Eventually, six weapons were aimed at their heads.

Jack glared at them. "Do you gentlemen mind? I can't remember the last time I had pizza this good."

A man, clearly in charge, stepped into the apartment. He walked over to the table and tore a slice off the pie. He took a bite then grimaced, tossing what remained back in the box. "I thought you said this was good."

Jack shook his head. "No, I said I couldn't remember the last time I had pizza this good. It's shit, of course, but pizza this bad truly needs to be experienced every once in a while so you can appreciate the good stuff."

"Bring him in," barked the new arrival, the order tossed over his shoulder toward the door. A moment later, the customs official that had let them clear the airport appeared in the door frame, terrified. He was beckoned over and the poor bastard reluctantly joined them. "You recognize these men?"

"Yes, Mr. Zaitsev."

"And this one said he was here for our fine Russian cuisine?"

"Yes, Mr. Zaitsev."

Zaitsev indicated the half-eaten pizza. "Does this look like fine Russian cuisine to you?"

"No, Mr. Zaitsev."

"And this one?" Zaitsev indicated Jack. "He's supposed to be here for a hot date?"

"Yes, Mr. Zaitsev."

"A busty blonde, if I remember. Do you see any busty blondes here?"

"No, Mr. Zaitsev."

"So, these two, who are not supposed to have known each other, who came in on separate flights, are sitting here together eating the worst pizza I've ever tasted, and we're supposed to believe it's coincidence?" Zaitsev turned to Jack. "Care to explain?"

Jack picked up a napkin and wiped his fingers clean before leaning back. "I can assure you they're going to get a horrible review on Yelp."

Zaitsev smiled. "Let me guess, you have a perfectly reasonable explanation for why the two of you are sitting here together."

"I have an explanation. Whether you believe it to be reasonable is up to you."

"Why don't you try me?"

"My friend here"—Jack indicated Zorkin—"spotted me after I left customs and said he had a rental car waiting. He offered to drive me into town as a thank you for helping speed up his own clearance. I accepted his generous offer, and then on the way here, my date canceled on me. Apparently, she got back together with her boyfriend, so my new friend said I could wait with him until I could arrange a flight back. And then we ordered this palate cleanser so that when we went out for dinner for some *authentic* Russian food, we'd truly appreciate what we were eating compared to this American shit."

Zaitsev smiled. "A well thought out story, and I have no doubt you even have text messages with the girl canceling the date."

"Of course."

"But there's one thing you didn't explain."

"What's that?"

Zaitsev leaned forward and pressed his index finger on top of the folder. "This."

Jack shrugged. "What about it? Some moron Americans nearly ran me down. I gave them a piece of my mind, then made them pay by grabbing a folder that the woman had that appeared important to her. I suppose I shouldn't have done that, but then the asshole who was driving should have been paying attention."

"So, you're telling me that you just randomly stole this paperwork from a woman in a van that nearly hit you at the airport. And then, coincidentally, this man you've never met before, offers you a drive into the city?"

"Yes, that's exactly what I'm saying." Jack indicated the folder with a tip of his head. "Is that what this is all about?"

"I think you know what this is all about."

Jack gave him a look. "If I knew, I wouldn't be asking now, would I? If I'm going to have guns aimed at my head, don't you think I have the right to a straight answer?"

"All right, I'll let you play dumb." Zaitsev picked up the folder and opened it without looking. "These documents are classified and were stolen from a state archive yesterday, but I believe you know that. It's been all over the news for almost twenty-four hours."

Jack shook his head. "Who watches the news? And besides, in case you didn't notice, I just arrived in the country. Unless it's international news, I couldn't have known about it now, could I?"

Zaitsev smiled. "You're good."

"It's not hard to be good when you're being honest. I have nothing to hide. Question me all you want. The only way you're getting different answers out of me is if you beat them out of me, and then I'll tell you whatever you want to hear. It won't be the truth, of course, but I'll tell you whatever you want to hear. This is, after all, the Russia we live in today, is it not?"

Zaitsev pursed his lips as he regarded him.

Jack shook his head. "I don't see what the big deal is. So, there are a bunch of papers about Stalin. Dude's been dead for almost seventy years, and those papers are dated a hundred years ago. How are they possibly a state secret? Wasn't everything regarding Stalin made public twenty years ago?"

Zaitsev said nothing, instead turning his attention to the papers gripped in his hand, and within moments it was clear it wasn't the contents of the pages that were of interest to him, but the pages themselves. He rubbed the top page between his thumb and forefinger then cursed as he glared at Jack and Zorkin. "Where are the originals?"

They both gave him a puzzled look. "What do you mean, originals?"

"The original papers. These are photocopies."

Jack shrugged. "I don't know. Ask that woman I took them from."

"You mean she was carrying copies?"

Jack threw his hands up in the air. "Copies of what? I have no idea what you're talking about. The van she was in nearly ran me down. We exchanged words, she pissed me off, so I took her file folder and walked away. My new friend here picked me up, we came back here after my date was canceled, we ordered the worst pizza in the world, then a bunch of Russia's finest burst through the door and began accusing us of stuff. That's the folder that I took from her. It's a bunch of papers about Stalin. Who cares? He's dead and gone. Now, can we finish our pizza in peace, or are you going to continue with these ridiculous questions?"

Zaitsev stepped back. "We're going to continue, but not here."

Jack sighed. "Fine." He reached out and snagged another slice. "I'm taking this one for the road. Something tells me prison food is worse."

"Only slightly," muttered Zorkin.

Federal Security Service Interrogation

Moscow, Russian Federation

Acton sat in an uncomfortable chair along with the others lined up to his left and right. The attack on the safe house had been swift. There had been no warning it was coming, though they had been told to expect it. The person who had met them for the transfer from the far too visible news van into a much more discreet SUV, indicated his orders were limited.

"We're to get you all out of the area and into a safe house. Extraction has been arranged for you, Professor Acton, and your wife. That's it."

Acton and Laura both firmly shook their heads. "We all go, or none of us go," said Laura.

The contact called for instructions then hung up his phone. "Okay, stay here until you hear from someone, but they will track us. It's just a matter of time."

And it hadn't been much time—less than an hour.

No one had resisted. At the first sound of the attack, they had all lay down on the floor, their arms outstretched, exactly as planned when the possibility of arrest had been suggested. And now they were here in downtown Moscow, two uniformed armed guards keeping watch, no questions asked beyond a demand for their papers. They had all agreed the truth was the best story, for it had the most likely chance of protecting them all. He just prayed Jack had gotten away with the documents and would safely get them out of Russia, because if he hadn't and had been captured, they might have to throw him under the bus.

It was the handover that protected them. If they went with the story that Jack was a stranger who had stolen the folder as he had made it appear to any cameras that might have been watching, then it provided them with protection. It meant that a random crazy man had the documents, and they were likely tossed to the wind or thrown in a bin somewhere, the secret preserved. But if the handover was intentional, it meant leverage.

"How long do you think they'll keep us waiting," asked Laura.

Acton shrugged. "The longer they do, the better chance those documents have of getting to safety."

"Jack as well."

"I'm not too worried about Jack. He can handle himself."

The door opened and a Russian official named Nikitin, who had been present at their arrest, entered. "Professor Acton, come with me."

Acton kissed Laura's hand that he had been holding and gave a reassuring smile to the young man and his two female companions. "Everything's going to be all right." He followed Nikitin down a corridor

319

and into what could only be described as a stereotypical interrogation room—a single metal table with two chairs, one on each side, bright, harsh lighting, and a large mirror with observers no doubt on the other side.

"Have a seat, Professor."

Acton sat, steadying his breathing as he attempted to control his nerves. But it was no use. He was scared. This was Russia, and they were involved in something that dealt directly with the president, who had proven he was willing to kill anyone anywhere, as there would never be any consequences for his actions.

Nikitin sat opposite him and opened a folder. "Professor James Acton, residing in St. Paul, Maryland." He tapped the top page. "You might notice this file is fairly thick."

Acton regarded the man, assessing whether he should play it cool and flippant, or take the situation seriously. He decided on a little bit of both. "I should hope so after what happened with the Japanese Imperial Regalia."

Nikitin stared at him for a moment. "So, you admit to your involvement in the theft of Russian property, in assisting a known criminal from escaping justice, and in the deaths of Russian soldiers?"

Acton leaned forward and tapped the file. "You shouldn't believe your own propaganda. If that's what this file says happened, then you and I both know it's a pile of bullshit." He leaned back and resisted the urge to fold his arms, instead keeping them open, indicating he wasn't on the defensive. "Now, why don't we discuss what's really going on here, not the propaganda version, but the truth?"

Nikitin smiled at him slightly as he leaned back and folded his arms. He waved a hand. "Fine, Professor Acton, why don't you tell me the truth?"

"Very well. Professor Orlov, a man I barely know and whom I haven't heard from in years, contacted me yesterday indicating someone had discovered documents that would rewrite history. They would only hand those documents over to him, and he needed an independent third party to hand them over to so they could safely be taken out of the country and then authenticated. He feared being arrested because of his escape from prison, something I wasn't aware of until yesterday. We agreed to meet him and take the documents. We were assured there was nothing illegal or nefarious going on, merely that they were important and needed to be authenticated by someone like myself or my wife.

"We arrived, we made contact with Orlov, we checked into our hotel, the same hotel he was checked into, then went to his room, and instead of finding him, found the others. They were terrified because you had their pictures plastered all over the news, apparently, with a ten-million-ruble reward, and they weren't sure what to do. Before we arrived, they had already reached out to every international reporter they could find, and at least one of them agreed to meet. When we saw what the documents were, as archaeologists and historians, we agreed that they were important and should be public, as was mandated by your government decades ago. They are historical, over a century old, so there is nothing national security related. It's simply diaries and correspondence between various people, long dead in a country that no longer exists. Why this is of such concern to the Russian authorities is beyond me."

Acton watched as Nikitin processed the story, all of which was true, except that he was fully aware why the current regime was desperate to recover the papers. But one thing had caught his attention as he testified, a slight flaring of the eyes at the mention of the contents of the documents.

Acton smiled slightly. "You have no idea what you're looking for, do you?"

Nikitin said nothing.

"You're just a patsy in this. You've been given orders to recover stolen documents, yet you have no idea what they contain. Would you like me to tell you what this is all about?"

Nikitin shifted in his chair, his mouth opening to respond, but Acton interrupted him, certain the man had received instructions to avoid viewing the contents.

"It's proof that Stalin murdered Lenin."

A quick inhalation was the only indication of surprise, Nikitin remaining otherwise remarkably composed. He leaned forward. "Professor, the contents of the papers are of no concern to me. All that is of concern is that they were stolen from the archive. They are the property of the Russian people, and I have been tasked with recovering them and those involved in stealing them. You and your wife are involved now, and you are foreign nationals."

Acton flicked a wrist. "That's right. We *are* foreign nationals, so keeping us for too long can prove problematic."

Nikitin chuckled. "Professor, I can keep you for as long as I want."

Acton smiled. "Perhaps you misunderstood. I'm not referring to you legally being able to hold us, I'm referring to the fact that you are on a clock."

Nikitin's eyes narrowed slightly. "What do you mean?"

"I mean, if my wife and I aren't on friendly soil before tomorrow morning, instructions have been given to friends of ours stateside to release all the information we have on the incident with the Japanese Imperial Regalia. Algorithms have been set up to ensure the information goes viral on social media. The narrative your government has been putting out there about that incident will be corrected permanently. Considering that happened in the past several years, I would think your government would be more concerned about preventing that from becoming public, than a murder a century old."

"Professor Acton, I fear you've misjudged the leverage you have. I am in direct communication with the President's Office, and met the president not even an hour ago. The rewriting of the narrative that you refer to has nothing to do with my country not wanting the world to know what happened with respect to the Japanese. It has everything to do with the fact that Russian soldiers were killed by Americans on Georgian soil. If the truth were known, my fellow citizens would demand a response that could involve an invasion of Georgia and perhaps retaliation against an American unit operating somewhere they shouldn't be. My government's discretion was in an effort to maintain the peace and save lives. If you want to go public with that and possibly trigger a war, then the blood that results is on your hands."

A wave of nausea swept through Acton at Nikitin's words. Was he being fed well-rehearsed bullshit, or was this the truth? Could the secret they hoped would protect them actually cost countless lives if revealed? Was the Russian government indeed keeping the truth of what happened secret so that its population wasn't riled up, demanding retribution? Georgia used to be part of the Soviet Union, it had a significant Russian-speaking population, and Russia had already invaded before. Could the Russian president be showing restraint?

Nikitin smiled broadly. "I see this never occurred to you. Like a typical American, you assume the worst of my country and her motives." He rose. "I'll give you a few minutes to reconsider your position, and then when I return, you're going to tell me exactly where those documents are." Nikitin left the room and Acton folded his arms, staring at the wall blankly, the conversation with Reading echoing in his head.

"There's one thing I think you're failing to consider."

"And what's that?"

"Whether the secret that Orlov has discovered is more important than the one you're relying upon to protect your lives."

Nikitin closed the door then glanced at the guard. "I'm leaving him in there to stew for a few minutes. I'll be back shortly."

"Yes, sir."

Nikitin went to the next room and stood in front of the two-way mirror, staring at Acton. The man was clearly uncomfortable, shifting in his chair, his fingers drumming on his arms. Acton clearly thought their knowledge of what had happened during the Japanese incident would protect them, and perhaps they were right. The explanation for what his government had done after the fact hadn't been made up on the fly, but it had been made up.

As soon as he had approved their visas, he had struggled to understand why they would take the risk. He had eventually concluded they must be relying upon the incident in Georgia and his government's denials of anything having happened. It didn't take him long to come up with a counter-story should it be necessary, and with the better part of a day to let it percolate, his delivery of the lie had apparently been convincing. Perhaps the thought in the back of his mind that it was indeed a legitimate reason for suppressing the truth could be why he was so convincing, for part of him believed the lie. He was counting on this being the only thing the professors were relying upon to protect themselves. If it were, any leverage beyond the documents they thought they might have was gone.

He shook his head. Until this point, he had no idea what the documents concerned. He had assumed they had something to do with Stalin, because of where they had been stored. But if Acton was telling the truth, that they proved that Stalin murdered Lenin, it was explosive. Yes, it could rewrite history as the professor had said, but more importantly, it would destroy the legacy of a man that had become a hero to his country. A man who had taken a fractured nation, still squabbling even under Lenin's leadership, and brought in the iron-fisted rule necessary to unite the country and create one of the strongest nations the world had ever known. A man who had inspired a nation to fight back and ultimately defeat Nazi Germany. A man who laid the foundations of a country that reached space first, that put the first man in orbit. A country that embarrassed the Americans at every turn until the ridiculously weak Gorbachev took over and decided peace and the abandonment of the ideals of Lenin and Stalin were the better way to go.

Nikitin didn't know life under communism when the Soviet Union had collapsed. He was barely out of diapers. But the stories told by his parents and grandparents made it out to be horrible, though he wondered if their memories were tainted by the final decade under Gorbachev's rule, then the decade of chaos that followed after the collapse. He didn't believe in communism. It had failed everywhere, the only state still clinging to it, North Korea, hardly a showcase for success. Cuba and Vietnam were already bringing in capitalist reforms, and China was becoming fully capitalist.

He admired their form of government, where the best and brightest were chosen to lead with a firm, unopposed leader at the helm. Civil discord was banned, with no tolerance shown for those who would oppose the state. Yet, if you were willing to work hard and had the brains, you could own a car, the latest cellphones and televisions, and live with all the trappings that those in the West claimed only a liberal democracy could allow.

A firm hand at the till, unopposed, unencumbered, leading a capitalist society, was the ideal. His country, still recovering from the mistakes of the eighties and nineties, was once again feared and respected. And his entire adult life, the president had been the one constant figure guiding them resolutely into a glorious future.

But if what Acton had said were true, and the stolen documents proved Stalin murdered Lenin, a man who was an even greater hero to many Russians, the strongman image could be shattered, and it could tarnish the president's image and hamper his efforts in creating the ultimate hybrid state—a permanent rival to America and its allies, with a strong economy that would no longer fear bankruptcy at the hands of its enemies.

He now understood the urgency. They had to recover those documents and suppress the truth from coming out. The problem was he had no idea where they were. The stories delivered by all of his suspects so far matched all the evidence they had, were all believable, and suggested far too many were innocent. The only evidence he had was camera footage. There was no doubt Volkov had been in the secret archive illegally. That had been established. Experts with the proper security clearance had confirmed that documents had been stolen from the room, though until this moment, he had no idea what those documents contained. Volkov had involved his ex-girlfriend, Katarina, and they were assuming she had seen the documents. They had enlisted the help of the hotel night manager, who he had to assume had also seen the documents. Orlov had apparently set up the professors, and they had obviously seen the documents, as Acton had just testified as to their contents.

All their stories were backed up by video evidence where possible. The big question was, did the other two they had just arrested know each other? One had a sealed record with a flag on his file indicating he was a hero of the motherland who should be left alone unless under the most extraordinary of circumstances, and the other was a young man with no criminal history, born just outside of Moscow, now working in Belarus as a social media expert. There was nothing connecting them. They had come in on two different flights, and all indications were that they had been caught up in the same security cordon he had ordered.

Yet they ended up in the same car together after a highly suspicious incident that was either an exchange or theft of the documents in question. And then those documents turned out to be photocopies of ones publicly available—nothing worth stealing. And if they were indeed copies of publicly available documents, then there was no theft whatsoever, which had already been confirmed as bullshit.

It had to have been a handoff, staged to look like an altercation. But if that were the case, why was it so clumsily done? They had to know they were on camera, and for two complete strangers to share a rental car, they had to know it would raise too many red flags, yet here they were with no real evidence against them. They had walked in on two men sharing a pizza, no weapons, no evidence of anything untoward, text messages that matched up with the story, the works. If they were telling the truth, then the documents they had stolen were decoys.

His jaw dropped.

It made sense. The documents had to be somewhere. Either Zorkin and his partner had indeed taken a handoff then passed them on before his team could get there, or they had never taken them, and had instead stolen decoys in an innocent altercation. And if that were the case, then either the reporter had taken them with her on the airplane, or the professors still had them after they left the airport, and passed them over to whoever had helped them hide.

And what he was supposed to do now, he wasn't sure, beyond sticking to his original plan.

None of these people had the documents, that much was clear. A hand-off had happened. Who it had been handed off to no longer mattered. So much time had passed, they were either already out of the country, or soon would be. There was only one way left to salvage his career.

He inhaled deeply and closed his eyes as he held the breath long enough for it to burn. He exhaled then stared back at the professor. The plan had already been approved by the president himself, but once he pulled the trigger on it, there was no going back. If it failed, there was only one person to blame.

And he could kiss all of his dreams goodbye.

Gorki Estate

South of Moscow, USSR

January 21, 1924

Bazarov sat in his friend's office. He had lost count of how times they had been together over the years, either here, at the Kremlin, or in surroundings far less ostentatious. He preferred the old days, like in Paris, sharing a room in exile, plotting the future in humble surroundings, rather than the trappings of kings.

Yet waste was to be frowned upon as well, and while this estate had once belonged to a wealthy family, it had been confiscated by the state, and now served a useful purpose rather than a vulgar one.

And his friend was once again talking of the upcoming Congress.

"It's been a long time, my friend. Too long. Comrade Stalin has tightened his grip on power while I recovered, and I fear it might already be too late, but if I still hold any sway in the country I helped found, in the party I helped create, then perhaps all hope is not lost."

Bazarov regarded the frail man, a shadow of his former self, the wheelchair that was now his home a fitting symbol of his confinement within these walls. He was entirely dependent on others, and appeared pitiable rather than powerful. If his words were to carry weight, it would only be if his past vigor were imagined, rather than his current witnessed. "You're still determined to go through with this?"

"I am. I know I won't make it to next year's Congress. My days are numbered, and this is my last opportunity to right the ship. I must deliver what will be my last testament before it's too late for our great nation."

"Stalin is too powerful to stop now, I'm afraid."

Lenin nodded. "You're probably right, my friend, but I must at least try. If it weren't for that damned stroke last year, I would have delivered my testament to the Congress and perhaps succeeded in implementing the changes I wanted to propose by now. Unfortunately, you are likely correct in that it is too late, however it is my duty to try."

Bazarov regarded his friend. "If it's too late, then why waste your time? You know you will be challenged, perhaps even killed. Why put yourself and your family through such a thing if it will result in nothing?" He leaned forward. "Why not rest? Enjoy your surroundings, spend your final days with your loved ones, and leave the country to those who have wrested it from you. They can never do as good a job as you, however perhaps they won't do so badly."

Lenin eyed him. "You say 'they' yet you know it is 'he' that we are referring to. Once he has control, there will only be one voice that is listened to. That was never the intent. That is not socialism. That is not communism. Committee, not dictatorship, that is what should be."

There was a knock at the door and the butler entered with a tea service. He positioned the cart nearby and Bazarov waved him off. "I'll deal with it, thank you. Our conversation cannot be interrupted."

"As you wish, sir."

The butler retreated, closing the door behind him as Bazarov rose. "Don't you worry about what might happen should your words create the very doubt you hope?" He lifted the tea pot, pouring a cup for his friend then himself.

"What do you mean?"

"I mean, if you sow enough division, could we not be looking at another civil war?" He added the milk and sugar his friend enjoyed.

"Yes, I have thought of that, of course. It is possible, in fact, it's quite possible, especially if enough are swayed. I no longer believe Comrade Stalin will go down without a fight, and he has many allies."

Bazarov paused, his back to his friend. "So, you would risk civil war, and the possible end to our grand experiment?"

"If Comrade Stalin is to lead that grand experiment into the future, then it has already failed. I would rather see it fail completely so someone else could try anew."

Bazarov reached into his pocket and retrieved the tiny vial he had purchased a year ago. "But that day may never come. We could lose all we built."

"Then we lose it. If we let someone like Stalin take the reins, then we deserve to lose it."

Bazarov's chest tightened with rage at his friend's words. This had become personal. Lenin was no longer thinking of the state, but of his hatred of the man who would lead it after he was gone. The Soviet Union must prevail, and Lenin would not be the man guiding it for much longer.

And his words sealed his fate.

He wouldn't be guiding it *any* longer.

Bazarov poured the vial's contents into Lenin's tea, then gave it a stir before returning the empty ampoule to his pocket. He turned with a smile, his friend's tea in his hand, and placed it in front of the man. "You are right, of course." He retrieved his own cup then returned to his seat, raising his tea in salute. "To the workers."

Lenin smiled. "To the workers." He took a sip, as did Bazarov, and the conversation continued. "My wife has transcribed and prepared my testament over the past year. She is as aware of it as anyone." He leaned forward, but not before taking another sip. "Should something happen to me, I have instructed her to keep its existence a secret until the Congress convenes, then she is to present it."

Bazarov's eyes widened slightly. "Is that wise? Perhaps someone else could. I would hate to see her suffer should there be resistance."

Lenin took another sip. "There is no one else I trust to do it."

Bazarov smiled. "Not even me?"

Lenin laughed. "My friend, if I felt you had any sway over these people, I wouldn't hesitate to ask you, however, unfortunately, you are little more than my friend in the grand scheme of things. Important to me, but few others." Another sip.

Bazarov tipped up his cup, draining it, then rose. "Another? It's particularly good today."

Lenin did the same. "Please."

Two more cups were prepared then Bazarov sat. "My friend, I must confess something to you."

Lenin adjusted his collar, shifting in his wheelchair. "What is it, Comrade?"

"You will never deliver that speech."

Lenin closed his eyes, sucking in a deep breath as he gripped the arms of his chair. "Wh-what makes you say that?"

"Because you won't be alive to attend the Congress."

Lenin's eyes shot wide. "What have you done?"

Bazarov removed the tiny vial and held it up. "Purchased a year ago, my friend, at great expense. Your stroke saved your life then, but now the original plan had to be carried out, as you still have not come to your senses."

Lenin collapsed on his desk, his chest heaving. "Why?"

"Comrade Stalin is the future, not you. Perhaps if you were healthy and strong, we could risk not having a man like him at the helm, but, alas, you are not. Your days were numbered regardless of this little poison, yet they were great enough in number to risk our nation's future. What we created is now bigger than both of us, and will outlive both of us with a man like Comrade Stalin leading. Your testament can never be heard. We cannot risk the chaos it might bring."

Lenin's head now lay on the desk, and he whispered something Bazarov couldn't hear. He rose from his chair and leaned closer.

"What is it, my friend?"

"You may have killed me, but my words will still be heard."

334

Over Russian Airspace

Present Day

Acton sat in their leased Gulfstream G5 business jet. Laura was beside him, and Volkov and Katarina sat in the row ahead of them while Alina sat on the opposite side of the aisle.

The speaker overhead crackled. "We've just cleared Russian airspace, Professors."

Everyone breathed an audible sigh. He was stunned they had let them go. The decision had been abrupt. Nikitin had left the room after mutual bombshells were revealed, then returned only minutes later telling him their visas had been revoked, and they were being put back on their plane. It meant safety for him and Laura, but not the other three. He had demanded to know what would happen with them, when the next bombshell dropped.

"They're going with you."

Acton had eyed the man. "We're returning to London, are we not?"

"Frankly, Professor, I don't care where you go, as long as you're out of my country."

"But they'll need British visas."

Nikitin laughed. "They don't need British visas to leave our airspace, they only need them when they land. Besides, after you tell the authorities what these poor, innocent people have been through, I'm sure the visas will be granted. Hell, have them declare refugee status. We just want to be rid of them."

Acton shook his head. "You do realize these are good people. Alina did nothing but try to help her friends, Katarina is completely innocent and only got involved because an ex-boyfriend showed up on her doorstep, and Dmitri was manipulated by his former professor, a man he idolized. You would destroy their lives over a hundred-year-old secret?"

Nikitin regarded him. "Are you really that naïve? Alina is anything but innocent. She's a known agitator and has been arrested on countless occasions in which apparently far too much leniency has been shown. Katarina could have refused entry to her ex-boyfriend, but instead she helped him transmit the documents then wipe all their electronic devices. And before you say he could have done it, you might not be aware that she's an IT expert and he isn't. There are no innocents here, Professor. Be thankful we're just ejecting you from the country and not putting you in prison to rot for a few years."

"And what of the news people that helped us?"

"The driver has had his visa and press credentials revoked as well, and the reporter is already on the ground with a message delivered that will keep her silent."

"And that's what you expect from us? To remain silent about what we know?"

"And just what do you know, Professor? A century-old secret that may or may not be true."

"Someone has those documents. If they were authenticated, then your secret is out with proof."

Nikitin smiled at him, as if at a child. "You academics are so naïve. You don't understand the human condition, you only understand books. Comrade Stalin had enemies, many enemies. That archive contains every record that even mentions the man. Nothing's been authenticated. For all you know, they're forgeries dating back one hundred years. You can do all the scientific tests you want on the paper and the ink, and everything will date back to that time. You should know your history, Professor. Around the time comrade Lenin was dying, there was a major power struggle over who would be his successor, including not just the members in the troika, but everyone in the politburo who had ever held ambitions to power.

"Don't you think it's a possibility that they took advantage of the situation and created a series of correspondence to make their opponent appear a murderer, then perhaps changed their minds? Or perhaps did attempt the deception but it wasn't believed, or failed because comrade Stalin was simply too strong? There's a reason why Russians admire the man, Russians like me. He was strong. Stronger than any of his opponents, and far more intelligent. He would have seen trickery like this from a mile away, as you Americans might say, and probably let it play through so that he could entrap all of those involved, even in the slightest of ways. What you have is an interesting piece of history that may or may not be true, that could easily be challenged. You have something that might create a little bit of buzz among those you socialize with, but it will be dismissed by the Russian public as yet another attempt by the West to discredit our glorious past. This is why we're letting you go. We don't care about you."

"Then why the ten-million-ruble reward? Why such a huge effort to capture everyone?"

"Because young Mr. Volkov stole, Professor. He stole from a locked room that only people with permission from the President's Office were supposed to have access to. In our country, that order makes anything beyond the door a state secret. Not all state secrets are important, but they are still secrets. We take the theft of state secrets seriously. And, as you well know, Professor Orlov is a fugitive. We had hoped that Mr. Volkov would lead us to him. Unfortunately, that hope was proved wrong, and instead, Professor Orlov revealed that he would betray even his own friends in order to get what he wanted. I'll give you one last chance. Do you know where Professor Orlov is?"

Acton shook his head. "Like I said before, I didn't even know he had escaped until yesterday."

"Then none of you serve us any purpose."

Acton regarded the man for a moment. "If all of this means nothing, then why exile Volkov and the others?"

"Their lives, as they know it, are over. The agitator, Alina, is now on every known list. If she gets arrested once more, she won't get a slap on the wrist, she'll be going to prison for a very long time, and I don't believe for a second she's capable of being a good citizen. As for the other two, with their faces plastered all over television for twenty-four hours, any future they hope to have is finished. They'll have much brighter prospects outside of their home country."

"So, they'll never be allowed to return?"

"I never said that. They can return, but only to uncertain futures."

"Unless there's a regime change."

Volkov smirked at him. "That's the first time you've revealed your agenda, Professor Acton."

Acton cocked an eyebrow. "Excuse me?"

"That's what this has all been about, isn't it? This is all a failed attempt to embarrass our president." Nikitin stepped closer. "Are you an agent of the CIA?"

Acton laughed. "Not bloody likely. I have no doubt you've seen my file. I'm a professor of archaeology, nothing more."

"Yet you seem to have friends who are well connected. Perhaps you're acting as an asset on their behalf."

Acton could sense the conversation had taken a turn and their free ride out of here could get canceled if he weren't careful. "Like I said, I'm a university professor and nothing more. And besides, if the documents are as worthless as you say, then even if I were CIA, it was a failed operation."

"Agreed, Professor Acton. You and the others will be escorted to the airport and put directly on your plane. Your pilot has already been notified, your flight plan has been filed for your return to London, and your visas have been canceled. I trust we'll never see each other again."

Nikitin left the room and moments later he was true to his word. The five of them were loaded in the back of what could be best described as a paddy wagon, taken directly onto the tarmac at the airport, and loaded onto their airplane with all but a boot to the ass. The pilot had been cleared for priority take-off, and since they had been in the air, little beyond explaining the conversation he had had with Nikitin had been said.

Alina was the first to break the silence. "Is it safe to talk now?"

Acton smiled slightly. "I think it's always been safe to talk."

Alina rolled her eyes. "You're so naïve. You don't think they planted bugs on this plane?"

Laura squeezed Acton's hand. "The bugs would still be working, my dear, even if we're not in Russian airspace."

Another eye roll. "Ugh! You professors have no concept of the real world. Before we left Russian airspace, they could have ordered us to turn around if they overheard something they didn't like. Now they can overhear it, but they can't turn us around. So now that you've been given an education into the real Russia, are we talking, or are we waiting until we land?"

Acton accepted her paranoia without judgment. "We're talking. We have nothing to hide, but to be on the safe side, let's talk about the future."

Alina shot to her feet then began pacing the aisle. "Yes, let's talk about our future. Who the hell decided that we had to leave Russia? Why didn't we get a say in it?" She spun toward Acton and stabbed a finger at him. "Was this your idea?"

Acton ignored the ungrateful little brat's accusation. "I expressed my concern for your safety, but they had already made the decision to put you on the plane."

"To never come back?"

"I asked him that, and he said, no, that wasn't the understanding. However, he did indicate that due to your history specifically, if you ever were arrested again, you'd be going to prison for a very long time, and he wasn't convinced that you could sit back and be a compliant citizen."

She growled. "Oh, he has that right, but I don't care. I have to fight for my country's future. I want to go back."

Acton shrugged. "I suppose that's your right, and if you want, we'll give you money for the ticket, though you might have trouble getting a copy of your passport and whatever other papers might be necessary, and you might find yourself arrested the moment you step off the plane. I highly recommend you take a few days to think about things." She opened her mouth to protest, but Acton cut her off. "A few days will make no difference in your cause, and it might just save your future." He turned his attention to the other two. "As for you two, he said you're free to return, however, because of all the publicity surrounding this, any careers you hope to have are likely destroyed, and he felt you'd probably have brighter futures outside of your country."

Katarina's chin slumped toward her chest as her shoulders sagged. "Just when I was starting to get some traction in my career, it's already over."

"How would you feel about living in the West?" asked Laura.

Katarina shrugged. "I never really thought about it much. Life's not that bad in Russia if you just keep your head down and ignore the obvious problems."

Alina spat. "That's the problem with sheep. As long as they don't go hungry, they'll follow the shepherd to wherever he herds them, even if it's to the slaughterhouse. People like you make me sick."

Volkov leaped to his feet, squaring off with Alina. "You have no right to talk to her like that!"

Alina glared at him. "You're just as bad."

"Go to hell! I tried to do the right thing and look where it got me. Banished from my own damn country, my family, my friends, my career. I've lost everything because I tried to do the right thing. She's lost everything because she tried to help me. Don't you dare call us sheep. We might have failed, but we still tried. And we got a lot closer than you ever did in any of your petty little protests."

Alina was about to deliver either a retort or a fist when Laura rose. "The two of you sit down now and stop acting like children. This is a serious situation and adult decisions have to be made. They don't necessarily have to be made right here and right now, but the thought process that will lead to sound, wise decisions has to begin here. And I think James is right. Everybody needs to take a few days to think about what they want to do. If you decide you want to go back to Russia, then fine, we'll work with you to make that happen. But if you decide to stay in the West and you're allowed to—because remember, we don't know what the British government will say when you land in London—we'll help you settle in. My husband and I have significant resources to help you. None of you should have been caught up in this but you were. That's the past. There's no point dwelling on it. We need to look to the future and see how we can make the best of a bad situation. Now, both of you sit down and let's discuss this calmly."

Alina growled but dropped back into her seat. Volkov returned to his own beside Katarina, and she took his hand as the flight attendant entered.

"Can I get anybody anything?"

"Vodka," echoed the three Russians, and Acton couldn't help but laugh.

"I think I'll just have a Diet Coke."

"Sparkling water for me," said Laura. "Oh, and ask the captain how long it'll be before we land in London."

The woman's eyes narrowed. "London? We're not going to London, ma'am. We're going to Frankfurt."

Over the Mediterranean

Command Sergeant Major Burt "Big Dog" Dawson sat in his seat in the C-5 Galaxy, loaded with priority evacuees from Afghanistan. It had been a last-minute Hail Mary Charlie-Foxtrot to get these people out as the entire damn country they had fought twenty years to free, fell in less than two weeks. There was plenty of blame to go around, but none of that mattered right now. Their mission was complete and had been a success, every name on their list now out. Unfortunately, that list had dwindled as the mission had been prepped.

Too many had died in the Taliban onslaught.

Under his command, Bravo Team, a group of America's most elite soldiers, part of 1st Special Forces Operational Detachment—Delta, had split into three groups and headed into enemy-controlled territory. Their mission, triggered by the outcry from veterans of that war which embarrassed administrations the world over, was to extract assets abandoned by America and its allies.

They had extracted their people with no problems, the Taliban spread thin, half a dozen people all it took to capture a town too terrified they would be skinned alive if they resisted. Too much of the country, including the capital city, had simply capitulated. He had fought here too many times to count during his career, and his heart ached at the price paid in human blood over two decades, all the gains lost in less than two weeks.

It was already taking an emotional toll on him and the others. He couldn't imagine how the hundreds of thousands that had served here must be feeling right now as they watched the news, especially those who had sacrificed their bodies, who had sacrificed their minds. Or how the families who had lost their loved ones felt with the knowledge their son or daughter, their father or mother, their brother or sister, had died for a lie.

They had been told by a grateful nation that their loved ones had died fighting to bring freedom and justice to the Afghan people. And where was that freedom, where was that justice, when in two short weeks it could all fall apart? Why was this country so ill-prepared? Why were their people willing to surrender to the Taliban so easily?

His comms squawked in his ear. "Bravo Zero-One, Control, come in over."

He activated his mic. "Control, Zero-One, go ahead, over."

"Zero-One, we're sending you an encrypted packet now. We're going to need your men for a covert op in Germany, over."

His eyebrow shot up as he pulled out his laptop and logged in. "Control, did you say Germany?"

"Affirmative, Zero-One. All the details are in the packet."

He looked at his exhausted men. They had been going at it non-stop for over 72 hours, only catnaps caught between hops. "Control, we're pretty burnt. Is there another unit available?"

"Possibly, Zero-One, but Bravo Team has been specifically requested for this. It involves some old friends of yours. Academic friends."

Dawson groaned, his head tilting back. "Let me guess, two professors?"

"Exactly. Looks like they're in some trouble with the Russians. They've been let go and are heading for Frankfurt now."

"Well, if they've been let go and are heading to Frankfurt, why do you need us?"

"Langley suspects they're being used as bait to recover some documents that could prove embarrassing to the Russian government, and to either eliminate or perform an extraordinary rendition on a fugitive. The bigger fear is that they could be setting everyone up to eliminate anyone exposed to the documents."

Dawson sighed. No matter how tired he was, no matter how tired his men were, the professors were friends, friends they owed. Friends they owed big. And the fact these same professors would drop everything, no matter how exhausted they were, to help him or one of his men, made the decision easy. "Copy that, Control. Has the pilot been informed?"

"Negative, Zero-One. You'll continue to Ramstein. There'll be a helo waiting to take you to your target."

"Copy that, Control. I'll read the brief then get back to you."

"Copy that, Zero-One. Control, out."

There was no privacy on a C-5 configured the way it was, so any of his men that had been asleep were now awake, woken by a comrade who had overheard his conversation. Everyone was either turned in their seats to face him, or standing close by.

"What's up, BD?" asked Sergeant Carl "Niner" Sung, the smart-ass of the group and the best sniper Dawson had ever worked with.

Dawson brought up the briefing notes. "Apparently, our professor friends have pissed off the Russians somehow. Langley thinks they're being set up for a possible clean-up operation."

The amply muscled Sergeant Leon "Atlas" James grunted, his impossibly deep voice drowning out the vibrations of the plane. "Those two do have a penchant for trouble."

Niner gave him a look. "Penchant? Did Vanessa get you a word of the day calendar or something?"

Atlas eyed him. "I read. You should try it sometimes. It's amazing how it expands the vocabulary."

Niner shook his head as he rolled his eyes. "You do know those letters aren't real, don't you?"

Master Sergeant Mike "Red" Belme snorted. "Do those magazines even exist anymore? It's all free on the Internet."

Sergeant Will "Spock" Lightman cocked an eyebrow. "But I thought everybody read them for the articles."

Dawson let the verbal sparring continue as he scanned the briefing notes. "Okay, if you ladies are done, here's the scoop. For those of you who were involved in the incident between the Russians and Japanese, you might remember the name Professor Arseny Orlov. While our

Georgian operation successfully rescued Acton and his friends with the imperial regalia, what you probably didn't know is that Professor Orlov was imprisoned. He escaped with the assistance of others who were involved, and has been living in exile in Germany since then under a new identity. He was supposed to never contact anyone from his past, but he broke that condition and reached out to Professor Acton, claiming documents that could rewrite history had been discovered, and he needed them to come and retrieve them in Moscow."

Sergeant Gerry "Jimmy Olsen" Hudson whistled. "'Rewrite history' are like trigger words for those two."

Dawson had to agree. "They went to Moscow to meet Orlov, but it turns out it was a set-up. He wasn't there. They found three young Russians who actually had the documents and yada yada yada, the Russians let them all go after capturing them, and they're now on a plane about to land in Frankfurt. Add to that, our friend Jack and the same asset that effected Orlov's escape were also captured and also set free."

"Did the Rooskies recover the documents?" asked Spock.

"Negative. The other asset managed to pass on the documents before they were arrested. Right now, even Langley doesn't know where they are, but they believe the Russians let everyone go in the hopes that someone would lead them to the documents and possibly Orlov."

"And just what are these documents?" asked Red.

"Apparently, they prove that Stalin murdered Lenin."

Niner's eyes narrowed. "Huh, wasn't that like a million years ago?"

"Not quite, but close enough."

"Then why the hell are they so determined to get their hands on them? I get why the professors want them, but why the Russians?"

"The analyst report suggests that their release had the potential to embarrass the Russian president, since he's been manipulating history so the Russian population has a favorable opinion of Stalin. That way he can use him as an example to pave his way to a permanent presidency, unencumbered by inconvenient elections."

"Yeah, you have to hate those pesky voters, always wanting you to be answerable to them," said Spock. "To call that country a democracy is a joke."

Dawson agreed. "You won't get any argument from me. Bottom line is, they're concerned this is some sort of set-up, and we've been specifically requested to provide protection. I know you're all tired after everything we've just been through—"

Niner interrupted. "Count me in. The Doc's wife is still my first love. If anything ever happened to her, I couldn't live with myself. And I'd probably feel pretty bad if something happened to the Doc, too."

Atlas eyed him. "I wonder how Angela would feel about that."

"Hey, I said *first* love. I didn't say current."

Jimmy leaned forward to get a better angle on Niner. "So, what you're saying is you love Angela?"

Niner froze. "Did I say that?"

"You definitely implied it," said Atlas.

Niner shrugged. "It's none of your business how I feel."

Atlas clutched at his heart, anguish on his face. "But I thought with all the times you tried to sport-hump me, I was your only love."

349

The men roared as Niner leaped from his seat and into Atlas' lap, wrapping his arms around the impossibly muscled man. "Say the word, big guy, and I'm yours."

Atlas hurled the tiny man across the cabin with an effortless shove. Spock and Jimmy caught their comrade and helped him back to his feet as Atlas jabbed a meaty finger at his best friend. "Didn't we just have a conversation regarding boundaries?"

Niner rose then dropped back to his seat. "I thought that was just foreplay."

"You're a troubled man."

"I am, but that's why you love me."

Spock cocked an eyebrow. "So, let me get this straight, you love the professor, you love Angela, and you love Atlas?"

"I have a whole lotta love in my heart that needs to be shared."

"Huh, a little man like you can love four people?"

Niner cocked an eyebrow at Spock. "Four?"

Spock jerked a thumb toward the massive Atlas. "I count him twice. Have you seen the size of that guy?"

Atlas extended a fist and Spock bumped it. "Thank you, brother."

"I wasn't talking about your junk."

"Oh, I guess I should have known, otherwise you would have counted me as three people."

Even Dawson joined in on the laughter before putting an end to things by raising his hand. "So, is everybody up for this?"

A round of "Yes, Sergeant Major!" was their response.

"Good, everybody get some rack time. We're going to be landing at Ramstein shortly, and who the hell knows when we're going to get our next chance at some shut-eye."

Frankfurt am Main Airport

Frankfurt, Germany

Acton and the others cleared customs in Frankfurt, Germany, not the expected London, England. The reason given by the flight crew was that they received last-minute instructions from the lease-share company with the new destination and no explanation. They hadn't bothered challenging the change in plans. There had to be a rationale for it, and the old man that approached them with a broad smile and a striking woman on his arm would hopefully provide them an explanation shortly.

The man extended a hand. "Professor Acton, I'm Alex West. I'm an acquaintance of Viktor Zorkin."

The woman pshawed that statement. "When are you going to acknowledge the fact that you two are friends?"

West granted. "Fine, I am a *friend* of Viktor Zorkin's, whom I believe you know."

Acton nodded. "Yes, we've met. You know Dylan?"

"Yes, I've had the pleasure of meeting him. A good man."

"Yes, he is. Not a very good archaeology student, but a good man."

West chuckled as he shook Laura's hand. Introductions were made and they were led to the parking lot where West waved a wand over them. "Just checking for tracking devices."

"Find any?" asked Acton.

West finished Alina. "Nope, you're all clean." He indicated a large SUV. "Let's get to our destination, shall we?" They climbed into the vehicle, the three Russians occupying the back row, Acton and Laura in the middle, with their two hosts in the front seats.

Acton leaned forward as they got underway. "Why were we diverted to Frankfurt?"

West glanced at him in the rearview mirror. "Because we believe Professor Orlov is still in the area, and we hope to draw him out. If you went to London and notified him that you had the papers, it would have taken too much time for him to get there, and we believe time is of the essence."

"Why is that?" asked Laura.

"Because this is likely a set-up,"

Acton tensed. "A set-up?"

"Yes, Professor. The Russians let you go too easily. They're hoping you'll lead them to Orlov and the documents."

"Then why play into their hands? Why not just have us contact Orlov and tell him we don't have the documents. He stays in hiding and we get on with our lives."

West shook his head. "Because that's not the way things work with Russia. You pissed them off, and those documents apparently have the

353

potential to embarrass the Russian president and worse, interfere with his agenda. If he decides to do a clean-up operation, you're all dead. It's best to nip this in the bud now."

Laura gripped Acton's hand. "And just how do you propose to do that?"

"We're going with your original plan. You're going to validate the documents, then we're going to make them public."

"But we don't have the documents. We passed them on to Jack."

Adelle leaned forward then raised a bag she had stowed in the footwell. "They arrived shortly before you did."

Acton and Laura exchanged relieved sighs. "Thank God! That means Jack's okay?" asked Acton.

"Oh, he was arrested along with Zorkin, but their covers are solid so they were released around the same time as you. Their involvement is finished, as they can't risk breaking their covers for now."

"Where are we going?" asked Acton.

"My place," replied West.

"Your place? Shouldn't we be going to a police station or something? If the Russians are coming after us, we're going to need some sort of protection."

"It's been arranged. I want you to send a message to Professor Orlov telling him that you have the papers and want to meet."

Acton pulled out his phone then hesitated. "Wait a minute. Isn't he under your protection?"

West grunted, clearly displeased. "He was until he went rogue."

"So, you don't know where he is?"

"No idea. We went to his house and every indication is that he's been gone for at least a week, if not two."

"But we didn't get a message from him until last night."

Volkov leaned forward. "And I didn't even find the papers until two nights ago."

Adelle retrieved her own phone and brought up some photos before handing it back to them. Acton flipped through the shots of a home, including a picture of rotting bread, lending credence to the claim Orlov had disappeared days before he should have. He handed the phone to Laura who swiped her thumb several times then paused, holding the phone up.

"Do you see anything wrong with this picture?"

He squinted at a photo of what appeared to be Orlov's living room. "Too many earth tones, not enough pops of color?"

She gave him a look. "If he's been gone as long as that rotting loaf of bread would indicate, those plants should be at a minimum showing signs of stress."

It was his turn to give her a look. "Plants can get stressed?"

"If you don't water a plant, things start to droop."

He suppressed the urge to make a joke about plant Viagra, and instead took the phone and zoomed in on several of the plants, all of which appeared healthy to him.

"Let me see that." Adelle reached back and took the phone. "I can't believe we missed that!" She held the phone up for West to see, but he shook his head.

"I'm driving here." He glanced in the rearview mirror. "Are you sure? Maybe it's a type of plant that can go for weeks without water."

Laura shook her head. "No, not these. If they go a week without water, everything will be drooping. These were all watered within a few days of you taking those photos, and besides, I'm British. We know our gardening."

West cursed. "That means he's coming back to the house!"

"That would be rather foolish, wouldn't it?" Adelle stared at the photos of the lovingly maintained plants. "Why would he risk being seen or caught? It makes no sense."

Acton had to agree. It didn't make any sense. He didn't know Orlov well, though he did know people who loved their plants as if they were people, talking to them, singing lovingly, maintaining them with care. Could Orlov have hatched his plan and disappeared only to return to take care of his beloved plants? It was possible, though if he feared his life was at stake, it was indeed foolish.

A thought occurred to him. After he and Laura had decided they were buying a larger home, his mind had occasionally drifted to what should be included. "How well do you know this house?"

Adelle twisted in her seat to make eye contact. "What do you mean?"

"I mean, the layout. How many rooms there are, how big they are, the basement, everything."

Adelle shrugged. "I don't know it at all. Alex?"

Alex splayed his fingers on the steering wheel. "Not very well. I've been to visit him, just to check in on him every couple of months, but it's usually just his living room. I've probably only been in his kitchen, main floor bath, and living area. That's about it. Why? What are you getting at?"

"What if he built himself a panic room? I know I would if the Russian government were after me." Acton glanced at Laura. "By the way, we're putting a panic room in the new place."

"Absolutely."

West turned to Adelle. "Contact the Network. We need the plans for that house."

Adelle went to work, leaving Acton to wonder what the hell the Network was, and whether West was no longer taking them to their planned destination where they had hopefully prepared for the Russians, but to Orlov's, where they might be sitting ducks.

Orlov Residence

Outside Schiltach, Germany

They were sitting ducks.

They were in a humble home, nestled in the woods outside of a small town. The nearest neighbor was only 100 yards away, but the thick trees of the Black Forest made it seem 100 miles. They wouldn't see anyone approaching, and nobody would be coming to help them should they fall under attack. They had to make quick work of this. Either find Orlov's hiding place, or disprove the theory that there was a panic room. They had split up and made a quick preliminary search of the house, pounding on walls and shouting his name, however there had been no response. The text message to the man had gone unanswered, which had Acton concerned.

Everyone regrouped in the living area. "Did anybody see anything unusual?" asked West.

Head shakes all around.

358

Laura stepped over and stuck a finger into the soil of a nearby plant. "This is wet. It's been watered today. He has to be here."

"But where? Everything I'm seeing matches the plans," said West. "Did anyone notice anything odd?"

Again, head shakes.

"I don't understand why he's ignoring my message," said Acton. "We've got what he wants. Why not reveal himself?"

"Could my government have already caught him?" asked Volkov.

West frowned. "Anything's possible, but I think we would have heard something."

Acton turned to Volkov. "You had some way to communicate with him. Why don't you try it? Maybe he'll listen to you, because he's obviously not listening to me."

Volkov retrieved the tablet from his bag and his eyes widened. "There's a message from the professor! It looks like it was sent just after you sent your message."

"What's it say?" asked Katarina.

"It says, 'tell Professor Acton to use this method of communication. It's more secure.'"

West rolled his eyes. "The fool. The contents of your messages between each other are barely of consequence. It's your location that is."

Acton's stomach churned. "They could track our phones."

"Of course they can track your phones. We're counting on that."

"What?"

"We want them to come to us so we can bring this to a head once and for all, but we wanted them coming to a prepared position, and this is anything but that." West jabbed a finger at the tablet. "You tell him to come out now, or he's never going to see those documents and he's going to be on my shit list permanently."

Volkov's thumbs tapped at the tablet's display. "I've sent it, though I'm not sure how to translate 'shit list' into Russian."

"He'll get the picture."

Acton looked around. "I don't understand why he can't see us. Normally, you have security cameras that you can watch from your panic room."

West shook his head. "Cameras inside your own home suggests the possibility that there *is* a panic room. He's obviously hidden it extremely well, and he doesn't want anyone to think there's even the possibility of its existence."

The tablet beeped.

"Is that him?" asked Acton.

Volkov nodded.

"What's it say?"

"'Back yard.'"

They all headed to the kitchen and West threw open the back door, giving them a view of the yard. A string of English, French, and Russian curses erupted as a chunk of the lawn rose and Orlov emerged.

Acton's eyebrow shot up. "Well, I can honestly say I never thought to look underground."

Orlov stepped onto his lawn, his eyes wide, a smile on his face. "Do you have the documents?" he asked eagerly.

Acton pursed his lips, slowly shaking his head at the man. "That's your first question? You don't even ask if everyone's okay? You do realize you put people's lives in danger."

Orlov stared at him blankly, then finally spoke. "What would you have me say? I'm sorry? Then fine, if that'll make you feel better, I'm sorry, but those documents are more important than anybody's life.

"Bollocks!" muttered Laura. "If I had known what kind of a self-centered piece of garbage you were, I never would have agreed to help."

"Me neither," agreed Acton.

Katarina growled and charged forward, punching the man in the nose. "You've ruined our lives! You've ruined all of our lives!" She hurled another haymaker, connecting once again, and everyone stood by as she continued to unload on the man who hunched over, protecting his head with his arms. Katarina finally stopped, exhausted, her chest heaving as her arms hung limp at her sides, her cheeks stained with tears. She turned and walked back toward Volkov when Alina stepped forward and hoofed Orlov in the balls. The man doubled over in agony and dropped onto the grass.

"That's for destroying my life too." She turned to Volkov. "Care to have a go?"

West held up a hand. "All right, that's enough. Everybody back to the car. We need to get to a secure location as quickly as possible. If they've been monitoring us visually, they know we've made contact with him and they're going to assume we also have the documents. This place isn't safe."

Acton agreed and stepped over to Orlov, extending a hand. "Let's go. You can explain yourself in the car."

Orlov took the hand and Acton hauled him to his feet. They rounded the side of the house, and as they approached the SUV, Adelle cursed and drew a weapon, firing two shots in the air. Acton and Laura grabbed the three young Russians, hurrying them toward the vehicle as a drone dropped from the sky beside them.

West stepped over and slammed the heel of his shoe into it, shattering what remained of the device. "Well, I think they know we're here."

Acton cursed. "What do we do? Make our stand here or try to get to your place?"

West pressed the button on the fob, the lights flashing. "We're dead here. This vehicle is at least bullet-resistant, and where we're going is only fifteen minutes away and is a prepared position."

Acton pulled open the rear door and everyone piled inside, Orlov joining him and Laura in the middle row. West fired up the engine and hammered on the gas, sending them surging toward the local road.

"Check right."

Adelle leaned forward. "Clear right."

West hurdled them onto the road, the vehicle rocking violently though never out of control. Acton gripped an overhead handhold as he twisted in his seat, peering out the back window for any pursuers. "How long before we get to your place, fifteen minutes?"

"Now, it's ten minutes, assuming we don't get stuck behind some old geezer."

Adelle flashed a smile at her partner. "Hon, you are the old geezer."

West laughed. "But I'm young at heart." He checked the sideview mirror and cursed. "We might have company."

Nikitin sat in the passenger seat, his plan so far working. And this was his plan. The president himself had ordered him to run with it, which meant one of two things. If the plan succeeded, he would be rewarded handsomely, and if it failed, his career was over. And depending on how spectacularly it failed, his life could be over as well. Fortune favored the bold, and he was fully committed. No matter what happened here today, he was either returning home a victor, or not returning at all.

He was on his own charter minutes after his suspects had taken off. The moment the revised flight plan had been filed, changing the professors' destination to Germany instead of London, he had known his plan was working and that he had been lied to. They knew exactly where Orlov was. New instructions had been transmitted to the private security team the President's Office had engaged for this situation, and a team had met him when he landed in Frankfurt.

They were mercenaries, of that there was little doubt, probably Wagner, a private firm that employed thousands of former Russian personnel. They were used as proxies by Moscow for small ops like this, and larger operations such as Ukraine, Syria, and Libya. They were professional, they were brutal, and he felt completely safe with them.

This operation would succeed. The drone deployed to follow his suspects from the airport had revealed they had met with two senior citizens and eventually Orlov. They would be easy prey for these men, filling two vehicles, armed to the teeth. All they needed was an opportunity to corner the suspects and not create a public spectacle by engaging them on the roadway.

"Back off. They're going to spot us," he said to the driver and man in charge, whose name he hadn't been given.

"I have done this before, sir."

"If you have, then why are you so close?"

"Because we were using the drone to track them, and that woman shot it out of the sky like it was nothing. Now we have to track them visually."

"Aren't we tracking their devices?"

"Yes, sir, but if I were them, the moment I knew I wasn't in visual contact, I'd be tossing them into another vehicle to send us off track."

"Deploying drone now," came a voice in Nikitin's earpiece. He glanced at the sideview mirror to see that the second vehicle had stopped at the side of the road. Moments later, the replacement drone sped past them as it gained speed and altitude. "I've got them."

"Backing off," replied the team lead as he eased off the gas, returning them to a regular speed. "Now, we let the tech do the work and see where they decide to hole up. We'll hit them fast and hard. I assume our orders still stand?"

Nikitin nodded. "Yes. As soon as we've confirmed they have the documents, everyone is to be terminated. Your men have acquired the other targets?"

"Yes, we have teams in position. Nobody involved will be alive by morning."

Nikitin smiled. "Perfect."

"They've backed off," announced West.

"Maybe it was nothing," suggested Laura. "You know how Germans drive."

West disagreed. "This isn't the Autobahn. They've probably deployed another drone. It's now following us."

Acton leaned closer to his window and peered up but saw nothing. "What are we going to do?"

West continued to exceed the speed limit. "We get to our house, we get inside, we activate the defensive systems."

"Defensive systems?" asked Alina. "Just who are you people?"

"I'm Alex."

"And I'm Adelle."

Alina frowned. "And *that's* not helpful."

West chuckled. "Let's just say we know what we're doing and we're well-prepared."

"So, what *is* your plan?" asked Acton. "Just for us to get to your place and wait for them to run out of ammo?"

"No. If we do that, we'll lose. The whole idea was to force them to play their hand, and they're playing it. Once we get you to the house and activate the system, all we need to do is hold out long enough for your friends to arrive."

Acton's eyebrows shot up. "My friends?"

Ramstein Air Base
Ramstein, Germany

Dawson was the last boot off the ground as per usual. One of the flight crew shouted the all-clear and the Black Hawk helicopter lifted from the ground. Dawson poked his head into the cockpit. "ETA?"

"Fifteen minutes."

"Copy that." Dawson took a seat among his men. "Fifteen minutes, ladies."

"Once more unto the breach." Spock checked his M4. "Any idea on numbers, BD?"

Dawson shook his head. "Zero to a dozen, I would imagine. We could be going in there to babysit, or we could be going into a hot zone. I'm guessing if the Russians are going to hit them, they're not going to hit them with their own personnel. They're going to use private security. Probably Wagner."

Red frowned. "That means seasoned personnel."

"Yes, we're not going up against Walmart security here. This is the real deal. Treat them just like you would any Spetsnaz unit."

"ROEs?"

"Once they fire the first shot at us or our people, shoot to kill."

Spock's eyebrow shot up. "The Germans are okay with that?"

"According to Control, everything has been approved. Apparently, the Germans are happy to have us deal with the problem."

Niner grunted. "Yeah, just in case it turns into a Charlie-Foxtrot, then they've got someone to blame other than themselves."

Dawson agreed. "Then let's make sure this doesn't turn into a Charlie-Foxtrot. As we planned, we'll insert in two teams. Red, your team will sweep the perimeter of the property and take down any targets of opportunity. My team will secure the main structure. If we're lucky, we'll get there before the Russians. If not, hopefully our people will be able to hold out long enough for us to eliminate the hostiles on the exterior."

Atlas checked his weapon. "And if they haven't been able to?"

"Then it could get ugly, but I've got a lot of faith in the docs."

"So do I, BD, but they're going up against former Spetsnaz. I love them, but I doubt they can hold out for very long against those odds."

"They don't have to. The structure has to."

Sergeant Eugene "Jagger" Thomas pursed his massive lips. "Let's hope the old man didn't just reinforce the doors and windows. If these Wagner guys are worth half their salt, they're going in through the walls, not the doors."

Dawson's comms squawked in his ear. "Zero-One, Control. Our targets have reached the property. Anticipate hostiles will engage within three minutes, over."

Dawson cursed and leaned toward the cockpit. "ETA?"

"Ten minutes."

He cursed. "Not fast enough. Show us what this bird can do. This battle begins in three minutes." He could hear more power going to the engines, but the pilot's reply was what he expected.

"There's no way in hell we're getting there in three minutes, buddy. The best I can give you is eight."

"Five minutes too late." Niner spat. "Five damn minutes. Is this thing armed? We could just hit the whole area around the house, shave at least a minute off."

"Negative," shouted the pilot at the front. "No weapons. The Germans would never go for it."

Dawson scratched his chin, an idea occurring to him. "What about defensive weapons?"

The pilot gave a thumbs-up. "Loaded to bear."

Niner eyed him. "What are you thinking, BD?"

"I'm thinking we go all Hollywood on their asses."

West/Bertrand Residence

Black Forest, Germany

West positioned their vehicle parallel to the front of the house then turned on the high beams, illuminating the forest on one side. "Everyone inside, now!" he ordered. Adelle was already out, heading to the front entrance, key in hand. Acton corralled everyone toward the door as West drew his weapon, scanning their surroundings. Acton peered up for a drone, but instead found a thick canopy of trees overhead that just might neutralize their opponent's advantage. West was the last inside and he closed the door behind him.

"Everybody step back from the walls!" he ordered as he entered a code on a security panel. It beeped twice then heavy metal plating rolled down over the windows and front door, creating an armored barrier between them and those outside.

Acton was impressed.

"What about the walls?" asked Laura.

"Reinforced. This home was designed from the ground up to keep people out."

"What kind of firepower can it hold back?" asked Acton.

"Small arms fire is nothing, even a fifty cal isn't getting through this. Hit us with a few RPGs in the same spot and they'll get through eventually, but I always figured if they sent that much firepower after me, no amount of protection was going to save my ass. I just assumed it'd be the lone gunman or a small team that I'd have to protect myself against."

"And what do you think we're facing tonight?"

"I'm guessing heavily armed private security that are limited only by what their orders are from Moscow."

Acton frowned. "So, we're screwed."

West nodded. "Basically, unless your friends get here in time."

"And when are we going to know that?"

West shrugged. "No idea, but why don't we go watch the show?" He led them into a small room filled with state-of-the-art equipment, at least a dozen camera feeds displayed on as many monitors.

Adelle pointed. "Camera three."

"Well, they're being pretty bold," observed West. He flipped a switch cover out of the way and pressed the button underneath. An explosion momentarily blinded the cameras, and when the lens recovered, the smoking wreckage of an SUV was revealed. "That should buy us a minute."

Acton shook his head. "Without knowing whether they're five minutes or five hours away, it's hard to get excited by that."

"Have faith, young man, and pray that they're *very* good friends of yours so they go the extra mile to get here as quickly as possible."

Acton said nothing and smiled at Laura as she took his hand and squeezed it. They both knew who the friends were, and they both knew Bravo Team would do whatever they could to get here in time.

Unfortunately, the laws of space and time often got in the way.

Outside West/Bertrand Residence

Black Forest, Germany

Nikitin cursed as the SUV flipped onto its side, the fireball from the explosion that had hurled it, quickly collapsing in on itself. Fortunately, the team lead had anticipated this, so nobody was inside, instead, the customized vehicle had been controlled remotely.

"Well, I think they know we're here," said the team lead.

Nikitin rose, having involuntarily taken cover from the distant blast. "Isn't that the same road they went up?"

"Yes."

"Then why didn't they blow up?"

"Either the mine was deactivated or it was manually triggered."

"Well, if they have this entire place rigged with explosives, how do you plan on getting in there?"

"By neutralizing their advantage." The team lead turned to the others. "All electronics in the cage."

Two more SUVs and another half-dozen men had joined them moments ago. All around him, gear was stripped and tossed inside one of the new arrivals, a customized vehicle unlike anything he had ever seen. "Just what the hell is going on?"

"No time to explain, but I suggest you put any electronics you have inside the cage."

"Cage?"

The team lead pointed at the odd vehicle. "The cage." He turned to one of the new arrivals. "Is the EMP ready?"

"Yes, sir."

"Make sure all the doors are closed."

The doors on the new arrivals were all shut. He had no clue what was going on. The two newly arrived SUVs were different. Customized. He noticed for the first time that the one all the equipment had been loaded into had windows that were now all covered with some sort of mesh, and the other one had a retractable roof now open, a strange tube-like device visible. "Did you say EMP?"

"Fire!"

A pulse reverberated through the entire area, his body tingling with static electricity. It lasted only a few moments, then it was over, with no evidence anything had actually happened.

"Gear up!"

The doors in "the cage" were opened and the men retrieved their equipment as the strange device retracted back inside the second vehicle.

"Will somebody please tell me what the hell is going on?" demanded Nikitin.

"It's an electromagnetic pulse powerful enough to knock out any electronics in the immediate area. Any cameras, remote detonators, anything that he's got is now dead, unless it was shielded against an EMP pulse, and something tells me they're not."

"But what about our equipment?"

The team lead strapped on his gear then tapped the customized SUV. "Faraday cage. Everything inside it was protected, and all of our vehicles have been customized to protect against the effects."

Nikitin cursed and reached into his pocket, pulling out his cellphone. It was dead. "You could have told me."

"I did. We're in a combat situation. You may be in command of the overall operation, but on the ground, you obey my orders without question or delay."

Nikitin didn't bother challenging the man. "Fine. What now?"

"Now we finish this without having to worry about any surprises. I suggest you stay back here, sir, and let my men take care of this. We should have this cleaned up for you in five minutes." The team lead turned to his men. "RPGs."

West cursed as Acton squinted into the darkness they now found themselves in. A lighter flicked and a candle was lit. "What the hell just happened?"

West's frown was revealed by the candle he held. "I'm not sure."

"Did they cut the power?" asked Laura.

"They did, but not in the traditional sense. The diesel generator should have kicked in and I'm not hearing it. And I've got a shitload of batteries that should have taken over the moment the power failed. This is something different."

Acton pulled out his phone to activate the flashlight feature. "My phone's dead."

Laura retrieved her own. "Mine too."

Adelle cursed. "EMP."

West glanced up at her from his perch behind the keyboard. "Is that even possible?"

"Yes, but it means they are extremely well-funded."

Acton stared at them. "EMP as in electromagnetic pulse?"

"Yes."

Alina tapped at her own dead phone. "I thought EMPs were caused by nuclear weapons. Are you saying a nuclear bomb just went off?"

West chuckled. "No, my dear, they're not trying to silence you with nuclear weapons. An EMP can be artificially generated. I just didn't think they had made it small enough to transport or cheap enough for mercenaries to have on-hand for a last-minute op."

Adelle squeezed West's shoulders. "Unlike my partner, I still like to keep up with what's possible. And yes, what just happened could absolutely have been caused by an EMP brought by our friends outside, though they're not cheap, which means they're extremely well-funded."

Laura took Acton's hand. "Well, it *is* the Russian president after us, after all, so their funding is likely unlimited."

Acton waved at the security setup, dimly visible with the candlelight. "I'm surprised that with all this, you didn't protect against an EMP."

J. ROBERT KENNEDY

West shrugged. "When this was built, the only risk from an EMP was if there was a nuclear blast overhead. I figured, if we got to that point, who would want to live, so why protect against something that just means you get to see the aftermath of nuclear war."

Acton had to agree with the man. He had often wondered what he would do if there were some disaster that could wipe out most of mankind, like an asteroid impact. Part of him wanted to simply stand outside and take the hit, ending it all. Another part wanted to fight every step of the way to survive the calamity and help rebuild. In the heat of the moment, he had no idea what he would actually do, and he hoped his character would never be tested. He understood West's position. This was a man who had likely fought against all odds for most of his life. This was supposed to be his retirement, his twilight years. Why would anyone want to live out their final days in a nuclear horror?

Another candle was lit and then another, Adelle having opened a drawer, retrieving a stack of them. West rose. "Well, there's no point in being in here."

"What are we going to do now?" asked Acton.

"There's nothing we can do. They're going to hit this place hard, unopposed." West opened up a weapons locker. "If they get inside, we fight. But if we're lucky and they didn't come equipped to get into a place like this, then maybe your friends get here in time to save us."

Laura gripped Acton's hand. "If they came with an EMP, something tells me they came with everything they're going to need to get in. Even if they don't have rockets, they might have cutting equipment. It's only a matter of time before they're coming inside." She stepped over to the

376

weapons locker and grabbed a Glock and several magazines, then an MP3 that she slung over her shoulder.

Adelle eyed her. "Do you know how to use those things, my dear?"

Laura shook her head. "Not a clue, but if we're going to die, my corpse is going to look badass."

Acton chuckled as he walked over to the weapons locker, retrieving his own set of weapons. "Don't let her kid you. We've been trained on pretty much every weapon imaginable."

West glanced at the three Russians. "I don't suppose you know how to fire a gun."

Head shakes all around.

"Then it's time for a crash course, because once they breach these walls, we're all fighting for our lives." West retrieved another Glock from the cabinet and held it up. "Now, this is a gun. It's used to shoot people. Everyone with me so far?"

The entire house was rocked from a massive explosion, cutting off any response.

"What the hell was that?" exclaimed Acton.

West quickly handed out weapons. "That was likely an RPG, which means they're going to be inside here any moment now."

Another explosion rocked the house and Acton readied his weapons as did Laura and their two hosts, the Russians awkwardly holding their handguns, terror on their faces. Acton shared the terror, but not the shock. He had been in situations like this before. Gunfire and explosions were no stranger to him or Laura. The key was to remain as calm as possible, as focused as possible, so as not to be overwhelmed by the adrenalin fueling your system.

Gunfire erupted from outside, several rounds breaching the walls, causing the Russians to drop to the floor and the rest to take a knee.

"This is it people," said West. "Shoot anything that comes through that door, and don't be a hero. Every wall in this place half-height or full is reinforced, so take cover where you can. Standing tall and proud while firing your machine gun only works for Stallone and Schwarzenegger."

"Don't forget the Rock," added Acton.

West eyeballed him. "This is no time for music."

Acton's laugh was cut off by a third explosion, light suddenly visible through the door to the living area. "Let's get the hell out of this room. It's a kill box."

Acton headed out, breaking left with Laura as West broke right with Adelle. He took cover behind a knee wall and aimed his MP5 at the gaping hole that once was the front door, the metal shield protecting them now a twisted wreck. But it was a narrow opening, and still a kill zone.

Something flew through the opening and rattled on the floor. "Flashbang!" shouted West.

Acton squeezed his eyes shut and pressed his fingers against his ears as he prayed for their friends to arrive, but his prayers were interrupted by the thunderous explosion that overwhelmed him in the confined space.

Hurry up, guys.

Dawson sprinted through the forest, having used the gunfire and explosions as cover to insert closer than initially planned. An EMP had gone off minutes ago, but most of their equipment and thankfully the chopper were shielded, so they were none the worse for wear, though Niner was pissed that his brand-new cellphone was fried. He had heard three explosions since they began their approach, and steady automatic weapons fire now sliced through the normally peaceful Black Forest. His briefing indicated the target building was fortified, but multiple RPGs to the same stress point would make quick work of most defenses, and the fact there was now automatic gunfire meant the breach had been successful, and the hostiles were directly engaging those inside.

"Zero-One, Zero-Two, we're in position. Commencing perimeter sweep, over."

Dawson acknowledged Red's signal as he continued toward the target structure, then triggered the next part of the plan. "Hawkeye Actual, Bravo Zero-One. Time to go Hollywood, over."

"Roger that, Bravo Zero-One, going Hollywood."

And moments later, the sky overhead turned into an alien invasion movie as flares and chaff erupted from the Black Hawk, its fully equipped defensive systems putting on a brilliant light show as it passed overhead.

Niner grinned. "We're doing the Mick Jagger."

Jagger eyed him. "Huh?"

"The Mick Jagger."

Atlas shook his head. "Nobody has a clue what the hell you're talking about, little man."

"That's it! The next time you and Vanessa come over for a movie night, you are not allowed to make out. 'Hobbs and Shaw' is a cinematic masterpiece that should have won an Oscar, but you two were snogging so much, you missed it all."

Spock's eyebrow cocked. "Snogging? I think you've been watching too much Harry Potter, son."

Niner glanced over his shoulder as they charged forward. "The fact you got the reference tells me you're watching it just as much as I am."

Atlas swatted Spock with the back of his massive hand, knocking him off balance as they sprinted through the mostly straight rows of trees, far too much of the forest replanted after World War II. "He got you there."

Dawson spotted something ahead and raised a fist as he came to a halt and took a knee. He pointed at Niner and Atlas then ahead. "Siskel and Ebert, we've got two men standing watch. Take them out. Silently."

They both nodded and rushed forward as their two targets stared up at the display overhead. By the time the Russians noticed, it was too late, and they were removed from the scene by suppressed weapons and bullets rattling in their skulls.

Dawson rose, indicating for the rest to follow, and as they charged forward, Niner grinned. "Two thumbs up?"

Dawson chuckled. "Two thumbs up."

The distinctive sound of an MP5 opening up, quite different than the SHAK-12s and AK-12s they had heard so far, confirmed his worst fears—those they were there to save were under direct fire. "Let's go!"

Nikitin took cover behind the SUV he had arrived in as he stared up at the sky and the assault from overhead. It took him a few moments to realize it wasn't weapons fire, but flares and chaff from a helicopter, and while it posed no danger, it could mean only one thing—troops had just been inserted into the area.

He gripped his weapon tight in his hand, debating what he should do. His bravado from earlier had him valiantly dying here if he didn't succeed, but now, in the heat of the moment, with explosions and gunfire pounding in the distance, the night sky lit up, it felt as if he were in a war zone, something he had never experienced before.

And he was quite certain he didn't like it.

He wasn't prepared to die. He had no intention of doing so today. Not over century-old documents that even if genuine could be discredited with ease. It had to be German police, but would they use what appeared to be a military chopper? And how would they have known to come? Even if their targets had made an emergency call, there was no way the Germans could have organized a response this quickly. A squad car or two, perhaps, but not a chopper with an assault team. It made no sense.

Though it did if he thought about it. Just who were Acton and Palmer? They were rich. They had been involved in the Japanese incident, but that involvement went far beyond Orlov handing over the imperial regalia to them. They had managed to get themselves through a security cordon and into Georgia. They had managed to get American Special Forces with air support to help them.

And again, it had all happened quickly.

They were people who could get visas in mere hours, who could fly anywhere in the world they wanted on their private jet, and appeared to have all the resources of the American government at their beck and call. Could there be more here than initially thought? The assumption had been that Volkov had stolen the papers for his professor, that Acton and his wife had come to retrieve those papers so they could be authenticated and made public. All fairly innocent.

Until now.

Why had their plane been diverted from London to Frankfurt? Why were they here where the entire area was booby-trapped and prepared for an assault? Who actually lived here? It had to be the old couple who met everyone at the airport, but who were they?

His jaw dropped. Zorkin had a flag on his file indicating he was a hero of the Soviet Union and was to be given wide leeway unless he did something truly outrageous. It had to mean he was former KGB. A spy. "Could these people be retired spies?" he muttered, then cursed as he finally put it all together.

The Gray Network.

He had heard of them, but their existence had always been denied. It was mostly former Western intelligence, with some KGB and FSB, whose members supported the concept of freedom. He had never encountered them, therefore had never paid them any mind, though it was a running gag among some in his business toying with the truly paranoid by pointing to someone with silver hair. "Careful what you say. They might be part of the Gray Network."

If this were indeed his first encounter with them, then it changed the equation. It meant they had connections that could get them resources. It meant there was a very good chance this Wagner team could be defeated. It meant he could be arrested at any moment, which would absolutely end his career, and depending on how badly the Kremlin wanted to cover up the involvement of the President's Office, they might claim he went rogue and have him imprisoned to satisfy the German government.

He had to get out of here.

Something moved in the trees ahead and his heart leaped into his throat as he readied his weapon. He had no way of knowing if it was a Wagner team member or someone sent to stop them. No code words had been given, no signals arranged, but no one had thought this was even possible. This was supposed to be a swift, uncomplicated mission.

He redirected his weapon at the ground. He didn't want to make himself a target. He wasn't here to fight, he was here to observe. He dropped the gun then rose slightly, peering inside the vehicle he was using for cover. He spotted the fob in the ignition and made a decision. He pulled open the door and climbed inside, slamming it shut, pressing down on the lock and breathing a sigh of relief at being inside the bullet-proof vehicle.

He started the engine and put it in gear, wondering what the Wagner personnel would think when they came back to discover they no longer had enough vehicles to escape with. He pressed on the gas. It wasn't his problem. He had to think of himself. He checked his rearview mirror and the gunfire and explosions lighting the forest behind him reaffirmed his choice. He redirected his attention to the road ahead, then cursed as he slammed on the brakes at the sight of two men in his path, aiming assault rifles directly at his windshield. He remembered he was in a bullet-proof vehicle and pressed on the accelerator. One of the men fired two rounds into the passenger side of the windshield, the rounds slamming into the empty seat beside him, reminding him why the term bullet-resistant was now more commonly used. He slammed on the brakes again and raised his hands.

"Turn off your engine!" shouted one of the men in English, and as he complied, fear gripped him with the realization that he wasn't dealing with German police at all, but with the American military.

West hid behind the kitchen peninsula, the opposite side reinforced underneath the wood paneling. It gave him a good angle on the door, an intentional part of the design. A body lay draped in the hole their attackers had blasted open, taken out by one of the professors who were proving they indeed knew how to use their weapons and, so far, had maintained a level head.

A smoke canister clanged on the floor, spinning as it spewed its contents into the air. "Watch your lines of fire!" he shouted as he squinted into the fog, ignoring the acknowledgments from the professors and Adelle beside him. He thought he saw something move and squeezed off two rounds. Someone grunted but continued forward, obviously equipped with body armor. An MP5 opened up to his left, one of the professors engaging. Two short bursts were followed by a thump as the target hit the ground.

He spotted more movement and again opened fire, emptying his mag in a left-to-right motion before ejecting it and reloading. He peered through the fog and reacquired the door as the smoke bomb spent the last of its chemicals. A shadow crossed the opening and both West and Adelle opened fire, but not before a hand whipped something inside.

"Grenade!" shouted Acton.

West cursed as he ducked, pulling Adelle down beside him, the sound of the metal casing bouncing over the floor then changing tone as he gasped in horror. The grenade had gone into the room with the Russians.

There was no way they would survive in the confined space.

"No!" shouted Laura.

West rose slightly to see Acton through the haze, diving toward the door with the Russians, his wife screaming after him. Shots erupted from his right, at least one hostile having made it inside in the confusion. Laura cried out and he heard her drop just as the grenade detonated.

Adelle gasped as Acton was tossed like a rag doll. West rose and opened fire, ignoring his own advice, now standing in the open, shooting at anything that moved and anything that didn't. Everyone was dead. Only he and Adelle were left, and as she rose shoulder to shoulder with him, spraying lead across the entire room from her MP5 on full auto, he fell in love with her all over again. They were exactly alike, and if this was to be their final stand, their final moments together on God's green Earth, then they were going out in a blaze of glory with no regrets. He switched to his own MP5, choosing quantity of shots rather than quality, when outside the gunfire changed. He grabbed Adelle by the back of her shirt, hauling her down with him and out of the line of fire.

Acton's friends had arrived.

Dawson signaled for his team to spread out on either flank as he rushed forward, his M4 hammering against his shoulder as he opened fire on the hostiles in his arc. Muzzles flashed to his left and right as the others engaged, the unsuspecting enemy dropping like flies with no place to hide, the area in front of the home cleared of any cover, making it a kill box as they were hemmed in by the house on one side, his men on another, with Red's engaging on the flanks. He continued to advance, keeping a mental tally of how many shots he had fired, and as the last one erupted from his weapon, he ejected the empty mag.

"Reloading!" he shouted so that Niner and Atlas on either side of him could temporarily cover his arc. He slapped a new mag in place, then resumed firing, but as they closed in on the house, he slowed up and raised a fist. "Cease fire!"

The battle outside was over, the enemy, unprepared for his team's assault, down. He continued forward, toward the hole blasted in the side of the house. "Is anyone alive in there?"

"Let me check," came a voice from inside.

Dawson chuckled. "I'll take that as a yes. Are you guys secure? Are there any hostiles inside?"

"None that are moving, but exercise caution on entry. A smoke grenade went off in here, so anything's possible."

"Copy that. Are the professors all right?"

There was a pause before the heartbreaking answer was delivered. "No, they're dead. Everybody's dead. I couldn't save them."

Dawson's chest ached as a lump formed in his throat with the knowledge two good friends were dead, and that he had failed to reach them in time. He activated his comms. "Zero-Two, Zero-One. Secure the structure perimeter. Making entry now, over."

"Roger that, Zero-One." Red's voice was subdued, and Dawson rushed forward in silence, his weapon directed at the blasted open door directly ahead. "Friendlies at the door!" he shouted, and someone inside acknowledged. He peered in to find it pitch dark and filled with smoke. He flipped down his night-vision goggles and squinted into the green haze. Several bodies dressed like those outside littered the entrance. To his left stood a man and a woman armed with Glocks and MP5s, though with their hands up. "Alex West and Adelle Bertrand, I presume."

"Yes, sir."

"Where are the professors?"

West pointed to Dawson's right. "Behind that wall."

Dawson stepped over cautiously, the half-height wall providing perfect cover should a hostile have made it deeper into the home. He peered over and his heart sank at the sight of the crumpled bodies of his two friends whose luck had finally run out.

"She's alive!"

Laura groaned as someone rolled her onto her back. She winced in pain and gasped for breath as someone tore her shirt off, someone else prying her eyes open and shining a flashlight in them.

"Speak to me, darling. Tell me you're okay."

She recognized the voice and smiled through the pain. "Niner, is that you?"

"Yeah, darling. It's all over. The bad guys are dead. You took a round to the shoulder, and it looks like you cracked your head on this little wall here. Now, you just lie still and let me take care of this. Medevac is on the way."

She slumped back onto the floor as she processed what was happening around her. "Manual releases are underneath each frame," she heard West say. The sounds of the metal barriers being lifted and windows thrown open were followed by the air rapidly clearing.

Dawson and Atlas came into sight. "How's she doing?" asked Dawson.

Niner maintained a smile for her benefit. "She's a tough broad. She's going to be fine. We just need to get her to a hospital."

"Chopper's already inbound."

Her mind replayed what had happened and she gasped. "James!" She bolted upright and Niner shoved her back down. "My God, darlin', stay still." He jabbed something into her arm and injected a plunger before wrapping a compression bandage around her shoulder. "Okay. Now, try not to move that too much."

"Just take me to my husband." She winced as Atlas and Niner helped her to her feet, and what was revealed on the other side of the chair she had been tossed over when shot, sapped her of all will to live. James was on the floor, his shirt torn open, his entire body littered with shrapnel, Jimmy performing chest compressions as Jagger hooked up a portable defibrillator.

"Is…is he…"

Jimmy glanced over his shoulder at her. "He ain't dead until I say he's dead!"

"Holy shit, BD, you gotta see this," called Spock from West's security room.

"Oh my God!" she cried. "The others! Are they all right?"

Dawson stepped inside the room and Laura tore herself away from the struggle to save her husband. She squeezed past the shattered door frame, the source for most of the shards embedded in her James. The grenade must have slammed the door shut when it detonated, absorbing much of the blast. But in the corner was a tangled mass of bodies, Orlov's bulky frame on top, his arms spread out enveloping the others like a human shield, his back and legs torn apart.

There was no way he had survived.

Spock grabbed the man by the collar and hauled him off the other bodies as Dawson shone a light on the scene, revealing the three young Russians, terrified but alive.

"He saved us!" cried Volkov as he struggled to his feet. "He saved us!"

A high-pitched whine then a thumping sound had Laura rushing back to her husband's side. Jagger shook his head and Jimmy resumed chest compressions. The machine beeped that it was ready again. "Clear!"

Jimmy backed off and Jagger zapped James again. She could see the line on the monitor and it remained flat. Her shoulders shook as she closed her eyes, tilting her head back and cursing God for letting her live.

"I've got a heartbeat!"

She opened her eyes and dropped to her knees as the beeping indicator steadied and Jagger checked James' pulse. "I've got a pulse. It's weak, but it's steady. We have to get him to a hospital STAT. I don't know how long he's going to last. He's pretty torn up."

Dawson walked out of the security room. "Copy that, Control. Bringing them to the LZ now. Let the Germans know we have one prisoner, a Russian named Nikitin. Looks like he's government."

Laura stared up at him. "Did you say Nikitin?"

"Yes, ma'am."

"I think he's the one in charge."

Dawson nodded as he climbed through the door, updating Control with the new information.

Niner helped her to her feet. "Let's get you outside."

West stepped over and pointed to the rear room where the grenade had detonated. "Inside the cabinet on the left are some collapsible stretchers."

Atlas disappeared and came back a few moments later with the stretchers. He laid one down beside James and handed the other to Niner who helped her through the door. He opened up the stretcher. "Let's get you on this thing."

"I can walk."

Niner shook his head. "No, you can't. You're running on adrenaline right now. As soon as that wears off, you're going to collapse, and I'd rather you pass out on a stretcher than while walking through these woods. Don't worry about the Doc. He's in good hands."

He helped her down to her knees then rolled her onto the stretcher. And the moment she was horizontal, a wave of weakness swept through her and she struggled to remain conscious.

A struggle she lost.

University Medical Center

Freiburg, Germany

Acton woke in a fog of confusion. He could hear beeps and whispers, and what he could only describe as a white noise that clouded it all. And then there was the pain. He struggled to recall what had happened, and at first drew a blank before remembering the attack and the grenade. Then it all flooded back.

His eyes shot wide and he bolted upright. "Laura!"

"I'm right here."

His head spun toward her voice and he breathed a sigh of relief at the sight of her. Then frowned at her bandaged shoulder. "Are you all right?"

She smiled as she stepped over to his bed and gently pushed him back on the sheets. "Don't you think I should be the one asking you that?"

He stared down at himself but couldn't see much beyond the dozens of abrasions on his arms, the rest of his body covered with a sheet. "What happened?"

"You died. Just like I said you would one day." Reading stepped through the door. "Let me be the first to say, I told you so."

Acton tilted his head slightly to the side. "I'll give you that one."

Reading patted Acton's foot. "I'm happy you're all right, despite your best efforts."

"Me too. But how about somebody tell me what's going on?" He reached out and took Laura's hand. "Let's start with your shoulder."

"I caught a round just before the grenade detonated. Niner patched me up and then we were medevacked to a hospital."

"So, they did arrive."

"Just in time."

His eyes shot wide. "The grenade! What happened to the kids?"

"They're fine. Orlov saved their lives by acting as a human shield."

"Is he…"

She nodded. "He's dead. Niner said he wouldn't have felt a thing. It happened fast."

"Well, thank God for that."

Reading frowned at him. "Aren't you going to ask about yourself? What this little stunt of yours did to you?"

Acton shrugged, waving his hands over his body. "I'm alive, aren't I? Isn't that all that matters?" He paused and wiggled his toes, breathing a sigh of relief. "Is there some piece of bad news you guys are hiding from me?"

Reading rolled his eyes. "You died."

"Did I?"

"Your heart stopped and they had to zap you twice to get it going again."

"Huh, I don't remember walking toward any bright light. I guess it wasn't my time."

Reading growled. "You're not going to learn a thing from this, are you?"

Acton laughed. "Trust me, I've learned not to run *toward* the grenade. So, what's the prognosis? What happened?"

"According to BD, it looks like the door to the room was caught in the blast wave, so it was blown shut, blocking most of the force. It was a wooden door so it splintered, and you've got fifty-some-odd minor wounds all over your body. The shock of the blast stopped your heart." Laura rubbed her head. "I was out cold, so, I'm not sure exactly what happened, but according to Alex and Adelle, Bravo Team arrived not even a minute later and immediately went to work on you."

"How long was I—"

"Dead?" finished Reading.

"For lack of a better term, yeah. How long was I dead?"

"A couple of minutes." Reading shook his head. "I'd wonder if you got some brain damage from the lack of oxygen, but I don't know if I'd be able to tell since you ran toward the grenade and not away from it."

Acton eyed him. "Are you trying to say that displays of bravery are actually acts of stupidity?"

Reading shrugged. "You said it."

Acton stared down at his body. "So, I take it I'm going to be fine?"

Laura squeezed his hand. "You're going to be sore for a while, but you'll be all right. You'll have some sexy new scars though."

Acton grinned, his eyebrows bobbing. "Yow, I didn't think I could get any sexier."

Laura leaned closer. "Neither did I."

Reading cleared his throat. "I'm still here. And if you mount him, he just might not survive in his condition."

Acton's grin broadened. "Totally worth it."

Laura slapped his hand. "Hugh's right. There'll be plenty of time for that."

Acton became serious. "Are Alex and Adelle all right?"

"Yes, they weren't hurt, though I think Alex is pissed that his house has been destroyed, especially because it was done by Russians."

"So, they were Russians?"

Reading nodded. "Mercenaries. Part of the Wagner group. They're all dead, but there was one government official with them. He was captured by the Delta team but released by the Germans because he has diplomatic immunity."

There was a knock at the door and everyone turned to see Nikitin standing in the doorway. "Yes, Professor Acton, diplomatic immunity. I'll be leaving for Moscow shortly, but I must insist you return what was stolen."

Acton held up his hands. "Sorry, I have no idea where the documents are."

"They're somewhere safe," said West as he entered the room with Adelle. "Somewhere your government will never find them."

Nikitin frowned. "That's most unfortunate. I fear this means this will not end well for you."

Reading turned to face the man, squaring his shoulders. "Is that a threat?"

Nikitin took an involuntary step back from the large-framed man. "Not from me, though I don't know what my superiors will want to do."

Laura shook her head. "After everything that's happened, your insane president would still threaten lives to get his hands on them? His obsession almost resulted in an airplane full of innocent passengers being blown out of the sky, young adults to be murdered, us to be murdered. Professor Orlov is dead all because of a buried piece of history. Why does your president care so much about the truth coming out? Does anyone today care that Stalin murdered Lenin besides historians like ourselves?"

"Many people care, Professor Palmer. Stalin is a hero to the Russian people. He symbolizes a period in our history where we defeated a powerful enemy and were feared and respected by the world."

Laura let out an exasperated sigh. "I don't understand this obsession of your culture. Why are you so concerned about what others think? You want others to fear and respect you. Why? If your country were an individual, I would say you had an inferiority complex. You need to grow up and put that type of thinking behind you. Relegate it to the history books."

Nikitin regarded her. "A decade ago, I might have, Professor, but these are uncertain times. The world is breaking apart. Countries that have been stable for decades no longer are, new alliances are forming, new power blocks. The days of liberal democracies determining the destiny of the human race are over."

"And you think that future is Russian, led by a man who would model himself after a brutal dictator?"

Nikitin shook his head as if pitying her. "No, Professor, though I believe for Russia to have a future, it must be able to stand on its own. It must be able to stand on its own with a man at its helm who is feared and respected so that our great nation can weather the coming storm. A century from now, when the dust settles and we see whether Western democracy even exists, or whether a country like China dominates, there's one thing I can guarantee you—Russia will prevail. She'll still be there strong and feared, and perhaps then can continue on with the failed democratic experiment."

Acton shook his head. "You're delusional. Russia was heading in the right direction. You just had to give it time, but you allowed a president to come to power who embraces the old ways. Your country is doomed to repeat history until the last Soviet dies. It's your generation that doesn't remember the Soviet Union, that should be fighting for what could be, not for what was. Remember, the Soviet Union might have been feared and respected, but it failed. Why aspire to failure when there are so many better options?"

Nikitin rolled his eyes. "You Americans think you're so superior, but look at your own country. It's tearing itself apart. You're no longer a beacon to those who would want to live in a free society, you're no longer an example for democracy. Why would anyone want to be like you? Russia will stand strong while America crumbles."

Acton sighed. "My country might not be perfect—it never was—but it's a hell of a lot better than most things out there, and we have an advantage that your country will never have if it continues down the path it's going."

"What's that?"

"A free and democratic society. While it might be broken now, eventually the population will smarten up and elect leaders who would work together to better their country than oppose good ideas merely because the other side thought of them first. A country can only save itself if its people have free will, and your country has lost that, though there's still time to get it back."

Nikitin chuckled. "You're mistaken, Professor Acton. Russia does have free will, and it has freely chosen our president to lead them." He dismissed the conversation with a wave of his hand. "Will you return the papers?"

Acton glanced at Laura who subtly shook her head. "No, they'll be authenticated and released."

Nikitin sighed. "I would hate to see your reputation destroyed, Professor Acton. I've read your file. You're quite well respected in your field, as are you, Professor Palmer. If you attach yourselves to this false narrative, I have no doubt the Russian government will do everything in its power to destroy whatever legacy you've built."

"False narrative?" asked Reading.

Nikitin addressed him. "The documents your friends have in their possession suggest Stalin murdered Lenin. It's the Russian government's position that these are forgeries created a century ago to implicate Stalin in Lenin's death. The plot was discovered, the documents were preserved, however the context of them has been lost. All your tests will show that the documents came from that period, but no amount of testing can show the context. You will never be able to prove that Stalin murdered Lenin because it's a lie. If you want to stake your reputations on this ridiculous notion, then so be it, I can't stop you, however, the Russian government will stop at nothing to make certain the truth comes out."

"Your version of the truth."

Nikitin smirked. "Professor, they're all versions of the truth, and unfortunately none can be proven." He held out his hands. "I have been authorized to make you an offer."

Acton frowned as he stared at the man. "And that offer is?"

"Keep the papers. As I've just explained, they're worthless. Meaningless. Whether they're fiction or not, no one could prove otherwise, so keep them, but keep them to yourselves. Professor Orlov is dead. He was my main mission, and that has been accomplished. Keep the papers secret, and the Russian government promises that no harm will come to Volkov, Rozhenko, or Abramov."

"They can return home if they want to?"

"Of course, though I would encourage them not to, as their reputations and prospects have been destroyed."

Acton looked at Laura who leaned in, her voice low. "He's right. There's no way we can prove that what's written on those papers is the truth. I don't care about my reputation, but if keeping secret what might be a lie allows those three young people to have a future without fear, I think it's worth the sacrifice."

He squeezed her hand and she stood back up. Acton regarded Nikitin for a moment then nodded curtly. "You have a deal. Can we get that in writing?"

Nikitin roared in laughter. "And they say you Americans have no sense of humor."

Acton raised a finger before Nikitin could leave. "One more thing."

"What's that?"

"The deal extends to everybody, including Dempsey and Doyle, the American reporters."

"Agreed." Nikitin eyed him. "What about your friends that you handed the documents over to at the airport?"

Acton shook his head. "Like I said before, I know nothing of that. The papers that crazy bastard stole were decoy pages we had printed up the night before. The real handover happened at our transfer point en route to the safe house that you raided. I lied so that I could buy time for them to get out of the country."

"Then Mr. Zorkin and his friend weren't involved?

"I don't know who this Zorkin is, or his friend, but no, not at all."

"Very well. I wish you both speedy recoveries." He stopped in mid-turn and pointed a finger at them. "And I hope to never see you again." He left the room and West closed the door.

Acton looked at the old man. "*Are* Zorkin and Jack okay?"

West nodded. "Perfectly fine. Thank you for preserving their covers."

Acton shrugged. "Least I could do."

"Are you going to keep the documents secret like you promised?" asked Adelle.

"Yes."

Adelle cursed as she turned to leave the room. "Then I better stop what's about to happen down the hall."

Acton's eyes narrowed. "What's that?"

"That reporter Dempsey is about to go live with an interview with our three young Russian friends telling the world why the Russian government pursued them and why a jetliner was almost blown out of the air."

Acton grunted. "That's one advantage Russia has over us."

"What's that?"

"No free press."

"Yes, they can be a pain." Adelle rushed out and West followed her.

Reading turned to them. "So, you mean all of this was over documents that might have been faked a century ago?"

Laura nodded. "It hadn't occurred to me until he said it, but yes, it's a definite possibility. And he's right, there'd be almost no way to prove it either way."

Acton closed his eyes, exhausted. "If you two don't mind, I'm just going to lie here and try to figure out how to increase the pain medication."

Laura leaned in and gave him a kiss, and Reading patted Acton's lower leg. They left the room, leaving him alone with his thoughts, wondering if the truth would ever be known.

Did Stalin murder Lenin?

Stalin Residence, The Kremlin

Moscow, USSR

January 22, 1924

"You did well, Comrade Bazarov."

Bazarov bowed as his eyes darted about the room, making certain they were alone. There was only one person alive who knew what he had done, and that was the man who now rose from behind his desk.

Joseph Stalin.

"Thank you, sir."

Stalin smiled broadly, extending a hand. Bazarov took it and let the man shake it vigorously. "I wasn't certain you'd have the courage to go through with it, but you did." He paused, regarding him. "You *did*, did you not? This wasn't simply a fortunate coincidence?"

Bazarov took the seat offered him as Stalin returned to his own. "Yes, sir, I did. I too was uncertain until my conversation with him. He was determined to deliver his testament to the Congress, and he didn't care about the consequences. He was clearly consumed with his hatred of you."

Stalin grunted. "It is a shame. We were such good friends, but once Russia was ours, he lost the nerve needed to rule what we had created. With his declining health, I knew he would die before his time. We needed a stable, guiding hand for the next several decades. I was willing for that to be him, but when it was evident it couldn't be, I knew I had to take action."

"Justifiably so, Comrade. And when I realized my friend was willing to tear down all that we built in a personal vendetta against you who would lead us after he died, I knew I too had to take action."

Stalin leaned back and turned his chair to the side, resting an arm on the desk, a finger tapping the blotter. "You were wise to come to me."

"You deserved to know. Our people need you, our nation needs you. He had to be stopped."

"And you did, Comrade, you did. And no one, of course, can ever know."

"Of course. You can trust me, I assure you, Comrade."

Stalin smiled. "I'm sure." He paused. "Have you told anyone?"

"Only you, Comrade."

"So, no one knows. No one at all. Not a confidante, a lover, a clergyman?"

"No one, I assure you. I suppose the man I acquired the poison from knows someone was to be poisoned, but it's been a year, and he assured me he was leaving the country."

"With the money I gave you for the poison, he could afford to. Fortunately, I've had him taken care of."

Bazarov's eyes narrowed. "Sir?"

"Did you think I'd hand over that kind of money to you, and not have you followed?"

Bazarov tensed. "No, I suppose not. But I assure you, I paid the man. I kept nothing of it."

Stalin smiled. "When my men killed him and retrieved the money, I was pleased to see every ruble was there. You are an honest man."

Bazarov relaxed. "Thank you, Comrade. I am here to serve."

"Yes, I believe you are." Stalin reached into a desk drawer then stood, a pistol in his hand. "And you will serve me once more, with your silence." He aimed the weapon and fired, the bullet slamming into Bazarov's chest. He grabbed at the source of the excruciating pain as the man he had sacrificed so much for stepped around his desk, the weapon still held high.

"W-why?"

"Because if I am to save what our mutual friend created, no one can know I had a hand in his death. The secret of his murder dies with you."

Two more shots were fired, and as the life rapidly drained from Bazarov's body, shouts in the corridor beyond the door erupted. Footfalls pounded toward them, yet it meant nothing. They weren't coming to help him. These were Stalin's men. They served him and no one else.

And as the last of his life faded, he took solace that this was exactly the act he would expect from a man who could lead Russia, the

Communist Party, and the Soviet Union, into the glorious future he and his best friend, Lenin, had dreamed of.

He was a true hero.

A selfless hero.

A hero the world would never know played a critical role in shaping the country he loved.

And helped kill millions long after his death.

THE END

ACKNOWLEDGMENTS

I loved writing this book. The subject matter was simply fascinating, and the idea was triggered by insomnia. I've been suffering from a lot of pain for decades, and it has affected my sleep patterns. Months ago, I decided to try settling my mind down at night by having my Kindle read books to me. I chose something I was certain would bore me to tears—the last thing I wanted was to get caught up in a good story.

I chose a biography on Stalin that I had bought some time ago.

And it worked. I fell asleep quickly, but through the night, during various outings for a squirt, I would hear another few minutes, and each night I would advance the starting point 10-15 pages.

And a fascinating history was revealed.

I of course knew Russian/Soviet history in broad strokes, but never the minutia. I wasn't aware of the rivalry between Stalin and Lenin in the final years, the rude phone call to Lenin's wife, the Last Testament and how it was ultimately presented—posthumously by his wife, its existence kept secret until she could deliver it.

In the end, it did not have the desired effect. It was too late. The Soviet Union was desperate for a leader after Lenin's death, and Stalin simply took what was to be had.

The history was fascinating, and the kernel of an idea was born.

What if Stalin found out what Lenin was trying, and killed him for it?

There are conspiracy theories out there that he did just that, though I didn't discover those until after I started working on the book. I like to think that I came up with a plausible scenario, for both the historical and present-day aspects of the book.

It was a lot of fun, despite writing much of it in agony, and I hope you enjoyed it—and if you did, please write a review!

As many are aware, I like to take little tidbits from my life and work them into my novels. This time, one of those things is almost unbelievable but true. Acton's science textbook that predated the moon landings? That was my textbook. In the mid-eighties. I wonder if that's why some people say the moon landings were faked.

As usual, there are people to thank. My dad for all the research, Michael Broughton for suggesting the movie, Marc Quesnel and Rob Carnell for some flying terminology, and, as always, my wife, my daughter, my late mother who will always be an angel on my shoulder as I write, as well as my friends for their continued support, and my fantastic proofreading team!

To those who have not already done so, please visit my website at www.jrobertkennedy.com, then sign up for the Insider's Club to be notified of new book releases. Your email address will never be shared or sold.

Thank you once again for reading.

Made in United States
North Haven, CT
20 July 2023

39315967R00253